Pel and the Paris Mob

Pel and the Paris Mob

by

MARK HEBDEN

HAMISH HAMILTON
London

First published in Great Britain 1986
by Hamish Hamilton Ltd
Garden House, 57–59 Long Acre, London WC2E 9JZ

Copyright © 1986 by Mark Hebden

British Library Cataloguing Data

Hebden, Mark
  Pel and the Paris mob.
  Rn: John Harris   I. Title
  823′.914[F]   PR6058.A6886

  ISBN 0–241–11764–X

Filmset by Input Typesetting Ltd, London
Printed in Great Britain by
St Edmundsbury Press, Bury St Edmunds, Suffolk

Though Burgundians will probably decide they have recognised it – and certainly many of the streets are the same – in fact, the city in these pages is intended to be fictitious.

1

Evariste Clovis Désiré Pel wasn't in the best of tempers. There was nothing unusual about this. There was plenty in the life of a chief inspector of the Brigade Criminelle of the Police Judiciaire to raise the blood pressure, and Pel wasn't normally in the best of good humour, anyway. Since his marriage, he liked to feel he was a new man who could look on the world with a kindly wisdom, but he wasn't really. Not by any means. He was still very much the old one and, being a little more advanced in age, had even suffered a further reduction in his threshold of tolerance. After all, people don't change. They just become more so.

Fortunately, his wife, formerly the Widow Faivre-Perret, was an understanding woman with a strong sense of humour. She hadn't managed to change Pel much – and didn't really expect to – but at least she managed most of the time to make him seem human, and his bad temper at the moment was attributable to the fact that he was away from home and far from her restraining influence.

Sitting in his bedroom at the Hôtel des Trois Faisans in the village of Quigny-par-la-Butte, where he was an unwilling resident for the night, he realised that for the first time in his life he had started to enjoy going home from work. Before his marriage he had lived a hand-to-mouth existence in a house as big as a dog kennel, his only companion a soured housekeeper who barely looked after him. Even his childhood had not been exactly full of comfort. His father, an irascible old man from whom Pel had inherited his doubtful temper, hadn't believed much in luxury and it had been a family joke that he liked to sleep on a concrete slab which was sluiced down every morning with the garden hose. When Pel had joined the force, the police barracks had actually seemed an improvement. And though the little home he had eventually set up in the Rue Martin-de-Noinville had been a further improvement, he realised now that he had never really known what comfort was until he had married.

He removed his tie and looked about him. The reception clerk of the hotel had given him what she said was their best room – on a corner facing the village square. It had windows on two sides, one looking across to the church forty paces away, the other facing directly along the road from Lyons which turned sharp left at the square and ran alongside the hotel. Quigny lay just off the N7 and the hotel was known throughout France as a gastronomic delight. Pel had decided he might as well temper his dislike of travel with the pleasure of a good meal.

Glancing out of the window, he saw people gathering near the church, more figures coming down the road to the square, and still more crossing the fields, all dressed in dark clothes because the occasion was the funeral of the Maire, Monsieur Robert Heriot. Pel was there because many years ago Monsieur Heriot had encouraged him to join the police and now, having long ago admitted – despite his complaints that he suffered from overwork, shortage of sleep, lack of money and a terrible tendency to smoke himself to death – that he would never have wished to be anything else, Pel felt he owed a debt of gratitude. What else could he have been? A schoolteacher? A man who could reduce policemen to tears would have terrified his pupils. A salesman in a shop? Faced with a difficult customer, he would have crushed him with a word. A civil servant? Restless as a flea, Pel could never have lived the soporific life of a government official. Aggressive, hostile, fond of minding other people's business, being a policeman was the only thing he was fitted for.

He fished a black tie from his overnight bag and tied it carefully, studying himself in the mirror as he did so. His hair, plastered across his skull, had ceased, he noticed, to look like wilting anchovies draped across the top of a pizza; these days it looked more like infant scratchings with a pencil on the shell of a boiled egg. He wasn't getting any younger, he reflected. It was a sad thought. Newly married and already on his way out. It was all those cigarettes he smoked. The number he put away in a day was enough to kill a carthorse.

Glancing from the window, he noted that the queue of

2

people entering the church had increased. He had already seen the Maires of two neighbouring villages, complete with their sashes of office, go in. Just time for a quick one, he thought, and headed for the bar. It was empty and he guessed that everyone except the barman was in the church because Monsieur Heriot was well known in the district and universally popular. As he sipped a Pernod and dragged at a hurried cigarette, he noticed the room was filled with old photographs of the village, the square, and the Trois Faisans. One of them attracted his attention. It was the church opposite, where he was bound within a minute or two, but it looked odd and it dawned on him that it had no steeple. The barman saw his look of puzzlement and explained.

'Taken in 1871,' he said. 'It collapsed into the nave. They had a battery of Prussian guns just outside the village during the Battle of Saulbrais. The Army of the Alps was trying to get up this way to lift the siege of Paris and they were firing all night. They said the vibration did the damage.'

Becoming aware of the church clock chiming four, Pel finished his drink and slipped across a sandy courtyard flanked by the ivy-covered wings of the hotel, and into the square. Though he barely noticed it in his hurry, the clock was still chiming four. The queue entering the church had thinned out considerably and he decided he had timed his entrance exactly. He had no wish to be obtrusive and didn't want to be among the family or official mourners.

There were now four Maires in the church but Pel found a seat among the people at the back, for the most part horny-handed men and women from the little farms and villages around, the women in out-of-date hats, the men in board-stiff black suits and heavy shoes, their faces devoid of expression. The coffin was covered with a tricolour. The priest moved forward to meet it, a tall thin man with a lined ascetic face and aggressive nostrils, as if he sniffed out sin with such constancy it had affected their shape.

Mercifully, he was not as ardent as a preacher as his features seemed to suggest, and he delivered an address blessed by its shortness, and everyone escaped thankfully into the bronze late afternoon sunshine.

As he left the graveyard, Pel debated going home. But he had calls to make the following morning on police matters

3

further south, so he gave himself wholeheartedly to commiserating with the relatives, raised his hat to the visiting Maires and a few other local officials, and smiled benignly – while hopping from one foot to the other in an effort to bolt – on the landlord of the Trois Faisans who insisted he had recognised him from his pictures in the newspaper. 'Inspector Pol, isn't it?' he said. 'Involved in that case in Corsica.'

'The name's Pel,' Pel said sharply. 'The rank's Chief Inspector, and the case you're thinking of was on the Ile de St. Ives.'

'Got you,' the landlord said. 'Evariste Clovis Désiré Pel. Easy to remember. Because of your name.'

Pel glared. He had never considered his name fitted the image of a successful detective. It was only with a great feeling of guilt that he had admitted it before his marriage, and even now he preferred not to be reminded of it. But it had a habit of cropping up again and again – every time he licensed his car, on every insurance he took out, during every case reported by the newspapermen who had somehow acquired it from police records. His wife, thank God, addressed him these days simply as 'Pel'.

He was barely civil for the rest of the conversation and escaped at last to light a cigarette to steady his nerves. He had intended to cut his smoking for this day at least, feeling that without the normal worries of a chief inspector of the Police Judiciaire he might be able to relax, but having his name trotted out like this was enough to up his intake from five hundred thousand a day to a cool million.

The cigarette worked wonders and he began to feel better, even a little smug with the sense of a duty well done. The bar had filled up quickly as the mourners, parched after the service, arrived to slake their thirst. Because he had no great fondness for his fellow human beings, Pel decided to sit on his own in the garden. On the whole – apart from what he considered to be an inferiority complex but, with his aggressive arrogance, couldn't possibly have been – he found that, even if he didn't like other people very much, he got on very well with Evariste Clovis Désiré Pel.

He chose a place as far as possible from the bar, situated between a row of sunflowers and a canebreak where the canes were as thick as his thumb. He was nicely screened there and

4

able to sit quietly with his apéritif until it was time to eat. Because it was warm and he felt pleased that he'd done his duty with as little personal wear and tear as possible, he had an extra drink and then, guiltily, another extra drink.

Only vaguely aware of other people sitting outside in the warm evening and the faint chimes of the church clock coming over the roofs, he ate what he considered a magnificent meal and drank rather more wine than he'd intended. Finally – not, of course, he persuaded himself, because he wanted one but simply to do justice to the chef – he had a brandy and an extra couple of cigarettes, guiltily aware that he'd already smoked more than his ration for the day.

He often wondered why he never managed to stop. Millions did. It cost him a fortune and without it he would doubtless feel healthier and smell fresher. Doubtless, if his wife ever decided to leave him, it would be entirely due to the dislike of kissing someone who smelled like an ashtray.

He decided abruptly that he'd stop there and then, and to celebrate the occasion he ordered another brandy. But the brandy made him feel like another cigarette, and he decided that he would stop not at that moment but the next morning when he would have had time to prepare himself for the ordeal. He sank the brandy and dragged the smoke down to his socks with a feeling of luxury.

Heading for bed, he had to admit that he'd thoroughly enjoyed the funeral, and he was just dropping off to sleep when the church clock opposite chimed the hour – eleven strokes. He waited patiently until it had finished and closed his eyes again. He was on the point of dropping off once more when it started again. Name of God, he thought, the damn thing was malfunctioning! He waited until the twenty-second stroke and composed himself again. This time he had just gone off properly when the quarter hour chimed and five minutes later chimed again and it dawned on him that he'd heard of this kind of clock before. Not six months before, in fact. Claudie Darel, the only woman on his team, had told him about one at Torcé-en-Vallée near Le Mans, which had kept her awake half the night while she was en route south for a holiday. She had even discovered one within a mile of Pel's office in the Hôtel de Police. This was another of the same kind – large, very loud and not forty metres from where

5

he lay. It chimed not only on the hour but every quarter, too, and its bells had been made loud because they had been cast in the days when farm labourers didn't wear watches and needed to be warned of the approach of matins and the angelus and the time to stop work, and to chime twice in case they'd been missed the first time.

The iron clangs sounded as if the clock were going off in the room with him and every time, as they started, he found himself tensing at the series of minor clonks, groans, creaks, grunts and shuffles as the mechanism got under way. After an hour he could have described in detail every single one, and was cowering with his head under the pillow, his face dark with fury. Why, he wondered, did God have it in for him so? He would have to organise a society for the removal of noisy clocks. Perhaps even a society for the blowing up of badly-planned hotels which didn't allow their residents to sleep, or the shooting of self-important landlords who inveigled long-suffering chief inspectors of the Police Judiciaire into their premises with the pretence that they served gourmet food. After four hours of the clock opposite, there was no place in Pel's mind for the memory of a splendid meal and no room in his heart for mercy for the man who had provided it.

Never a good sleeper – for most of his life Pel had gone to bed early in the belief that he needed sleep when, in fact he needed remarkably little – his mind was busier than ever through being kept awake and he recalled again, with the landlord's insult at calling him Pol, the priest's nostrils, the coffin covered in a tricolour, the visiting Maires in their sashes, the sombre interior of the church, even the story the barman had told him of the church spire collapsing into the nave because of the vibration of the Prussian guns at the Battle of Saulbrais.

He dropped off at last only to be awakened almost at once by an appalling crash. He sat bolt upright immediately, convinced that the guns of Saulbrais were firing, or that the church spire had collapsed again, or both. But, as he glared through the window, the clock chimed defiantly back at him. Then he became aware of voices coming through the other window overlooking the road and, crossing the room to stick his head out, he discovered the trouble had been caused by

6

a fire engine returning from a fire, which had taken the corner into the village rather too sharply and had removed every single ground-floor shutter from the outside of the hotel.

As he peered out, he saw one fireman stacking the shutters neatly against a wall, and another two endeavouring to wrench the wing of the fire engine off the wheel while their officer urged them to get a move on so they could be away before anyone arrived to see what had happened. It was a vain hope, because just then the landlord arrived, in pyjamas and dressing gown and looking half-asleep – doubtless, Pel thought bitterly, *his* room was well away from the church clock at the back of the hotel. Taking in what had happened at a glance, the landlord sailed into the firemen with every scrap of vituperation in his possession.

By the time Pel turned from the window, the staff and several residents had also appeared. It looked like turning into a riot. Pel gave up trying to sleep and, putting on his clothes, decided he might just as well go home.

He reached the Hôtel de Police long before anyone else and in a thoroughly bad temper because the Bar Transvaal opposite, where he often took his breakfast of a coffee and croissant, wasn't yet open. He told the policeman at the desk to let him know as soon as they opened their doors and, when the call came, stalked out, bought a newspaper, and found a corner of the bar where he might recover.

By the time he returned to the office, his team were beginning to appear – first Sergeant Bardolle, big as a brewery dray, his huge iron voice setting Pel's head ringing; De Troquereau, slight, handsome, his aristocratic face full of intelligence; Darcy, Pel's deputy, as well-dressed as if he were about to attend a levée at the Elysée Palace and smiling with those strong white teeth of his that captivated the girls so much; Lagé, plump, slow and hard-working; Aimedieu, looking like a choirboy; Brochard and Debray, the Heavenly Twins, pale hair, pale eyes, looking as if they were related; Lacocq and Morell, recently arrived from Uniformed Branch; Claudie Darel; and Martin, the cadet who ran the errands. Inevitably the last to arrive was Misset, running rapidly to seed, his good looks beginning to disappear, struggling with a failing marriage and a dislike of hard work. Only Nosjean, who was on leave, was missing.

Within ten minutes the Chief's conference started. Judge Brisard was there and he began a long discussion on the aspects of a case that was about to come before the magistrates and the suggestion that had been made that one at least of the defending lawyers had an interest in it that was more than merely legal. Pel disliked Judge Brisard, who was a tall pear-shaped youngish man with a nice line in marital fidelity which was a load of hypocrisy because, as Pel well knew, he had a woman in Beaune. Brisard returned the dislike, which made everything easy because neither expected compliments, but Brisard was a judge nevertheless, and Pel promised to check on the backgrounds of the lawyers involved in the case they were discussing.

Back in his office, he discovered that Judge Polverari, another of the juges d'instruction, had borrowed his copy of *La Liste des Avocats et Juristes Français*, so he walked across to the Palais de Justice to collect it. He could just as easily have sent Cadet Martin, but he liked Judge Polverari, who also disliked Judge Brisard and insisted from time to time on buying Pel lunch just to hear his latest pithy comments on him. They chatted for half an hour and the judge brought out a bottle of brandy. Cigarettes were offered and Pel accepted one before he remembered he'd decided to stop.

When he returned to his office, Darcy was waiting for him. He offered a packet of cigarettes.

Pel shook his head. 'I don't smoke,' he said.

Darcy's eyebrows shot up. 'I just saw you put one out, Patron.'

'That was a mistake. I've just stopped. I decided last night. What's on?'

'We are, Patron. There's been a robbery.'

'Big one?'

'Very.'

'Who's involved?'

'Baron and Baroness de Mougy.'

Pel frowned. He knew the Baron and the Baronne de Mougy well because they'd featured in an enquiry of his some time before.* The Baron was a cold-eyed man, tall and thin as a lath, and his wife was twenty years younger and as beautiful as a film star. Their land marched south towards Quigny where he'd spent the night.

'What have they lost?' he asked.

'A lot of money and valuables,' Darcy said. 'Traffic have set up road blocks and are stopping all cars for a search. I've sent De Troq' along, but I think you and I had better put in an appearance. De Mougy has a lot of influence. We'd better spend the night over there and have a chat with their staff. Martin's arranging accommodation.'

As Pel returned to his office, Cadet Martin appeared. Due any time for full police duties, Martin liked to run Pel's life as if he were an aide-de-camp.

'Off now, Patron?' he asked.

'Yes. I have the names and I know the château at Mirebeau. What's the hotel?'

'It isn't at Mirebeau,' Martin corrected him. 'They aren't there. They were held up as they were on the way to the airport to fly to Deauville for a holiday. They're staying with friends nearby until you arrive. At Quigny-par-la-Butte. You'll have no difficulty finding the hotel. It's right opposite the church.'

Martin never understood why Pel threw the List of Barristers and Lawyers at him.

*See *Pel and the Faceless Corpse*

2

As Pel climbed into Darcy's car, Darcy was just lighting a cigarette. Pel drew a deep breath.

'I'll have that cigarette after all,' he said.

'I thought you'd stopped.'

'I've decided to take it up again.'

He explained about the hotel and Darcy laughed.

'Soon sort that one out, Patron,' he said. 'We'll let De Troq' stay there instead. He'll be useful when it comes to dealing with De Mougy's staff because he's a baron, too, and they'll all drop on one knee. *We*'ll come home.'

The Baron de Mougy was seated in the salon at the home of his friend. Judging by the surroundings, his friend had as much money as the Baron de Mougy.

Two metres of bone, muscle and sinew despite his advancing years, the Baron had been a champion fencer, a dead shot and an utterly ruthless Resistance leader. His wife, blonde, the daughter of a financier who was reputed to have sold her to the Baron in return for payment of debts, sat alongside him in a deep chintz-covered armchair. To Pel's surprise, neither of them seemed desperately upset. He had expected tears and temper but the Baron showed only cold fury and his wife only indignation. He had to assume they had so much money the theft troubled them only in so far as it was an inconvenience that had delayed their journey north.

There was no hand-shaking. The Baron didn't believe in shaking hands with inferiors in the form of policemen. He conceded a small nod of his head.

'Pel,' he said, his face as unyielding as a granite slab. 'I think we've met.'

The Baronne gave Pel a scared look before composing her features into a mask of indifference. She knew Pel had once caught her out in an affaire with another man and she was afraid he might let the cat out of the bag.

'How much, Monsieur?' Pel asked.

'There were five hundred thousand francs worth of jewellery,' De Mougy said. 'And twenty thousand francs in cash.'

'What happened?'

'We were on our way to the airport at Dijon. We were to fly to Deauville. A friend had put his aeroplane at our disposal.'

Some people were lucky, Pel thought.

'And?' he said.

'We were on the road from Mirebeau past Quigny towards the N7. Just outside Quigny we had to stop for a man who was standing in the middle of the road with a bicycle. He had his back to us and it seemed that his chain had broken and he was mending it. As we approached he put the bicycle down and waved and we thought he intended to come and apologise. But then I saw he was wearing a stocking mask and he pulled out a gun. Another man in a mask appeared from the bushes and they took my wife's jewel case and my wallet. As they were doing this, a car appeared with another man in it. He also wore a stocking mask.'

'What were they like. Build? Colouring?'

'The man with the bicycle was small, dark and narrow-faced. He might have had a moustache, I think.'

'Height?'

'About one metre sixty-five.'

'Did he say anything?'

'Nothing. Everything was done by signs. They slashed the tyres of my car, jumped into the waiting vehicle and disappeared. It took us some time to call help.'

'You walked to a telephone?'

Baron de Mougy's eyebrows shot up. 'My chauffeur walked to a telephone,' he corrected. 'On my instructions, he also got in touch with my friend here, who collected us. I would be grateful if you could hurry your interrogation, Chief Inspector. We would very much like to be on our way.'

Marvellous, Pel thought. Just like that. Over half a million francs light and all they could think of was being on their way.

11

'Doubtless you made a note of the number of the car they drove off in, Monsieur?' he said.

The Baron gave him a blank stare. 'Never occurred to me,' he admitted, as if taking the numbers of cars whose occupants had just robbed him of a fortune were a job best left to servants.

'Perhaps Madame la Baronne?'

'Never thought about it.' She still kept her face averted from Pel.

'Then, surely the chauffeur?'

'He's outside,' the Baron said. 'You can ask him but you won't get anywhere. He didn't.'

Pel scowled. Name of God, he thought, three intelligent people and not one of them had thought to take the number of the getaway car. Not that it would matter because without doubt it would have been stolen, but it seemed to show how indifferent the wealthy could be, not only over the loss of half a million francs but also about being helpful to the police who were trying to recover it. If the aristocracy had been like this in 1789, he thought, no wonder there'd been a revolution.

'Did they touch your car at all, Monsieur?'

The Baron looked puzzled then light seemed to dawn. 'Ah, fingerprints you mean? No – ' he frowned. 'Come to think of it, they were very careful. They made Josso – that's my chauffeur – get out and open the doors for us. They didn't touch a thing.' He looked pointedly at his watch.

Pel saw the movement and deliberately took as long as he could, delaying his questions and dealing with trivialities which could easily have been found out by other means.

The Baron was growing more and more restless and in the end the cold eyes flashed. 'Pity I hadn't my gun with me,' he growled.

'What would you have done, Monsieur?'

'Shot him, of course.'

'That would have been most unwise.'

'Doubtless. But it would have given me a lot of pleasure.'

They questioned Josso, the chauffeur who could add nothing.

'Better write down a description of the three men, Daniel,' Pel suggested to Darcy. In an undertone, he added maliciously, 'And don't hurry.'

They learned that the De Mougys had been invited to a house party in Normandy, with a large and expensive get-together that evening to start off, and sailing, the Casino and the races to follow.

They learned that the man with the bicycle had worn a blue windcheater. The man who had appeared from the bushes had been taller and worn a red windcheater – it was thought, but nobody seemed sure – while the man who had brought up the getaway car had been wearing a leather jacket – black or brown, again they couldn't be certain. Since he hadn't got out of the car they had no idea how tall the third man was, and no idea what he looked like because in addition to his mask he'd worn a large flat cap that had hidden his face. Most people, Pel knew, went about with their eyes shut and wouldn't have noticed if Brigitte Bardot had appeared alongside them in the street, but these three seemed blinder than usual.

As he left, he heard, with a certain amount of sly pleasure, the Baron discussing the possibility of staying overnight because the delay would mean that they wouldn't reach the airport until almost dark and would arrive in Deauville too late to attend the function that evening.

It cheered him up. Anybody who could shrug off half a million francs *deserved* to be delayed. Pel would have been hopping about like a chicken on a hot tin roof over the loss of a mere five francs, let alone five hundred thousand.

They drove to the spot where the robbery had taken place. The car, a large black Citroën, was still where it had been stopped and a man from Fingerprints was working over it. De Troq' and Aimedieu were also there with Lagé and two of Leguyader's men from the Forensic Laboratory. Another man from Fingerprints was bent over a battered green bicycle lying by the side of the road. A local cop, who had turned up from Quigny in a cream van, recognised Pel from the funeral the previous day.

One of the Forensic men had found a footprint and was trying to take a plaster cast of it. With tweezers he had plucked out the grass and twigs from the imprint in the soil and was running into it a thin mixture of plaster of Paris. Unfortunately a dog had appeared from somewhere. It was large, young and friendly and as Pel arrived it had its head on its forepaws, its tongue hanging out, and was regarding Leguyader's man with clumsy affection. If he wanted to play with sticks and twigs, it was more than willing to join in.

Leguyader's men glared at it. 'Va-t'en,' he snapped.

As the dog sprang up, barked and galloped round him in a circle, he snatched up a thick stick and hurled it at it, but the dog decided it was part of the game and chased after it, grasped it between its teeth and tore back towards him, stirring the earth with its clumsy paws.

'Whose is this damned animal?'

'It comes from the farm down the road, I think,' the local cop said.

'Then you'd better remove it or I'll have it shot.'

It took three men to ambush the dog, and the local cop, his handkerchief through its collar, set off for the farm looking acutely uncomfortable.

Pel studied the footprint. 'Think you'll get something?' he asked.

'It's not a bad print, Patron,' Leguyader's man said. 'Of course, it isn't a scrap of use unless we find the shoe that caused it and the man who was wearing it.'

Pel turned to the man working over the limousine who shrugged.

'Nothing, Patron,' he said. 'Chauffeur's dabs – most of them made with gloves because I gather he always wears them when he's driving, and a few which seem to belong to the owners.'

'What about the bicycle?'

'We found prints on the bell, Patron. Nothing else worth having. Somebody's handled it with gloves and it looks to me as if several people have had their mitts on it, but most of them seem to be kids.'

'Kids?'

'They're not fully developed male prints.' The Fingerprint man stared at the bicycle, which was scarred and scratched, its drab green paint flecked with patches of rust. 'It's an old bicycle, Patron,' he pointed out. 'There should be a number on it but I think it's been painted over so often it's disappeared. Racing saddle but not racing handlebars. And – ' he added ' – it isn't a man's bicycle. Fourteen-year-old's. Something like that.'

'They said one of them had a moustache,' Darcy put in. 'He doesn't sound like a fourteen-year-old.'

'He doesn't have to be,' Pel said. 'They probably brought it here lashed to the back of the car and just used it to stop the car. I expect we'll find it's stolen.'

'We'll have all known bike thieves in,' Darcy suggested. 'There's one in Talant who's just done time for an attic full of missing machines. He can't even ride a bike, either. He just likes the colours.'

'This one isn't missing,' Pel pointed out gently. 'It's *here*. We'll just have to wait until someone reports it missing and see if there's a connection.'

They left De Troq' and Aimedieu to look after things, and headed homeward. De Troq's title was as old as Baron de Mougy's, and was usually enough to flatten any attempt at snobbery. But De Troq' was still only a sergeant, and wealth had great influence, and the absence of a senior officer might well have suggested an indifference equal to the Baron's, with the difference that police indifference might have raised a howl of protest whereas the Baron's only raised indignation in police breasts.

'It sounds like a gang job, Patron,' Darcy said. 'A tip-off.'

'I imagine it must have been,' Pel agreed. 'We'd better look into our old friends. Not just the local boys. Outsiders. Pépé le Cornet, Maurice Tagliatti. This place is just about halfway from Paris where Pépé operates, and Marseilles which is Tagliatti's stamping ground. From time to time they seem to like to pay us a visit. De Troq' can keep an eye on it for the moment and we'll tackle the staff tomorrow. In the meantime, let's have the owner of that bicycle identified. Look for a fifteen-year-old. But let's do it quietly. If professionals are involved, and I suspect they are, I don't want to frighten them off.'

3

The afternoon sun was streaming over the city, catching the varnished tiles for which it was famous, and touching with gold the roofs of the Palais des Ducs and the church of Notre Dame. Though it was still only spring, the city was trying its best to look as if it were summer.

The station was jammed with people, many of them tourists heading for different parts of France – red-faced English ladies delighted to have found that French lavatories were an improvement on those they'd found in Italy, fat Germans loaded with gold jewellery, and steeple-tall Americans trying to decide what in the name of God had persuaded them to come to a country where the people stared at you as if you were mad when you demanded coffee or a Coca Cola with a four-course meal.

Sergeant Josephe Misset stared round him, bored. He felt he didn't fit very snugly into society. A policeman's pay provided him with sufficient money to paint the town red only at irregular intervals and now, with pay-day still some time away and his car broken down, he was finding life somewhat oppressive. Spontaneity, he felt, was not the strong point of the Burgundians. He himself came originally from Paris and sometimes he found the city where he had chosen to live hard to endure. Lack of money and difficult girlfriends sometimes also made it very awkward, because while he hadn't enough of the first he had rather too many of the second, with the result that his affairs were becoming not only tangled but well-nigh insupportable.

In addition, his eyesight was beginning to go and he had had to take to wearing spectacles. Because he was vain, he'd had them tinted so that he appeared to be wearing sunglasses which was the habit of film stars, spies and men in television commercials advertising deodorants. They gave a fellow a

16

mysterious look and could disguise the fact that he no longer saw as well as he used to, something Misset was anxious to hide. Aimedieu had already twice called him 'Four-eyes', and Misset had no wish to see the end of the days when girls were interested in his bulky if fading good looks.

He had often thought of resigning from the police and starting a business, but businesses needed money and Misset hadn't got any, and he had no experience except as a cop and – he had to admit it – not a lot of that. He didn't fancy the hard work and discomfort that went with being a private detective. Or for that matter, the poor pay. Money was something that always worried Misset. It had led him more than once to pass on to the press tips on what the police were up to, but he'd long since guessed that Pel had found out and he knew he wasn't trusted much any more and was even at times in danger of being returned to the Uniformed Branch.

He frowned. Complete chaos in his affairs had never been very far away and he had an uneasy feeling that it was stalking him again. He had married in haste and fathered a family which had seemed to increase with every year but, as his family grew, so his finances had dwindled and, as his finances had dwindled, so his wife's complaints had increased.

Having just come off duty, he was waiting at that moment to meet his mother-in-law off the train from Metz in Lorraine on the frontier with Germany. He wasn't looking forward to it. Lorrainers were said to be as wooden as their own trees and were known derisively to the rest of France as the Boches d'Est. Misset could well understand it. His wife and mother-in-law were perfect Boches and they had a habit of ganging up on him whenever they were together. It would be worse this time, too, because over the first cup of coffee they'd be discussing the fact that Madame Misset had recently seen him with not one girlfriend but two. Trying not only to keep the girlfriends from Madame Misset but also from each other was becoming a little like being a bad juggler trying to keep four china chamber pots in the air all at the same time.

The train was late and he moved down the platform slowly, eyeing the girls, then, tired of waiting, he strolled to the entrance of the station. The forecourt was full of cars containing people waiting to meet relations.

Heading for the bar, he ordered a beer. Misset liked his

beer and it had long since given him a belly and blurred what had once been good features. Over his drink he tried to chat up the barmaid but she had a boyfriend further along the counter who was much younger than Misset and she wasn't interested.

Back on the platform, he pushed through the growing crowd. The arrival of any train always ended in a shoving match and this one was late. The waiting travellers were already growing restive and ill-tempered and he noticed a little man in a light-weight brown suit run through with gold threads standing in one of the telephone booths in the entrance. He seemed to be nervous and Misset wondered whom he was waiting for – his mother-in-law, too, perhaps, or his boss's wife, his girlfriend, his mistress. Perhaps even, he conceded with the broadmindedness of one who could see *any* possibility – a mere male.

An official hurried past, trying to look as if he were invisible, and Misset asked him what had happened to the train. The answer was brusque.

'Un défaut électrique,' he said. 'In the Morsard tunnel.'

Misset's heart sank. Name of God, he thought, a hold-up in the Morsard tunnel! It would mean hours of waiting and his mother-in-law arriving hungry, thirsty and in a foul temper, ready to find fault with everything. There was as much chance of persuading her that the fault wasn't his as there was of trying to teach a cow to dance the polka.

An hour and a half later, with the city lights beginning to throw a glow in the sky, the platform was jammed with people. The southbound train from Paris which should have followed the one held up in the Morsard tunnel was also delayed by this time and there were now two lots of waiting passengers and they were beginning to eye each other with the blank hostility of bank robbers.

Misset found a wall to lean against and opened his newspaper. There was another financial crisis looming, he noticed, and somebody had robbed the Baron de Mougy. Misset knew about that because Pel, Darcy, De Troq' and several others from Forensic and Fingerprints had shot off to attend to it. Misset was pleased he hadn't gone or he'd still have been there, his feet aching and nowhere in sight to buy a drink. On the foreign page, China was accusing Russia, someone was passing counterfeit notes along the border and a Russian agent had defected to the West with a secret file that threatened to blow sky-high the whole network east of the Iron Curtain.

As he lowered the paper, the signals indicated that the train was due at last, and there was a movement towards the edge of the platform. There wasn't a railway official in sight.

'You never know,' one of them had said to Misset as he'd hurried past, 'they might take it into their heads to lynch us.'

The train swept round the curve into the platform and there was an immediate and ominous surge forward. The little man in the gold-thread suit began to push through the throng with a desperate look on his face that suggested he was afraid of missing someone. The train arrived with a howl like a banshee and the riot started at once. People on the platform were determined to get to their seats and began scrambling aboard even before the train had stopped, and the corridors were jammed with passengers trying to get into compartments that hadn't yet been evacuated. Suitcases were passed through windows and an argument in a second class corridor turned into a screeching bedlam.

Over the heads of the struggling people, Misset vaguely thought he saw his mother-in-law. Advancing warily, he found himself in a shoving match at the door of one of the first-class compartments where a stout stubborn man about to descend had met a stout stubborn man about to climb aboard. Around them a minor riot was building up. A fist flew, somebody poked somebody else with an umbrella and officials started shouting as they tried to bring order.

Misset caught sight of the little man in the gold-thread suit fighting his way forward, then he lost him again as a pile of suitcases was knocked off a trolley. A hat box rolled across the platform and fell on the line and more luggage was knocked between the carriages by the feet of the struggling mob. It was then that Misset saw the woman at the window. She was pleading for help and pounding on the hat of the man in front of her who was trying as hard as she was to get out.

'Mon mari!' she was wailing. 'My husband!'

She was in her middle thirties, he judged, was dressed in black, with a scrap of black lace on her head, and she had the sort of red hair and green eyes that made Misset go weak

19

at the knees. At once several of the men around her stopped shoving but Misset was nearest and her appeal was to him.

'Help me,' she begged. 'Help me! My husband!'

She was speaking in heavily-accented French.

Never behind the door when it came to helping damsels in distress, Misset yanked a couple of elderly gentlemen out of the way, and the woman, pressed from behind, burst on to the platform like a pip from an orange, dropping her handbag and gloves and losing a shoe as she arrived.

Misset scrambled for the handbag and gloves as she struggled to slip the shoe on again, clinging to his arm as she hopped on one leg.

'My luggage,' she said. 'My husband! Please get my husband!'

Misset thrust the handbag at her and looked round, expecting to see some short stout foreigner advancing through the skirmish.

'My husband,' she said again, gesticulating beneath the coaches.

Misset stared. On the line were two or three suitcases and a brass-bound box.

'Down there,' she said.

Deciding that she'd been travelling so long that she'd slipped her trolley, Misset fixed his glasses firmly on his nose and looked round for help. He had no intention of climbing under a train but if she wanted the box off the line she was good-looking enough to have it.

He got hold of an official who was trying to bring some order by the carriage door and indicated the box. A porter appeared and the official nodded and summoned two or three more officials. One of them went to the engine and another to the end of the train, and, assured finally that the train wasn't likely to decapitate him by moving off, the porter slipped to the track and began to throw the lost luggage to the platform, the suitcases first.

'My husband,' the girl said, gesturing furiously.

'For God's sake,' Misset said, 'where?'

'In the box,' she snapped.

The porter's head popped up, his eyes like saucers. 'In the box?'

'Yes.'

'Why doesn't he travel in a compartment like everyone else?'

'Oh, *please!* He's dead! Those are his ashes!'

Misset's jaw dropped and he stared at the porter who ducked out of sight once more. When he resurfaced, the uproar on the platform had stilled. The word had got around and the presence of death seemed to have brought everyone to their senses.

The scrap of lace on the woman's head was over her face now and it dawned on Misset that she was in mourning. The crowd opened up for her and the men, still a little ruffled, stood silently with their hats in their hands.

The box was heavy and the porter slammed it to the platform with relief. The official winced at the bang and Misset saw a few scowls.

'Sorry,' the porter apologised. 'No disrespect. Heavy, that's all.'

The official gestured and the porter regained the platform. Reverently he laid the box on a flat trolley.

'My luggage,' the woman whispered.

A leather valise and two white suitcases, a little oil-smeared, appeared, were passed awkwardly hand-to-hand by men holding their hats across their chests, and were finally placed alongside the box.

The woman looked about her helplessly and, as Misset stepped forward, to his surprise she took his arm.

'Thank you,' she whispered. 'Thank you.'

'Taxi,' Misset said imperiously, and the little procession started off like a cortège down the platform, first the porter pushing the trolley, then the woman with Misset. What a way to come home, Misset was thinking. On a trolley with a bunch of suitcases, as if you were a lot of dirty washing.

Nobody else seemed to think it odd, however, and hats came off along the platform in a shower as they moved to the exit. There was a taxi waiting and, as the box was placed gently in the boot, Misset gave the porter a walloping great tip he couldn't afford and helped the woman in.

'Thank you, Monsieur,' she said. 'You have been very kind. I can manage now.'

Because she looked defenceless and was beautiful enough

21

to make a strong man sob, all Misset's gallantry came to the surface. He brushed her protest aside.

'That's all right,' he said, without even thinking. 'I'm a policeman. I'll see you safely to where you're going.'

'I have a suite reserved at the Hôtel Centrale,' she said.

Even as he turned to pass on the address to the driver, whose face also now wore an expression of extreme solemnity, it registered on Misset's mind that the Hôtel Centrale was no tourist hotel and the girl was obviously no tourist.

The driver fished under the seat and put on a peaked cap he probably hadn't worn for years, and the taxi moved off. Vaguely Misset felt there ought to be sorrowing relatives and the smell of lilies but instead there was the scent of Dior perfume and the girl beside him, curiously exciting even in her silence. He swallowed uncertainly, feeling like a mourner himself, especially with the porter and the railway officials standing alongside holding their caps to their chests.

It was as the car swung out of the station towards the Porte Guillaume that he caught a last glimpse of the man in the gold-thread suit bursting like a bomb through the throng and staring about him before running backwards and forwards across the station forecourt looking for a taxi. Then, as he disappeared into the moving mass of people, Misset's eyes fell on a woman in fawn coat staring about her hostilely, and he remembered with a shock that his knight-errantry had made him forget all about his mother-in-law and the job he'd arrived at the station to do.

As the taxi drew up outside the Centrale, Misset jumped out, his mother-in-law pushed hurriedly to the back of his mind. Misset had the gift of pushing to the back of his mind anything that worried him. Dusk had arrived and the city was covered with a gaudy velvety purple slashed with the red, green and yellow of neon signs. The woman in black had said nothing since they'd left the station. With the occasion as sombre as it was, it obviously wasn't the time to make conversation, but in the dark interior of the taxi Misset had a feeling that her brain was racing and that her thoughts were more than merely contemplative. She seemed different suddenly, no longer in need of help. In fact, there was an air of marked self-assurance about her that gave him a startled feeling that her defencelessness had all been part of an act.

As she followed him from the taxi, he noticed that the black lace was up off her features again and secured by a comb, so that it looked more like a neat small hat now than a mourning veil. Her face was pale and expressionless but there was something about her eyes that was anything but lost.

As the taxi driver opened the boot, a small army of porters appeared under the direction of a major-domo dressed like a general, who began to direct operations with the aplomb of a traffic policeman.

'Vocci.' The girl gave her name briskly and with no trace of helplessness. 'I have a suite reserved.'

'Of course, Madame.' The major-domo jerked a hand and the hotel porters descended on the luggage. The taxi driver, his cap off, was lifting the wooden box to the pavement, his face rigid with an expression of sorrow. The hotel porters failed to notice his solemnity and picked up the box cheerfully, their reverence for what was inside not very deep.

'Steady with that!' Misset moved forward quickly, bristling with officialdom. 'It's – '

'Thank you, Monsieur!' The woman's tone was peremptory and cold and cut him off sharply.

Misset felt flattened. Suddenly she didn't seem in need of assistance any more and there was no longer the slightest sign of distress on her face. 'If there's anything I can do, Misset's the name. Detective-Sergeant Josephe Misset. You can get me at the Hôtel de Police. Perhaps I can – '

'I don't think so, Monsieur. Thank you for your help.'

Misset stopped dead again. He could see the box containing the ashes standing in the hallway of the hotel with a suitcase on top of it, almost as though it were just another piece of luggage.

'Thank you,' she said again, more firmly, and as Misset stepped back she swept into the hotel.

The taxi driver was still staring at the large tip he held in his hand, then he shrugged and turned to Misset. 'What do you do with a thing like that?' he asked, indicating the brass-bound box. 'Stand it on the mantelpiece with an inscription on it?'

4

When Pel returned to his office there was a message for him to see the Chief. In the Chief's office was a squarely-built man in a blue suit with his hair cut en brosse.

'This is Inspector Briand,' the Chief introduced.

As they shook hands, Pel eyed Briand warily, wondering what was about to appear.

'Briand's from Paris,' the Chief said. 'From Counterfeit Currency.'

Briand produced a list from his pocket with the masterful dignity of an Italian customs official sorting through a caseful of lingerie. 'There's been a sudden rash of counterfeit dollars,' he said. 'It started first in Belgium, Holland and Lorraine but since then they've started to appear in Alsace and Champagne and now here in Burgundy. I know local Crime Squads usually handle this sort of thing but it's pretty big so we're dealing with it. So far it's merely an enquiry. We don't know where the notes are coming from but they're large notes and they're troubling my department.'

'It's possible that the money's made in France,' he went on. 'But,' he added with the sort of shining French honesty that always started a guilt complex among visiting foreigners, 'we don't think so. It could also be a deliberate coup by a German or an Italian Syndicate. On the other hand it could be a much smaller affair operated by tourists.'

Pel sniffed. He didn't think much of tourists either.

Briand frowned. 'We can't overlook the possibility and we're therefore visiting every police headquarters and issuing warnings. If you should spot large quantities of new notes, perhaps you'd inform us because, with the French border touching on Belgium, Germany, Luxembourg, Switzerland and Italy, we have our work cut out.'

'I think we should have a look at it, Pel,' the Chief said

24

slowly and without enthusiasm. Like the heads of all provincial forces, he didn't like people from Paris arriving and telling him what to do. It was always the same. They asked assistance and ended up issuing orders.

'Perhaps,' he suggested to Pel, 'we could arrange to visit the hotels, the tourist organisations, the travel bureaux, the information centres and the exchange offices and banks. I think we'd better have one of your men. Whom can you spare?'

Pel was nothing if not cunning. 'We've got that hold-up at Quigny,' he said. 'The Baron de Mougy. It's a major crime with a lot involved.' And if they didn't sort it out, he thought, the Baron de Mougy would start using his influence to make sure that a few heads would roll. 'I think it's a gang job and Marseilles or Paris is involved.' He paused, trying to look helpful when in fact he was just being crafty. 'Perhaps they could have Sergeant Misset, though. I think I can spare him.'

The Chief caught on quickly.

'Very well,' he said. 'Sergeant Misset. He can keep his finger on things. We can just catch him before he goes off duty.'

Misset couldn't believe his ears. A free hand! Just walking round the city paying calls at offices which, for the most part, employed women – young women at that!

It didn't take him long to convince himself that he'd been chosen because of his fine male presence and his gift for getting along with girls. Even Pel admitted Misset's skill with women.

Besides – Misset grinned to himself – it would provide him with a good excuse to see Madame Vocci again. He'd discovered her gloves in his pocket where he'd stuffed them during his rescue act at the station, and had been looking for a chance to return them.

The receptionist at the Hôtel Centrale fell for Misset's smile, as they all did, but she was thoroughly confused.

'Madame Vocci?' she said. 'We have no Madame Vocci here. Only a *Mademoiselle* Vocci.'

Misset adjusted the dark glasses, trying to appear masterful and, looking over her shoulder at the hotel register, managed to catch an interesting glimpse down the top of her dress.

'You sure?' he asked. 'She arrived a few hours ago. She had her husband in a box.'

She stared at him as if he were mad. 'A little while ago,' she said. 'That's right. Mademoiselle Vocci.' With a long white finger she indicated the name on the fiche d'hôtel she passed across.

Misset found the woman from the station reading *Elle* in the lounge. She was no longer in black, and she looked up as he stopped alongside her. A flicker of recognition passed across her face but her expression didn't alter and he had the feeling she hadn't expected ever to see him again.

'Madame Vocci,' he said.

'I am *Mademoiselle* Vocci,' she corrected him firmly. 'Lucrezia Desiderata Ada Vocci.'

Disconcerted by the coolness in her voice, Misset adjusted his glasses and pressed on, determined not to be put aside. 'Nice name,' he commented.

'All Italians have nice names.'

It was becoming hard work and his smile was already a little forced. 'Just happened to be here on duty,' he explained. 'Police. Making enquiries.'

'Oh?'

She turned back to the magazine, trying without putting it into words to suggest she had never seen him before. She was doing very well at it, too, and her unrelenting hostility made Misset feel vaguely insanitary.

'What happened to – er – ?' He gestured lamely. 'I got the impression you were married,' he said.

'I am *Mademoiselle* Vocci.'

Misset gazed at her expressionlessly. There must be some good reason why she was fibbing and he decided she didn't wish to be recognised by him. He was fully aware of what she was up to: Deny everything until you could come up with a thumping great lie that was good enough to cover everything. He'd done it often with his wife.

It seemed to be time to twist her arm. Standing there, ignored, Misset was beginning to feel like a piece of discarded soap. She was pretending to read her *Elle* again. He laid the black gloves alongside her on the arm of the chair.

'You forgot them,' he said loudly. 'Two hours ago. When you were a widow.'

Although she kept her eyes on her magazine, she was sitting as still now as the statue on the lid of a stone coffin. Misset saw one of the waiters watching them.

'The police in France take a poor view of the falsification of documents,' he continued loudly and she finally put down the magazine.

'What are you after?' she asked. When he didn't answer, she stared at him a moment longer, then she picked up her belongings and rose abruptly. 'Perhaps you'd better come to my room,' she said. 'We can talk better there.'

She had a suite at the back of the hotel overlooking the garden where it was quiet and there was a warm air of luxury about it that appealed to Misset. As she put down her bag, he moved about the room, trying to look sinister behind his dark glasses. The settee was large and wide and the bed, which he could see through the open door to the next room, looked big enough to hold a circus in.

She stared at herself in the mirror, giving a few casual pushes at her hair. She was tall, built like Sophia Loren, and she wore a contemplative expression as she turned towards him, as though she were weighing up how to approach him.

'Nice little place you've got here,' Misset said.

She stared at him for a moment and he noticed how cold the green eyes were, then she turned to the sideboard.

'I expect you'd like a drink,' she said.

'I'm not often known to refuse.'

She poured two whiskies. 'Sit down,' she said.

Misset sat on the edge of the settee.

'Now, Monsieur – ?'

'Misset. Detective Sergeant Misset. Police Judiciaire. You can call me Josephe if you want to.'

'Most people call me Ada. You deserve an explanation.' She tried a smile. 'My name really *is* Vocci,' she explained. 'All I've done is change my title from Madame to Mademoiselle.'

'To make the running easier?'

She smiled properly for the first time and immediately the room seemed warmer. 'I suppose so,' she agreed. 'After all, I'm young and not unattractive.'

Misset nodded in acknowledgement of the fact.

'You know how Italians regard death,' she went on. 'I see no reason why I should be treated as though I've got a disease. I was never in love with my husband and his death doesn't mean much to me.'

'So why bring him home in a box?'

This time she laughed. 'There's a little trouble over a will. A lot of money is involved and I am the sole beneficiary.'

'And you like to have him around to make sure of getting it?'

She nodded. 'His family are being difficult, you understand. They want proof of death. I went to Poland to bring his body home, together with the documents that prove he's dead.'

'What was he doing in Poland?'

'He was on business there. I got permission to bring his ashes out. The Communists were helpful and an American friend at their Embassy in Warsaw made all the arrangements.'

'And now?'

She opened her handbag for a cigarette. 'I'm going to enjoy myself.'

'Marry again, for instance?'

She shrugged. 'First of all, I'm going to have some fun. So, as the Italians have such a depressing attitude towards widowhood, I prefer to be unmarried.'

'It certainly improves your chances.' Misset looked about him. There was no sign of the brass-bound box. 'Where's Himself?' he asked.

'Serafino?' She smiled and, crossing to the mantelpiece, indicated a small decorated urn.

'Is that him?'

'Yes.'

'Is *that* all there was in that damned great box?'

'There were marble chippings.'

'To make him feel more cosy?'

She laughed again. 'You are not respectful, Sergeant Josephe Misset,' she said.

Misset was staring at the urn, fascinated. 'Seems funny to think he's in there,' he said.

She picked up the urn and crossed to him. 'Take a look.'

There appeared to be nothing inside but grey dust and a few crystals.

'I didn't know they could crystallise them,' Misset said.

She laughed again. 'The crystals provide perfume,' she explained. 'They use them for embalming. Smell.'

Misset sniffed, then stared, interested. 'And which is Himself?'

'Serafino is just – among them.'

Misset studied the contents of the urn thoughtfully, then he looked up. 'You'll have to be careful you don't use him in mistake for bath salts,' he said. 'It'd be awful to think he'd gone down the plughole.'

She laughed again and the slanting green eyes lost their chill. Putting the urn back in its place, she sat down opposite him and crossed her legs, so that he had a view of a handsome slice of thigh.

'I like you,' she said impulsively.

Misset wasn't neurotic about having friends.

'Now that we have cleared up my little mystery, what are *you* doing here?'

'Job I'm on.'

'May I know?'

Misset put on his 007 face. 'Can't tell you. Secret.'

She smiled at him again, this time warm and encouraging. 'We should see more of each other.'

Misset was all in favour of that. 'I have a few small trips to make. But otherwise – '

She changed her seat on the settee, moving against him so that he felt his arteries swell disconcertingly. 'Serafino was a wealthy man,' she said. 'His solicitors have already paid out something on account. Can one enjoy oneself here?'

Misset gestured. He never seemed to. 'Bit dull,' he said. 'They take the sidewalks in at ten-thirty. But you can get around if you're with someone who knows the place.'

'Would you like to show me, Sergeant Josephe?'

Misset hesitated only for a moment. A quick whip round the night clubs, he thought, then oops into bed.

'Be my guest,' he said.

She smiled. 'Do I seem wicked to you?'

Misset gave what he considered to be a modest smile. 'I'm

a bit of a specialist in the more subtle varieties of sin myself,'
he said. 'How about tonight?'

5

'I'm going home,' Pel said, closing the drawer of his desk. 'I haven't seen my wife for two days.'

Darcy fished out a packet and handed over a cigarette. 'Before you go, Patron,' he suggested. 'It'll be one less you'll need to smoke around the house.'

Pel nodded. The last cigarette before he headed for home had become almost a ritual. His wife was well aware that his efforts to stop smoking weren't meeting with much success but she was a tolerant woman who turned a blind eye to his bad habits. She knew he smoked too much, had an uncertain temper and was inclined to be mean with his money, but she was wealthy enough in her own right not to need his money, he was never bad-tempered with her and it was clear he made an effort to cut his smoking down whenever she was around.

He lit the cigarette and drew the utmost enjoyment from it while he could. 'I'll really give them up one of these days,' he said.

Darcy smiled. He didn't believe a word of it.

For a while they stood by Pel's car discussing the De Mougy robbery then Pel threw down the cigarette end and carefully placed his foot on it. 'There's just one thing,' he said thoughtfully. 'De Mougy has a reputation as a gambler and there's just a possibility he might have lost a lot. Let's check, shall we, Daniel? It might be he's in difficulties.'

'With what *he* possesses?'

'A lot of it's in property, paintings and so on. There might be problems with cash and it's the oldest dodge in the world to recoup your losses by saying you've lost something or had it stolen and then claiming the insurance on it. It's virtually impossible for an insurance company to prove you haven't, unless you're stupid enough to be caught selling it later. Let's find out how much it was insured for and if he *is* in difficulties. Let me know what you turn up. Soon as you can.'

Climbing into his car, Pel set off home with a feeling of a day well spent. He hadn't enjoyed it but, then, he didn't expect to enjoy his days. Pel never considered things should be easy. Life, he believed, was hard work. Being alive took nerve. If you lost your nerve, you might as well curl up and send for the undertaker. Nevertheless, there was a certain smug feeling of satisfaction at having suffered for the sake of the security of the Republic. Though he complained enough about it, Pel never really objected to hard work done to bring criminals to book. For Pel, being a detective was a crusade. Criminals were a blot on the fair land of France and it was his duty to remove them from circulation – preferably for as long as possible.

He drove slowly, his mind busy with what he'd been doing, enjoying the fact that he was well off enough now to live in a pleasant area outside the city. Since his marriage to Madame Pel, who ran an expensive hairdressing salon in the Rue de la Liberté near the Hôtel de Police and was wealthy beyond the dreams of a normal policeman – whose pay always precluded a life of sybaritic luxury – Pel had actually begun to his surprise to enjoy his leisure. What was more, he no longer had to struggle with a car whose doors might drop off at any moment. Madame had persuaded him it was time he abandoned the ancient Peugeot he drove – despite a life-time of squirreling his savings away, he had always considered himself too poverty-stricken to risk it – and he now drove a splendid new one. Modest in size, of course – the wrench of forking out always almost gave him heart failure – but new, nevertheless, so that he no longer suffered the insults of lorry drivers who liked to pull up alongside him at traffic lights and ask what sort of bottled gas he ran on.

Moving from the centre of the road where he'd wandered, deep in thought, he concentrated on his driving. He wasn't the world's best driver and had been known to run into ditches when his mind was occupied. Madame Routy met him at the door as he put the car away. Before his marriage, in the house in the Rue Martin-de-Noinville, Madame Routy, who had appeared to be the only bad cook in a country that prided itself on its culinary expertise, had been his housekeeper. She had been addicted to the television, so that even her bad cooking was rushed. Since his marriage – thanks to his wife's wealth and the new large house at Leu, near Fontaine – by some miraculous arrangement Madame Routy's television viewing had been restricted to the evenings in the small flat she occupied at the back of the building, with the result that she had amazed Pel by proving she could cook as well as anybody when she tried. He could only assume – grudgingly, mind you, as a good male chauvinist pig – that, since Madame Pel had worked this wonder, there were certain things that women could do better than men.

However, being Pel, he was never prepared to give much away in the way of friendliness, while Madame Routy's scowl indicated what she thought of him. She would have lain down and permitted Madame Pel to walk up and down her in spiked heels if necessary, but there was no relaxation of her long-held dislike for Pel.

'Wipe your feet,' she snapped.

Pel kept her waiting while he spent as long as he could at the job. 'What have you spoiled for dinner today?' he asked. Honours, he felt, were even.

Madame Routy's nephew, Didier Darras, was in the kitchen. As Pel appeared he stood up politely, a tall, sturdy boy with the sort of good looks that were going to make him a lady-killer before long. He had been a tower of strength to Pel in the days before his marriage. His grandfather was a sick man whom his mother regularly had to visit, so that for odd meals Didier had tagged on to Madame Routy in Pel's old house in the Rue Martin-de-Noinville. Pel never minded because Didier disliked Madame Routy's television as much as Pel did and had a great fondness for boules, fishing, and eating out, and they'd often disappeared into the blue just as Madame Routy finished cooking one of the disgusting dishes she had prepared in those days so that she'd had to eat it herself.

'I'm going to join the police,' Didier said.

'Already?' Pel was startled.

'I'm old enough.'

With a little mental arithmetic, Pel had to accept sadly that he was. Which meant that Pel had also grown older and

33

was probably even – Pel was never one to be optimistic – rapidly approaching the period of decline.

'Louise Bray says she'll be proud of me,' Didier went on. Louise Bray lived next door to him and had been his steady girlfriend from the day she'd first hit him over the head with her doll. 'I thought you'd tell me how to go about it.'

Pel sniffed. He could put a lot into a sniff and this one indicated doubt. 'Wouldn't it be better to go to university first?' he asked. 'Promotion's quicker.'

'You always said experience counted most.'

Pel agreed. He had never been over-fond of the young men who arrived on the force expecting rapid promotion simply because they had a degree. Some of them turned out to be awful and, because Pel had had to struggle to the top the hard way, he was sour enough to think everybody else should too.

'You'll need to submit a summary of your background,' he advised. 'What you've done. Sports. Exams you've passed and so on.'

'I've written it out. I've got it here with me.'

Pel read the sheet. 'You could have mentioned you know me,' he said. 'It might help.'

'It doesn't matter,' Didier said. 'They said so.'

'Who did?' Pel felt miffed.

'The type I saw. "Why make a fuss," he said, "when you know everything's all right? When you're aiming for something and can reach it easily, just go straight for it." That's what he said.'

Madame Pel was in the salon listening to Mahler. Everybody listened to Mahler these days, Pel noticed. He'd been suddenly discovered as if he were an old sock left lying around at the back of a cupboard and had suddenly fallen out. They said the fashion had been started by an English politician. Pel, who didn't think much of Mahler, decided that the English must have dull politicians.

Madame was looking beautiful. It wasn't too hard for her, of course, because she owned the most expensive beauty salon in the city. Brave women broke down when they couldn't afford to use it. Her salon was so successful, in fact, there was a story that a farm sow once wandered in by mistake and came out looking like Catherine Deneuve.

Without letting her see him, Pel poured apéritifs and sat down by the door to wait, not interrupting the music. He regarded his wife warmly. Some cops, he thought, fell for lady cops, some of whom these days managed to be attractive – take Claudie Darel, for instance! Some fell for the typists employed about the Hôtel de Police. Some fell for the lawyers' secretaries they bumped into in their work, even occasionally for lady lawyers. Misset fell for anything in skirts and Nosjean, it had to be admitted, also found it hard to resist a pretty girl – especially if she looked like Charlotte Rampling. The number of Charlotte Ramplings Nosjean had fallen for, in the guise of librarians, shop assistants, and secretaries, was nobody's business.

Some cops fell for people they'd interviewed, some for witnesses, some were even stupid enough to fall for women they'd arrested. Pel felt he'd been wise. His wife had her own business – and a lot of money besides, he thought comfortably – and, what was more, knew how to run it in such a way as to make colossal profits. She had her own interests and therefore didn't feel deserted and resentful when he was busy.

He waited for Mahler to finish. It seemed to go on for ever, but as it drew to a stop Madame looked round, saw him and turned her head so he could kiss her. She wasn't wearing her spectacles, Pel was pleased to note. Since she was inclined to be short-sighted, he always felt he could be seen to greater advantage without their assistance.

As he handed over the drinks, he described his activities for the last forty-eight hours – with more than a few sharp words about the church bells at Quigny. Madame listened with interest. Though she wasn't involved with Pel's work, she always liked to know what was going on. It was, she considered, much more exciting than watching elderly ladies have their hair shampooed and set.

'Who was it?' she asked.

'The Baronne de Mougy. She's one of your clients.'

Madame's salon didn't have customers. It had clients and they were so proud to be allowed to use it they happily paid not prices but fees.

'Road blocks were set up at once,' Pel went on. 'We stopped and searched cars but nothing turned up. I expect the gang were already clean away with the loot.'

'Unless,' Madame commented, 'it's still there.'

'Still where?'

'In the area where it was stolen. Perhaps they had someone waiting nearby they handed it to. Someone who knew the woods, for instance. Isn't that the way they work?'

It was indeed, Pel had to admit, and it might be an idea worth following up. Madame hadn't been married to a policeman for long but she was already catching on to the methods of criminals.

They had just settled down to enjoy their drinks when the telephone went. It was Darcy, and Pel exploded at once.

'You didn't have to telephone me tonight!' he snorted. 'De Mougy will keep until tomorrow!'

'It's not De Mougy, Patron,' Darcy explained. 'There's been a shooting.'

Pel sighed. 'Where?' he asked.

'Montenay. I've informed the office of the Public Prosecutor. Judge Polverari will be out there.'

'Casualties?'

'Two, Patron. One serious. Name of Huppert.'

'Do we know who did it?'

'No, Patron. I'm going along there now. It's that little metalwork factory just off the main street. The house adjoins the yard. Bardolle's out there.'

'I'll join you there.'

Madame raised only a token protest when Pel announced he was going out after he'd eaten. 'What is it?' she asked.

'Somebody's been shot at Montenay.'

'Just be careful.'

'I'm always careful,' Pel said. 'Especially with guns around. When I was a young cop, whenever guns were involved I always used to utter up a little prayer. "Don't let me get shot, Lord, because of my mother." I never was.'

She laughed and reached out to hold his hand for a moment. 'Don't stay out too late, Pel,' she said.

She was so easy-going about his disappearances, he felt it was about time he suggested they had a holiday. He hated holidays but he was unselfish enough – but only just – to be aware that his wife might feel differently.

'One day,' he said, 'we'll have a day or two off. Get away from things.'

She smiled. 'You'd die of boredom. That's why I've never done anything about that weekend house in the Jura.'

Pel was faintly shocked. In addition to the splendid new house at Leu, she had already converted rooms over her salon in the city so they could use it as a flat if anything big cropped up to keep Pel in the city too long. But she'd also talked of a weekend house by a lake so he could do some fishing and the idea of owning not two but *three* properties had appealed to Pel. He'd always fancied being a plutocrat.

'I like fishing,' he said indignantly.

'But not in the Jura,' she said placidly. 'On the River Orche. You'd die if something happened and you weren't involved.'

It was late when Pel reached Montenay. Fabrications Metaux de Montenay occupied a set of old buildings in the Rue Bucha, and all the lights were on. Alongside was the house belonging to the owner, an ugly red-brick building with a small and very formal front garden surrounded by a high fence and a gate which could only be opened by a key or by pressing a button inside the house. In effect, however, it was valueless because the small metalworks could be entered via two large red-painted wooden gates which filled an arch in a blank wall through which vehicles had to pass, and these led to a yard which backed on to the house. As Pel arrived, one of the gates was ajar and nearby, the pressmen, Fiabon, of *France Dimanche*, Henriot, of *Le Bien Public*, and Sarrazin, the freelance, were waiting. Sarrazin moved forward at once.

'Got anything to tell us, Chief?' he asked.

'I don't know anything myself yet,' Pel snapped.

A policeman was standing by the gate. 'Look out for the dog, sir,' he advised.

It was a timely warning. As Pel stepped through the gate, a lean-looking young Alsatian, attached to a ringbolt set in a wall by a long chain that gave it the run of a large part of the brick-paved yard, hurtled from the shadows at him, to be stopped only a metre short with a neck-breaking jerk. The clamour as it leapt up and down with bared fangs made Pel jump back into the forge. The desire to take a flying kick at it was only restrained by the fear that it might have his leg off. Pel had no high regard for dogs, not even police dogs, which, he felt, did little more than fight every other dog they came across.

He made threatening noises at the animal – having first made sure that the chain didn't allow it within reach – and, advancing warily round it, headed for the door. Darcy appeared.

'What happened?' Pel asked.

Darcy shrugged. 'Hard to tell, Patron. A major battle. We've already picked up seven or eight ejected cartridges.'

'Seven or eight? Who was hurt?'

'Owner and his wife.' Darcy glanced at his notebook. 'Jacqueline Huppert. Jacques Huppert. He says he heard someone in the yard and, because he found an intruder there three or four weeks ago, he went out. He says he was shot at on the other occasion – one shot. Tonight he was shot at several times and this time he fired back. When things had quietened down he turned round and found his wife lying in the doorway – with a bullet in her back.'

'Dead?'

'No. The local doctor – guy called Lachasse – sent her to hospital. He's still here.'

'Have someone sit alongside her bed, Daniel. In case she saw something. I'll see the doctor.'

Just inside the house, the owner of the yard was sitting in a chair. He looked deathly white and clutched a crimsoned towel. His jacket was on the chair back and he was wincing with pain. His shirt was stained with blood and the doctor was standing over him with cotton gauze, bandage and plaster. Judge Polverari was with them.

Pel introduced himself, and the doctor gestured at the wounded man. 'Huppert,' he said.

'Is it serious?'

'No. Slight. A flesh wound. Painful but not much more. He'll be using it more or less normally in a few days. It's his wife I'm worried about.'

'Is he in a fit state to tell me what happened?'

'Oh, yes. Bit of shock, that's all. He's all right. Good as new now.' The doctor patted Huppert's shoulder and moved away.

Huppert rose and with his good hand hung his jacket behind the door.

'Inform me,' Pel said.

'Well – ' Huppert drew a deep shuddering breath ' – my house adjoins the metalwork factory, as you can see, and I was sitting in the office going through the books when I heard a noise in the yard. So I grabbed my gun. I have one – '

'May I see it?'

Huppert fished one-handed in a drawer and produced an automatic in a holster attached to a belt. The dull blue gun-metal of the barrel was dark against the paler leather. 'FAS Apex 6.35,' he said. 'I've had it a long time. I'm allowed one because I have money on the premises occasionally. I bought it some years back from the owner when he left the country.'

Pel studied the gun. 'Only you ever touch it?' he asked.

'That's right. My wife's frightened to death of guns.'

'I'd better keep it for the time being.'

'Why? That's *my* gun. What if he comes again?'

'You'll be all right. There'll be one of my men handy. For a while, anyway. Until we've reassured ourselves that you're safe.' Pel gestured. 'Please continue.'

Huppert drew a deep breath. 'Well, as you know, someone shot at me about a month ago. Same sort of thing. I heard a sound and went out and a shot was fired.'

'At you?'

'Yes.'

Pel glanced at Darcy who nodded. 'It was reported, Patron,' he said. 'We have the details at the office. Nothing was found and we had to assume that it was somebody who'd let off his gun by accident. A bullet mark was found on the wall above the back door. It *could* have come from outside and that's what we had to assume. Nothing turned up. Nosjean went over it carefully. It was put on the file.'

Pel turned to Huppert and gestured to him to continue.

'It *must* have been someone shooting at me, mustn't it?' Huppert said. 'It frightened me. That's when I dug out the pistol. I haven't had it out of the safe for years but after that I thought I'd better. Then when I heard this noise tonight – '

'What sort of noise?'

'A sort of clink. As if something in the foundry had been moved. Something like that. I called to my wife to come down because there was somebody in the yard. She was reading in bed. Then as I went outside I was fired at from the darkness

39

– more than once. I fired back at the flash. I thought he'd gone into the forge so I went after him. It was then he hit me. I staggered to the house and that was when I found my wife lying in the doorway with a wound in her back. I telephoned the police and the doctor.'

'Where did the bullets that were fired at you come from, do you think?'

'Near the forge.'

'How near?'

'Near the old pump.'

'This intruder. What do you think he was after?'

'It could only be money. Wages. That sort of thing. He wouldn't want to cart away lumps of iron or metal sheeting or strips of brass, would he?'

'When do you pay your people?'

'Tomorrow.'

'And you have the money in the house?'

'No. I pick it up tomorrow from the bank and pay it straight out. It's not a lot anyway. We only have twenty employees.'

'Could anybody think you'd drawn it today?' Huppert looked puzzled. 'Have you been to the bank, for instance? Have you been out and come back carrying a bag that might seem to contain money?'

'Not today.'

'Who knows when you pay your people? Apart from them.'

'Only the bank. And Connie Gruye.'

'Who's Connie Gruye?'

'She comes here to do the accounts. She does the wages.'

Pel was silent for a moment. 'This intruder,' he said. 'Did you see him?'

'No.'

'Could your wife have? From her bedroom?'

'I shouldn't think so.'

They went upstairs and, looking from the window, decided it was unlikely. The bed was disturbed and the book Madame Huppert had been reading was still open alongside the telephone on the bedside table.

'Do you have much occasion to use the telephone at night?' Pel asked.

Huppert shrugged. 'Not much. Just once in a while. But it saves coming downstairs if the bell goes. Sometimes a

40

customer telephones late to save money. You'd be surprised how mean some of them are.'

Returning downstairs, Pel stared about him. 'Did you hear the intruder himself at all?' he asked. 'His footsteps, for instance.'

'Not really. I thought he was in the forge but I didn't see anything and I didn't hear anything after the first clinking sound until he started shooting.'

'Any indication where he got in?'

'Through the gates. They're secured by a chain and padlock but the chain's been cut.'

As Huppert passed a hand over his forehead and seemed to sway, Pel gestured. 'I think that'll do for the time being,' he said. 'I'll see you when you're over it a little. And you'll be wanting to see your wife, I expect.'

'Is she bad?'

'She's not good,' Doctor Lachasse admitted.

As Huppert disappeared, Pel turned to the doctor. 'How soon after it happened did you arrive?'

'Within minutes. Quarter of an hour at the outside.'

'On your own?'

'Of course.'

'I'm surprised the dog didn't bite you.'

'I was aware of it. I've been here before.'

'It nearly bit *me*,' Pel said. He turned to Darcy. 'Let's have enquiries made at the hospital,' he suggested. 'For dog bites. If there *was* a man in the yard he's probably in hospital minus a leg.' He turned back to the doctor. 'Where was Madame Huppert when you arrived?'

'She was lying in the hall. On her side. The wound was in her back, just below the shoulder blade. The bullet's in the upper abdominal region and I think it's perforated the liver. Huppert told me he found her lying on her face and was going to turn her on to her back when he saw the wound, so he propped her up on her side. It couldn't have been easy with only one hand.' Doctor Lachasse indicated a pile of bloodstained cushions lying in the corner of the kitchen. 'Then he telephoned – for me and the police.'

'Was she unconscious when you arrived?'

'Yes. But she rallied a little. She opened her eyes.'

'Say anything?'

41

'She muttered something I couldn't hear. Then she called for her husband. "Jacques," she said.'

'Anything else?'

'No. Just "Jacques". Twice. "Jacques", then a pause and "Jacques" again. She tried to say something else but then she became unconscious.'

'Know anything else about them?'

'They've been my patients for some time. Huppert's a hard-working man. His wife's probably the brains, though. There's also Madame Gruye – Connie Gruye – who comes in to do the books. She's a widow who lives next door.' The doctor gestured. 'That side. The other side's Arthur Démy. I gather he's just gone to Paris. He goes a lot. He's a computer expert. A bit of an odd type.'

Judge Polverari interrupted. 'What's this Connie Gruye like?' he asked. 'Young?'

The doctor gave a sad smile. 'I can see the way your mind's working. But I doubt if there was anything between her and Huppert.'

'Why do you doubt that?'

'Because I know her. She's older than Huppert and hardly ever speaks. What you'd call solid. Good with figures, though, I believe. She worked for the original owner and I think she was once hoping to be taken into the firm as a director. But he let her down, sold out to Huppert and went to live in the south. She got over it, though, and stayed with Huppert. She comes in two days a week to do the accounts and type letters. I expect she'll be around before long. I can't imagine her missing a thing like this. This place has been her life.'

6

As he did first thing every morning, Darcy appeared next day for a chat in Pel's office. They liked to call it a conference but it was really just a get-together to swop ideas. Claudie Darel arrived with coffee and Darcy fished out his cigarettes. Pel eyed them warily.

One of these days, he promised himself, he'd clear everything connected with smoking out of the house, empty the drawers where he kept his spare cigarettes and the cupboards where he kept the spare spare ones in case, by some mischance, he should run out not only of cigarettes but of spare ones too.

He took Darcy's cigarette sadly. It was a problem getting over smoking and unfortunately it was a problem that required a cigarette to help solve it.

'Pity you can't breathe through your ears, Patron,' Darcy said. 'It would save the smoke going down into your lungs.'

He sat back, enjoying his cigarette in a way that made Pel envious and set him wondering why he couldn't also be a devil about it and ignore the dangers, why he always had to worry about dying of lung cancer when Darcy obviously never gave it a thought.

They discussed Montenay. Bardolle was still out there.

'We've asked at the hospitals,' Darcy said. 'They all had a quiet night. No emergencies. No dog bites.'

'Which,' said Pel, 'is strange. I'd have expected something. How about local doctors?'

'They report none either.' Darcy frowned. 'What was he after?' he said. 'There couldn't have been much of any value about the place because they seem to be running on a shoe-string. Bardolle's talked to all the workers. They can tell him nothing. It's true what Huppert said. There was no money on the premises.'

'Somebody seems to have thought there was. Has Bardolle checked the backgrounds of the people who work for Huppert?'

'Yes, Patron. Still at it. All straightforward. One or two motoring offences. One assault. But that was years back when the guy was twenty. He's forty now and he's lived a blameless life ever since. One other – ' Darcy paused ' – drugs. Four years back. He told Bardolle he's kicked the habit now, but you never know.'

'Got the name?'

'Charles Tehendu. He's twenty-five. He's clever. Went to university but dropped out. Madame Huppert took him on because he's good with his hands.'

'*Madame* Huppert?'

'She seems to have done the hiring and firing. She even seems to have been the expert. Huppert runs the buying and selling, and if anything big comes up they contract it out. It's a bit of a Mickey Mouse outfit, with a lot of homemade gadgets. This Connie Gruye does the letters and the books.'

'Have you seen her yet?'

'Yes. Funny-looking dame. Looks like that terrifying aunt everybody claims to have but never does. Tall. Bust like a frigate under full sail. Doesn't say much. She turned up very early. Just after you left. Said she might be able to help. She didn't have much to offer, but she was useful for making coffee. Bardolle and the boys were beginning to feel the strain by then.'

'What about the bullets we found?'

'Ten altogether.'

'Ten? Was someone putting up an anti-aircraft barrage?'

'Ten, all the same, Patron. And all 6.35s.'

'All of them?'

'All of them. Whoever it was, he had the same calibre gun as Huppert. We found a 6.35 slug in a wooden beam near the door of the forge and another one in the plaster nearby. One of them must have been the one that nicked Huppert's arm. The other must have missed. There are also marks on the walls outside. Two of them on the wall near the Hupperts' back door. And three in the outside wall of the forge. It looks to me as if, when Huppert came out, three shots were fired at him. Two missed and one hit Madame Huppert. He fired

44

three shots in return. Then he went into the forge and two shots were fired at him there. The one in the beam and the one in the plaster. He fired two shots there, too. We found them at the opposite end of the forge, as if he'd fired from the doorway where he was standing. Ten in all. And all 6.35s.'

'Where did these 6.35s come from, do you think?'

'Could be anywhere but – ' Darcy fished among the papers on his desk ' – a consignment of 6.35s from Fabrique d'Armes Automatiques de St. Etienne's just gone missing on the way to Paris.' He tossed down a sheet. 'It came in a week or two ago.'

'What do Forensic Ballistics say?'

'They haven't finished yet. They'll let us know.'

'Can Bardolle handle it for the time being?'

'Yes. I've got the boys out there searching the place still. Until they've finished there's not much we can do.'

'Right. So for the moment let's go and see the De Mougy staff. We can't leave that too long in case whoever was involved gets busy working out an alibi.'

There seemed an incredible number of people at the château at Mirebeau to look after a family of two. The Baronne had done her duty and provided the Baron with a son who was away at school so that the château was occupied – when they weren't living in their apartment in Dijon or the chalet in Switzerland or the house they owned on the Promenade des Anglais in Nice – only by the Baron and his wife. But it wasn't a big château – nothing like Bussy-Rabutin or Ancy-le-Franc or the châteaux of the Loire – and there had been no question of it being allowed to decay.

The baron's butler let them in. He obviously didn't approve of them. Police tramping round the château could get the place a bad reputation. Pel returned his icy look with a glare. Pel wasn't very big or very prepossessing and, with his eccentricities, could well be considered a subject for being locked away somewhere quiet, but he was never one to be put on. Especially by a butler. Or for that matter a baron either. He wasn't a Socialist who objected to people with wealth or even to people like butlers living on the outgoings from wealth. He wasn't politically inclined at all, in fact, and considered all politicians – if they weren't crooks – to be half-

45

witted. But he didn't like self-importance and he made it clear to the butler that he was in danger of being charged under the Penal Code of obstructing the police in the performance of their duties. After that the butler became more helpful and produced a full list of the staff, together with their ages and length of service and a résumé of their backgrounds.

Pel studied it carefully. 'You've missed one,' he pointed out.

The butler studied the list. 'I don't think so, Monsieur,' he said coldly.

'Yes,' Pel insisted. '*You*. What's your name?'

The butler sniffed. 'Algieri,' he said. 'Hubert Algieri.'

Pel's head jerked up. 'That's not a local name.'

'No, sir. My family comes from Marseilles.'

Pel added the name to the list. 'Age?'

'Fifty-one.'

'Length of service?'

'I came here as a young footman. I was nineteen at the time.'

Only three of the staff had not been with the Baron for most of their lives – one of the under-gardeners, a scullery maid and Josso, the chauffeur. The scullery maid, who was seventeen, was a country girl who was terrified of being put in prison. But you could never tell these days, Pel thought bitterly. She might well be the mistress of Maurice Tagliatti or Pépé le Cornet's kid sister. After all, everybody watched television and, since these things were possible in the minds of script writers, people went out of their way to make them possible in reality. The under-gardener, a thin man with a face like a ferret, looked so evil that it would have been easy to charge him on the spot with conspiracy, but it was never as simple as that. He was probably as honest as the day was long because appearances were nothing to go by and one of the biggest con men Pel had ever come across had had a face so innocent he was in the habit of posing as a priest.

It looked like being a long haul.

Stomping through the hall, Pel gestured. 'I'd like somewhere we can talk to the staff,' he announced curtly.

Algieri's eyebrows raised. 'Talk to the staff?' he said.

'It's usual when there's been a robbery.'

46

'I don't think you'll find any member of *this* staff involved in it, sir.'

'I'll be the judge of that,' Pel snapped.

Algieri sketched what was nearly a shrug. 'You'd better use my sitting room,' he said. 'I can occupy myself for a while.'

'After we've talked to you.'

'Me, Monsieur?'

'You can be first.'

They worked through the staff carefully, concentrating, after Algieri, on those who hadn't been long at the château.

Algieri himself answered their questions carefully, giving a great deal of thought to them in a way that had Pel on the edge of his chair with impatience.

'How long had you known the Baron would be going to Deauville?' he asked.

'Two months, Monsieur. The Baron always informed me first.'

'After you, who else did he tell?'

'Madame Gracy, the housekeeper, of course.'

'What about the estate manager?'

'The Baron manages the estate himself.'

'What about the Baronne's personal maid?' Pel glanced at the list he'd acquired. 'Suzy Vince. She'd be informed, of course, wouldn't she?'

'Of course. But not immediately. Her interest would be solely in the clothes the Baronne would be taking with her.'

'And the jewels?'

'I beg your pardon?'

'The jewels. She'd know about those, too, wouldn't she?'

'Ah! Of course.'

'Where are the jewels kept?'

'In the safe, monsieur. It's a very good safe, I can promise you.'

'Who has the key?'

'It's a combination.'

'Who knows it besides the Baron?'

'Nobody, Monsieur. The Baron's a very cautious man. He was a leader of the Resistance during the war and learned to keep secrets. The habit's remained with him.'

'Surely the Baronne would know?' Pel was banking on the idea that the Baronne might have communicated it to her maid.

'No, Monsieur. The Baronne does *not* know. She always has to ask the Baron for her jewels and he always fetches them personally for her.'

'But the maid would know what the Baronne was taking with her, wouldn't she? She'd wish to know, because of the clothes that would be worn with them.'

'The other way round, I think, Monsieur. The jewels are worn to match the clothes, not the clothes to match the jewels. The Baronne has great taste and she's a very beautiful woman.'

'I know the Baronne,' Pel snapped.

Well enough, in fact, to wonder if she could have tipped somebody off. If she was devious enough to have an affair with someone, as she had, was she also devious enough to insure the jewels privately under a false name and then arrange to have them stolen and handed back to her? It wasn't a bad idea. The insurance money and the sale of the jewels afterwards – because she'd *have* to sell them – could bring in a small fortune.

Algieri insisted on being present when other members of the staff were interviewed. It was in the Baron's interest, he said. Pel didn't argue.

Josso, the chauffeur, seemed to have an impeccable background, with a whole array of references. The butler, the housekeeper and Suzy Vince, the personal maid, seemed so loyal it was painful; while the under-gardener with the evil face turned out to be simple-minded; and the scullery maid burst into tears and had to be allowed to go.

When they returned to the Hôtel de Police, De Troquereau was in the yard talking to Prélat, of Fingerprints. In front of them, propped against the wall, was the green bicycle used by the man who had stopped the Baron de Mougy and his wife.

'How did you get on?' Pel asked.

De Troq' looked round. 'Oh, no problems,' he said.

'At the hotel, I mean,' Pel said maliciously.

De Troq' frowned. 'No problems, Patron.'

48

'Sleep well?'

'Excellently.'

It turned out that De Troq' had reconnoitred the ground better than Pel had. He had noticed the church clock very quickly and had found, instead of the main hotel, an annexe at the bottom of the garden with a room on the far side that looked over the river.

'Why, Patron?' he asked, smiling. 'Did the bells worry you?'

Pel scowled. 'Let's get on,' he said, indicating the bicycle. 'Any dabs?'

Prélat shrugged. 'Just the kid's I told you about, Patron,' he said.

'It's got a name, *Intrépide*, on the frame,' De Troq' added. 'Some kid who likes to think he's riding it in the Tour de France, I suppose. We've also found a number under the saddle. It's not very clear but I think it's 784326. It's hard to tell. Do we put it out to the press and appeal for the owner?'

Pel frowned. The De Mougy robbery was big-time and the people who'd planned it were equally big. It would pay to tread warily.

'Not yet,' he said. 'It'll be stolen. They wouldn't use one that could be traced to them. Let's wait and see if anyone turns up asking for it. This was a planned job and those boys who stopped De Mougy and his wife knew they had those jewels with them when they left for Deauville. We have to find the connection. Have you tried Georges Ballentou?'

They all knew Georges Ballentou. Every police force had its Georges Ballentou – someone they were always arresting but someone for whom they managed somehow to maintain a certain amount of respect. Ballentou was – or had been – a criminal, but never a dangerous one, and he was a man who always accepted his punishment without whining, was always polite and never gave trouble, and he was a man moreover who managed to have a sense of humour.

'Ballentou's going straight, Patron,' Darcy pointed out.

'Do they ever go straight?' Pel growled. As far as criminals were concerned, Pel was an arch-cynic.

'Armed robbery's not the sort of thing he went in for.'

'He did once.'

'He was pushed into it by that type he was working with.'

'He was a busy little burglar in his day, though, wasn't he? He's spent a lot of time inside.'

'Not for two years, Patron. I think his spirit's broken. His wife died while he was doing his last stretch. Cancer. And now his daughter's just died, too. Soon after he got out. Effects of drugs. She got on them while he was in gaol. They knocked a bit off so he could be with her at the end. He blames himself, because he wasn't in a position to help her. It's what made him go straight.'

Pel gestured. 'Bring him in all the same,' he said.

Ballentou was a small man with a long face, and sad bloodhound eyes outlined with purple circles. He stood up politely as Pel and Darcy appeared.

'Why have you brought me in?' he asked. 'I've done nothing.'

'Gone out of business, have you?' Pel asked.

'For good.'

Pel waved to him to sit down and perched on the edge of the table. 'Know Quigny, Georges?' he asked.

'Of course I know Quigny. My wife came from round there. We lived there for a while. What are you after?'

'There's been a bit of trouble there,' Darcy said.

'What sort?'

'Armed hold-up. Baron de Mougy lost the family jewels.'

'Well, it wasn't me. It's not the sort of thing I go in for.'

'You did once, Georges.'

Ballentou looked sullen. 'That was the only time and I didn't pull the trigger. I've never used a gun since.'

'All right, Georges, I'll take your word for it.' Pel offered cigarettes and Ballentou took one. 'I'm sorry about your daughter.'

Ballentou's eyes flickered, then he shrugged. 'That's the way it goes, isn't it? She got in with a stupid lot who introduced her to drugs. Soft ones, of course. No harm, they said. But that's how it starts, isn't it? Soft ones lead to hard ones, and somebody was quick to supply her.'

'All the same, I'm sorry. You've never given us much trouble.'

Ballentou managed a smile. 'Except for a bit of breaking and entering now and then.'

'We always knew it was you, Georges.'

'At least I was tidy. I never wrecked the places I worked over.'

'Pity you wasted so many years doing something you weren't very good at.'

Ballentou smiled again. 'Perhaps if I'd realised a bit earlier,' he said, 'I might have tried something else.'

'You were good with electricity.'

'I wasn't thinking of electricity. I was thinking of bank robberies.' Ballentou's sad smile came again. 'Only I never had that much courage and guns scared the living daylights out of me.' He gestured. 'All the same, I'm told you can get used to them if you try. You never know, if I'd tried I might have been good at it.'

'Come off it, Georges,' Darcy said. 'It was never your scene.'

'Perhaps not. So why did you bring me in? Surely not to discuss what I might have been? I might have stood for the district in the House of Representatives if I'd given it my attention. I might even have been President of France.' Ballentou's smile came again. It was a frail sort of smile but it was sweet and gentle and genuine.

'Know where Maurice Tagliatti's operating these days, Georges?'

'Is that what you're after? Information?'

'It might be. You're far from stupid – except about being dishonest – and you've been inside. People who've been inside hear lots of things from other people who've been inside with them. A lot of plans are made inside. People inside don't have much else to do except make plans. What about Maurice? Heard anything of him lately?'

'I never worked for Maurice Tagliatti. He's big time. Casinos chiefly.'

'Jewels, too, Georges. Where's he operating these days?'

'Where he's always operated, I suppose. Nice. Marseilles. South coast. It's a long time since he had any interests round here.'

'He ran a wine business and used to come up here to buy his stocks.'

'Not lately. He's acquired a taste for the dolce vita. He stays where it's comfortable.'

And where the pickings were good, Pel thought. Where the jet-set operated, people with more money than was good for them, people like De Mougy who had enough possessions to be careless about them. Ballentou was right. Maurice Tagliatti, with whom Pel had tangled on more than one occasion, preferred these days to live the velvet life. He was more than likely driving a Cadillac with a bright little thing alongside him swathed in mink and dripping in diamonds.

'What about Pépé le Cornet?' he asked.

'Now you're talking,' Ballentou said. 'It's more his line.'

'What about that type who used to work for him? A strong-arm boy. Pépé began trusting him with jobs. Only he wasn't as clever as Pépé thought and he did a stretch for a bank robbery when he was a bit careless.'

'Nick the Greek.'

'That's the one.' Why did all Greeks seem to be called Nicou, Nicos, Nicolaou, Nicolaidis or Nicopopoulos, so that they all carried the same nom de guerre? 'Nicopopoulos. Arion Nicopopoulos. Likes guns. Mixed up in those hold-ups near Rheims. Where's he? He's disappeared.'

Ballentou shrugged. 'He was never picked up for the robberies. I expect he's in Rheims.'

'He could be here, too.' Pel paused. '*He* was never slow to use a gun. Know anyone else who uses a gun? We've heard that a consignment from Fabriques d'Armes Automatiques de St. Etienne has disappeared in Paris. Heard anything about that?'

'Not till you just told me.'

'Who took it?'

'I can guess, but it would be worth my life to tell you.'

'Was it Pépé le Cornet's lot?'

'You said it, not me. What are you after?'

'A gun was pointed,' Darcy said. 'Some type's also been pulling triggers round Montenay.'

'Who're you thinking of? Apart from Nick the Greek?'

'I'm thinking of Patrice Trafault. Known as Pat Boum – Pat the Bang. Good with clockwork. Explosives expert. Likes guns and armed robberies. He was in when you were in.

52

Same time as Nick. He came out a fortnight ago. Same time as Richard Selva, who was sent down for handling drugs.'

Ballentou looked up. 'Is *he* out?' he said.

'Did you know him?'

'In the same block.'

'Did *they* know each other? Selva, Pat the Bang and Nick.'

'They detested each other. Selva thought Nick had been trying to muscle in on his scene – the drugs game.'

'Had he?'

'He might have been.'

'What about plans? To hold up the Baron de Mougy, say, and relieve him of his valuables? Heard any whispers about that?'

Ballentou shook his head. 'They weren't planning together. They didn't get on well enough. They were all running rackets inside and they didn't trust each other. Anyway – ' Ballentou shrugged ' – De Mougy won't miss what he's lost. He can afford to replace it. In fact, it's a pity I didn't know where he kept them. I might have had a go myself.'

'You'd have been caught, Georges.'

Ballentou nodded. 'Yes, I expect I would'

'What are you up to now, George?'

'Working as an electrician at Metaux de Dijon. I'm too old now to do much else but go straight. Besides, my wife – and then my – Michelle – ' Ballentou lifted his face, his expression full of sadness. 'She was a good kid, you know,' he said.

'I met her, Georges,' Darcy said. 'Last time I picked you up, remember? I had to wait. She gave me coffee. Pretty girl. Who's looking after you now?'

'Her cousin. My niece. Kid called Wathus. Imogen Wathus. My sister's daughter. I always hoped – ' Ballentou stopped and sighed ' – I ought to have been a better father, but it's too late now.'

7

It hadn't been the best of days for Misset. His mother-in-law had seen him at the station with Ada Vocci and he had had to offer a long story about having to chase a pickpocket. Neither his mother-in-law nor his wife had believed him and things had been tense ever since. In addition, the children were whining and he was short of cash. However, after a couple of drinks he was in a more mellow mood and changed into his best suit slowly and with pleasure.

'Where are you off to?' his wife demanded as he appeared in the kitchen.

'On the job,' he said. 'Shadowing.'

'In those clothes?'

'It's an inside job. Hôtel Centrale. Got to be decently dressed.'

Misset avoided her eyes. Annette Misset was a good-looking woman, if on the large side. There were times when Misset looked at his wedding photograph and saw them both, slim and handsome, and wondered where they'd gone to. Things were closing in on him, he felt. He needed elbow room. In Misset's world, it was always the firm upstanding man who made the running while the women were always small dark-eyed houris with the submissiveness of geisha girls; and the life they inhabited was always one without kicks in strong male teeth or a wife with a face as wooden as the trees of Lorraine to ask questions about where they were going.

At the Hôtel de Police he managed to borrow money from Lagé. Lagé was approaching retirement and was easy-going enough even to help other people with their work, something Misset never hesitated to take advantage of.

'I'll see you get it back,' he pointed out earnestly.

Lagé nodded expressionlessly. He'd lent money to Misset before.

Misset's car was still at the garage so he took a bus. It seemed slow and old and he was in a bad temper by the time he arrived, but the smile with which Ada Vocci rose to meet him made him feel better at once.

They ate at a small restaurant near the Church of Notre Dame and, though the bill took Misset's breath away, she was holding his hand as they left.

'We'll walk, shall we?' Misset was still reeling from the cost of the meal.

'When we're dancing,' she smiled, 'why arrive tired?'

Misset's smile was a little forced but the taxi arrived almost before the door closed behind them. Ada indicated it with her handbag. 'Almost as though they were expecting us,' she said.

Misset gave the name of the night club and they roared out of the Place Notre Dame into the Place de la Libération at top speed and manoeuvred for a right turn.

'He's shifting a bit,' Misset observed. His voice grew louder. 'And, name of God, he's taking us the long way round!' Alert at once, the man of the world, he thought how much it was going to cost.

The taxi was swinging in a wide circle, its tyres whining as it roared dangerously across the stream of traffic, and Misset reached forward to air his protest. But, as he half rose, he was thrown off-balance as the taxi swerved violently with screaming brakes to avoid a big Mercedes which shot across their path. The crunch as the wings of the two vehicles touched flung him to the floor and, as their speed caused them to swing, he rolled over on to his back. By the time he'd regained his seat, an argument had started between the taxi driver and the owner of the Mercedes. Misset was just about to climb out and arrest everyone in sight when Ada spoke.

'Let's try another one,' she said coolly.

It was typical of her that, as she stepped from the taxi, another one happened to be passing and they climbed into it at once. Immediately, the driver of the original taxi broke off his argument in alarm, but his arm was grabbed by the driver of the Mercedes. Misset saw him break free and run across the Place de la Libération towards a telephone box.

They danced for a while in the semi-darkness. Ada was clinging to Misset as if she'd fall down without him and, although the invitation to take the last lingering drink in her room at the Centrale was not uttered, it was as real as if it had been printed on a piece of pasteboard and decorated with RSVP. Misset's breathing had become slightly constricted. The whispers in his ear and the silk dress, cut low at the top, were almost too much for him and his dark glasses persisted in steaming up.

He was on the point of swinging her out through the front door and into a taxi before she could change her mind, when he saw the man in the gold-threaded suit, sitting by the bar and talking into the telephone. Misset's pleasurable anticipation changed to a chilly alarm and then to annoyance, as he decided he was a private detective put on his tail by his wife. She was a good Catholic with firm ideas about morality and liked to keep a sharp eye on Misset, so that he could only suppose she had finally decided to make the shadowing professional.

As they headed for the entrance, he saw without surprise the telephone slammed down but, as the little man in the gold-thread suit swallowed his drink and dived out ahead of them, Misset swung Ada round abruptly and led her to the side door. A taxi was waiting across the road and he pushed her into it quickly.

'Aren't you coming?'

'Later,' Misset said, doing his James Bond act. 'You go along and keep things warm. There's a little chap here I ought to see. Police business,' he added portentously. 'I'll be there in a few minutes.'

There were only a few late-night taxis about as he slipped round the corner to the front entrance of the club. Moving quietly under the trees, he found the little man in the gold-thread suit waiting by the bus shelter across the road from the front door, trying to see what was going on inside. Misset took off his glasses and slipped them into his pocket.

The little man was lighting a cigarette but at the last moment he heard Misset approaching and swung round just as Misset's hand shot out and grabbed him by the collar.

'Police officer,' Misset said. 'Did Annette Misset put you up to this?'

The little man was choking on the smoke he'd swallowed. 'Who's Annette Misset?'

He tried to wriggle free and Misset slammed him back against a tree but then, from across the road, he heard running feet and whirled in alarm. Misset wasn't half as tough as he liked to think.

As he turned to see what was coming up behind him, he felt the glowing end of the cigarette pressed against his hand. He yelled and let go, only to receive a violent and very professional clout at the side of the head that made his eyes feel loose. The little man slipped between his fingers. Stumbling to his knees, half-dazed, Misset saw him join another man and together they vanished between the trees.

As Misset rose to his feet, an elderly Peugeot pulled up alongside him.

'They've gone.' The voice came from the dark interior. 'Jump in.'

Misset remembered Ada Vocci waiting for him, but a hand reached out and dragged him into the car, which started immediately with a speed which made Misset think he was being kidnapped or that his wife had planned some sort of beating-up to pay him back for all his wrongdoings.

They drove for a while away from the Hôtel Centrale then, as they rounded the corner, the man in the driver's seat, a short thickset military-looking man with spectacles, turned and smiled.

'We'll not catch them,' he said. 'So you might as well relax.'

Misset stared. 'Are you in on this as well?'

'I was watching you.'

'Why?'

'I need to talk to you.'

Misset's anger was coming back, now that the danger had passed, and he was beginning to remember Ada Vocci's low whispers and the vast bed at the Hôtel Central. 'What about?'

'I've got your name. Detective-Sergeant Misset, isn't it?'

'Who put you on to this?'

'Chief-Inspector Pel. I also talked to an Inspector Darcy. They agreed.'

'Agreed what?'

'That I could pick you up.'

'Are you a cop, too?'

'Well, sort of. Name of Chaput. Major Chaput. Service de Sureté de la République.'

Misset gave up. 'Who sent you?'

'Never mind who sent me.' Chaput stopped the car and offered a cigarette.

Misset was convinced now that Pel and Darcy were after him for neglecting his duty, for corruption – he'd accepted one or two small bribes in the past – or for dispensing to the press information he picked up at the Hôtel de Police.

Chaput lit a Gauloise that made the car stink like a Paris taxi. 'Josephe Misset, isn't it?'

'Look,' Misset said. 'What *is* this? I've never met you before, have I?'

'No.' Chaput gestured. 'But your activities have recently crossed the operations on the periphery of a search area I'm concerned with.'

Misset dragged smoke down into his lungs. Somewhere, he had always felt there was a golden future for Josephe Misset and perhaps this man, Chaput, who was obviously someone important, held the key to it.

'Don't tell me you're going to offer me a million francs to become a spy or something,' he said.

'Not exactly,' Chaput said. 'On the other hand, I think you ought to know what's going on.'

'You'll be telling me *you*'re a spy next.'

'Let's say I'm an agent – of sorts.'

Chaput had an ominous stillness that was vaguely perturbing. He didn't move much and he spoke in a low voice as though he had denied himself instinctive reaction – as though years of caution had kept his eyes and hands and mouth expressionless under any emotion.

'Some of us play small but important rôles,' he said. 'At the moment I'm wanting to enlist your help. I should have thought being like James Bond would appeal to a man like you.'

Misset wasn't so sure. He remembered the film where Bond was strapped to a table with a circular saw coming up between his legs.

'There's nothing very dangerous in what I want you to do,'

Chaput went on. 'You're acquainted with a lady at the Hôtel Centrale, I believe?'

Ada Vocci swung abruptly back into Misset's memory, all warm arms, low-cut dress and bedroom eyes.

'You're not telling me – '

'A Russian agent has just crossed into France via Poland, Germany and Belgium. Name of Spolianski. Haven't got the details yet. Just the name.'

'Sounds like a violinist in a symphony orchestra.'

'Isn't. Assure you.' The comments were rapped out like coins dropping from a slot machine. 'File on Soviet network crossed at the same time.'

'I read about it. In the paper.'

'Been traced to France. We think this agent's the lady you've been spending your time with.'

'Ada Vocci?' Misset wanted to laugh.

'Spolianski,' Chaput corrected him. 'The route's the same. Poland, Germany and Holland. Dates are the same, too.'

'What about the Patron? Where does he come into this?'

'He knows about it. I talked to him this evening. Not very long before I picked you up.'

'What did he say?'

'He said they were fully extended but he was agreeable to me using you.'

I'll bet he was, Misset thought. Misset was under no delusions about how he was regarded by Pel.

'He said you were already making enquiries in the area I'm interested in. Is that so?'

Misset remembered Inspector Briand. 'Yes,' he said. 'I suppose so.'

'And those two gentlemen you were having trouble with just now were part of it, I suppose? Right, then. Apart from those enquiries, you're answerable only to my department. Chief Inspector Pel will want to know what you're up to, of course, but you'll take your orders from me.'

Misset still wasn't convinced. 'You're not kidding me, are you?' he asked.

'Why not ring Chief-Inspector Pel and find out? There's a phone in the bar over there.'

Misset shook his head. The one thing he wasn't prepared

to do was ring Pel at home. He could just imagine the blast he'd receive.

'Then try headquarters. They know about it.'

Misset headed for a nearby bar and used the telephone. Darcy happened to be still in his office and he confirmed what Chaput said.

'He says I'm to take orders only from him,' Misset said.

'That's right,' Darcy agreed. 'You're nothing to do with us while he's here.'

Misset was annoyed to hear the relief in Darcy's voice but he was reassured nevertheless. He returned to Chaput's car and climbed in. 'What am I supposed to do?' he asked.

'What do you know about her?'

'Nothing except what she's told me. She went to Poland to fetch her husband out. He's a Milan businessman. Serafino Vocci. He died there.'

'You sure?'

'I saw him. At least, I saw what's left of him.'

'It's a good story,' Chaput said after Misset had explained. 'Do you believe it?'

Misset considered. He was always one to give credit for a thumping good lie. 'I must admit it sounds a bit steep,' he admitted.

Chaput gestured with his cigarette. 'What better place to bring out a bulky file than in a coffin? Border guards are human and inclined to be moved by the sight of grief.'

'There wasn't a coffin. Just this little urn.'

'Nothing else?'

'Only suitcases and the box she brought the urn in.' Misset gestured with his hands. 'About this size. She says it's full of marble chippings.'

'And under the marble chippings? Couldn't she have a false bottom?'

Misset grinned. 'There's nothing false about *her* bottom.'

Chaput cleared his throat. 'Stay friendly with her. But don't get involved. I want to know where the file is. It's a pretty bulky package, I gather.'

'What do I do when I find out? Report to you?'

'Through your office. Just be careful.'

'Why? Is anybody else interested in this file?'

60

Chaput managed a smile. 'Well,' he said, 'the people who lost it will be, won't they?'

As Chaput's car vanished, Misset stood on the pavement for a long time, staring after it. To his surprise, his knees felt as if they'd come unhooked and he had to pull himself together with a jerk.

The zest had gone out of the evening. Chaput's talk and the men who had attacked him had left a nasty taste in his mouth, so that the lust had drained out of him. It was a long walk to the Hôtel Centrale and by now, he decided, Ada Vocci would be asleep. The frustration almost choked him.

On the other hand – he paused, a half-smile on his face – this really was one for the book. Trailing a foreign agent! If he found out where that file was, Pel couldn't refuse him the promotion to inspector he'd been chasing for years.

Misset smiled to himself. Josephe Misset, he thought proudly. The well-known spy. It was one in the eye for Pel. He was free to move where he liked. Turn up at the Hôtel de Police when he liked. Leave when he liked. Doubtless there'd be expenses too. The Paris set-up was never afraid to cough up. A bit different from the penny-pinching methods of local forces. Misset straightened his shoulders. Tomorrow was another day and Ada Vocci would still be around.

He thrust his shoulders back. What was more, he thought, it ought to shut his wife up, too. There could be no comeback from her because for once, weird as his story would seem, it was true and she could prove it by contacting the Hôtel de Police.

8

When Pel appeared next morning, his wife was drinking her coffee in the morning room. A morning room! Sometimes Pel was staggered at the advance in his fortunes. Where once he had eaten in the kitchen, he now had the choice of two rooms, neither of them the kitchen.

As he sat down, Madame Routy appeared with fresh coffee and croissants. The coffee tasted like real coffee and the croissants were that morning's.

'The Baronne de Mougy,' Pel said.

His wife smiled. 'Friend of yours?' she asked.

Pel frowned. 'Geneviève de mon coeur,' he said. 'There is only one woman in my life.'

She leaned over to kiss him. 'What about the Baronne de Mougy?'

'Is she up to anything these days?'

'Up to anything?'

'A man? Something like that.'

Madame smiled. 'Nadine de Mougy is always up to something. Any woman married to that old stringbean would inevitably be up to something.'

'Her jewels are worth around half a million francs.'

Madame's eyebrows lifted. 'And you think she might have sold them and *claimed* to have been robbed?'

Once more, Pel noticed how quickly she caught on. 'The Baron was with her when it happened,' he said. 'It's possible, however, that one of them's working a fast one with the insurance companies. De Mougy's pretty mean.' Pel was mean, too, but he preferred to think of himself as careful. 'That's how people become wealthy, of course. And it's also been known for women to *arrange* to be robbed. To spite their husbands. To get money. Because they've overspent. Because they're being blackmailed. There are a lot of reasons.'

62

'And you wish me to keep my ears open?'

'You did once before. You discovered she had a lover.'

'That was when we first got to know each other.'

Pel's stern face dissolved in a smile of pleasure. It wasn't used to such extravagances and it made him look bilious.

'I'm wondering if she has another,' he said. 'I imagine cuddling the Baron would be about as exciting as cuddling a desk lamp. Perhaps you could keep your ear to the ground.'

Madame Routy had just appeared to clear away and was listening avidly.

'Paul Morey on television,' she pointed out, 'says that *most* police cases are solved from the gossip of passers-by.'

Pel glared. 'The world of the media,' he observed acidly, 'is full of people who can't do things commenting on the work of people who can.'

Madame Routy gave him the benefit of a sneer and disappeared.

Madame Pel laughed. 'You really shouldn't torment her like that, Pel,' she said.

Pel was unrepentant. 'She shouldn't offer observations on things that don't concern her.'

He kissed his wife and headed for the door. Madame Routy was waiting with his brief case. She held it as if she hoped it contained a bomb.

Taking it, Pel emerged into the sunshine as cautiously as if he were appearing for a *High Noon* confrontation with a baddy with pistols in the main street. He didn't like mornings very much. On the whole he didn't like afternoons a great deal either.

Despite being called to the Hôtel de Police in the middle of the evening, however, he had suffered no pangs of resentment at finally getting rid of Misset. Misset was the most troublesome member of his team and on more than one occasion had been within an ace of being returned to traffic duty. At least, for a while he was out of Pel's hair and they could get on with the job without fear that he'd bungle it.

He'd heard Major Chaput's story and was happy to let him share Misset with Briand of Counterfeit Currency. Somehow, some instinct – no more – made it hard to believe what he'd been told. Beautiful spies! It only happened in novels. Besides, he had no wish to be involved with spies. His job was

63

stamping out crime – the more crime was stamped out, the better he was pleased – and it was none of his brief to get involved with international to-ings and fro-ings.

From time to time, of course, the Secret Service did turn up in their diocese and wasted their time looking for something that didn't exist. Last time it was an American sergeant who had gone missing in Germany and was believed to have crossed into France with secret documents. But there had been no case in spite of the top priority classification given to it. No secrets. No spies. Nothing. Just a lot of work with nobody really knowing what they were after because the people who were employing them refused to tell them anything beyond a lot of hazy names and addresses that had caused them to tramp around for days until they'd finally been told the alarm was false. The American sergeant hadn't disappeared with secrets at all. The secret documents had been put in the wrong file and the American sergeant had fallen into a dam after celebrating too well.

No, he decided, let the people in Paris handle the spies. If they didn't see through Misset within twenty-four hours the French Security System wasn't what it was cracked up to be. They might even, he thought with some pleasure, recruit Misset and send him to Moscow.

The last thing he wanted was interference from Paris. Burgundy – on this Pel was adamant – was for Burgundians – not for members of Security or Counterfeit Currency. They didn't understand Burgundy. They expected Burgundians to behave like Parisians, who always felt that Paris reflected the whole nation and that anywhere else was pioneer country. They regarded people who returned to Paris from the provinces, in fact, as if they were as daring as Christopher Columbus, and were lucky to have survived the experience. For outsiders, Pel had little love and at the moment there wasn't just *one* outsider, there were two. The damned place was being invaded.

When he arrived at the Hôtel de Police Claudie Darel was waiting for him. Her first words made his face grim. The hospital had telephoned. Madame Huppert had died during the night.

When Darcy appeared he looked like a Chasseur Alpin

spruced up to do a guard of honour for the President. Pel took the smile off his face.

'Madame Huppert died during the night,' he said.

Darcy frowned. 'So now,' he said, 'instead of an assault with an offensive weapon, we're investigating a murder.'

Pel nodded. That always made things different. 'We'd better get out there,' he said. 'What about De Mougy? Found anything?'

Darcy nodded. 'He's been losing a lot. He was in Monte Carlo recently and he lost heavily. He's also been backing losers at the races, and a couple of companies he invested in – ' Darcy tossed a file on the desk ' – those are they – have just folded. *And* – ' Darcy's smile came back ' – that jewellery *was* insured, Patron. Heavily. Think he's working a fast one? He was pretty calm.'

Pel shrugged. 'We'll have to give him the benefit of the doubt, of course, because he's influential and wealthy enough to take a few losses without panicking. All the same, if he *is* trying to defraud the insurance company, we'll haul him in, influence or no influence. What do the insurance people say?'

'They're sending down their best man from Paris.'

Name of God, Pel thought. Another one! Soon, they'd be falling over them in the street!

With the sun out, the Hupperts' gloomy old-fashioned house managed to look more cheerful.

As Pel stepped inside the yard, the guard-dog came to life at once. As it leapt forward, the chain sprang taut, almost throttling it. It danced around, barking as if it were crazy. Pel stared at it, white-faced. 'One of these days,' he said, 'I shall bring my gun and shoot that thing.' He paused. 'At least, I would if I thought I could hit it.'

Huppert was in his shirt sleeves in the kitchen drinking coffee. He looked pale and shaken, and they found he'd heard from the hospital. With him was a woman who was standing by the stove. She was older than Huppert, blonde, heavy-featured and with a lowering presence that made Pel feel ill-at-ease. Huppert introduced her as Connie Gruye.

'She lives next door,' he said. 'She's come in to give a hand.'

The telephone went and Madame Gruye went to answer

it, and returned almost immediately. 'It's the undertaker,' she said. 'He wants to make some arrangements with you.'

Huppert rose. 'Forgive me,' he said to Pel.

The woman placed two glasses on the table, poured wine into them and gestured to Pel to drink. It tasted like iron filings and he wondered if she made it with the leftovers from the forge.

Huppert seemed to be doing a lot of arguing on the telephone and Pel became heavily aware of Madame Gruye's presence in the room. She said nothing, as though she'd never been in the habit of saying much.

'Did *you* see the intruder?' Pel asked, more in an attempt to break the silence than anything else. 'From your window next door perhaps.'

'No,' she said.

'Did you hear him?'

'No.'

Pel sighed. It was heavy going but he struggled on.

'I suppose the dog woke you.'

'No.'

'It looks a good guard-dog.'

'It is. It nearly bit your Inspector.'

It nearly bit me, Pel thought. The woman was staring at her feet and for a moment Pel decided she'd gone to sleep standing up.

'But perhaps I wasn't awake,' she said as if it were an afterthought. 'And it woke me, and by the time I'd come around it had stopped barking. Or Monsieur Huppert had managed to shut it up.' It was quite an unexpected speech.

'Doesn't it shut up for you?'

'No.' They were obviously back to square one. 'Only for her.'

'Her? Madame Huppert?' Pel tried a little light-heartedness. 'I expect you're afraid of it,' he said. 'They always know when you're afraid.' They certainly always knew with him.

'It wants shooting,' she said.

Pel looked up, startled to discover such a brooding personality was capable of so much anger, so much emotion.

'You don't like it?' he asked.

'I hate it. Everybody does.'

66

'Why does he keep it then?'

She gestured to the hall where they could still hear Huppert talking into the telephone. 'He says it keeps intruders away.' Her face lifted unexpectedly in the ghost of a smile. 'It didn't keep this one away, though, did it?'

Men were still carefully searching the place, going through the yard and the forge as if with a fine-toothed comb.

'How did he get into the yard?' Pel asked.

Bardolle gestured. 'He broke the chains on the gates. Then he cut a piece of the grille out of the door of the forge.'

'What with?'

'There are bolt-shearers in the forge. Then he reached through the hole he'd made and slipped the bolt.'

When they went back into the house, Huppert was in the kitchen again. He had his jacket on now.

'How's the arm?' Pel asked.

'Better. Still stiff. Still stings a bit.' Huppert's gloom returned. 'I don't know what I'm going to do,' he said heavily. 'My wife almost ran this place. I'll have to rethink the thing through now, because she was the expert. I only attended to the details.'

'Tell us again what happened.'

Huppert sighed and, watched by the woman, tried to explain. 'I heard the noise,' he said.

'What did you do?'

'I called to my wife to come down because there was a man in the yard.'

'Why?'

'To telephone the police.'

'And then?'

'I grabbed a towel and put it round my neck. As a scarf. It was cold. Then I grabbed the gun.'

'In your hand?'

'Not at first. I put on the belt with the holster. Then I went outside to the forge.'

'With the yard light on?'

'No.'

'I'd like to have a look at the forge,' Pel suggested. 'Do you feel like showing us round?'

Outside Darcy counted the marks the bullets had made in

67

the brick walls of the rear of the house and the forge. There were five of them.

'The sixth hit my wife,' Huppert said heavily.

'He wasn't exactly a good shot, this intruder,' Darcy observed quietly to Pel. 'He must only have been standing by the pump there. And why shoot, anyway? If he'd kept quiet, he might not have been noticed because it would be dark there without the light.' He looked at Huppert. 'What happened then?'

'He went into the forge,' Huppert said. 'I went after him. I fired. Twice. And he fired back. One of them hit me.'

Darcy frowned. 'I wonder what he was after? What's made here isn't easily carted away.'

'Perhaps it wasn't that he was after,' Pel said.

Huppert didn't think it was either. 'Who'd want to steal a wrought-iron gate?' he asked.

'What about the pay for your staff? It's today, isn't it?'

Huppert sighed. 'Connie's let everybody know what's happened and not to come in. She'll take their pay to them later in my car.' His sigh came again. 'Perhaps I should pay them by cheque. But just try to suggest it. The types who work for me are old-fashioned and they like to feel the weight of their wages in their pocket.'

'How often are they paid?'

'Every fourteen days. *They* decided that. Some people pay every month.'

'Any enemies you know of?'

Huppert pulled a face. 'None.'

'Then why should someone want to take a shot at you?'

'Ask me another. I can only think he got inside thinking he might find something of value and when I appeared he panicked and shot at me.'

'He – if it was the same man – came once before,' Darcy said. 'He didn't find anything then, so why come again? Burglars don't operate that way.'

Pel was sniffing round the workshop now. It contained all manner of things to do with the business. 'Show me where you were standing when the shots were fired?' he asked.

Huppert led the way across the yard. Pel followed, keeping well out of reach of the dog. Huppert stopped by the back door of the house. 'I was here,' he said. 'I suppose I must have just come out of the door.'

'What's through there apart from the kitchen?'

'Nothing. Just the house. The office, of course. It's next to the kitchen.'

The telephone went again and Madame Gruye's head appeared in the office window. 'It's the florist's,' she said. 'They want to know what you want?'

'I think you should know,' Darcy pointed out, 'that the burial might have to be postponed until the body's released. It might take time.'

Huppert gave him an agonised look. 'Is that what happens?'

'Usually.'

'I'd better tell them.'

As Huppert vanished again, Bardolle was staring about him, frowning. 'There was no trace of fingerprints or foot-prints, Patron,' he said. 'No sign of the intruder. As far as I can make out, he took his time, too. After he got through the gates, he searched the forge until he found the bolt-shearers. Then he cut a hole in the grille leading to the yard itself, then – it doesn't make sense, Patron – he put the bolt-shearers back in their place. He must have. They're there and we've checked the bite. It matches the mark. Then, when Huppert heard him, instead of disappearing as he ought, he hid in the forge. Huppert followed him and when Huppert was inside he came to life and fired at him. *Twice*. Only then did he disappear.'

'No fingerprints on the shears?'

'Nothing, Patron. He used gloves.'

Pel was standing by a bench. Hand tools lay about on it and a vise was bolted to one end. Pel stared at the floor. It was black in colour, and seemed to be compounded of dirt, soot and grease in equal quantities.. Near the bench, close to the vise, there were marks that looked as if they were made by chalk. An attempt had been made to erase them but they were still visible. Two of the marks were arcs, about the size of the toe of a boot and just in front of the right hand one was a straight line with right-angled marks at each end. There were other chalk marks, the width of a man's hand apart, on the bench.

'What are those?' he asked.

Bardolle shrugged. 'I asked. Huppert said he thought someone had been making something. Measuring. That sort of thing. And he made them to save measuring over and over again.'

'Did he say what he was measuring?'

'He couldn't remember. They're all craftsmen here and all have their own way of doing things.'

Pel studied the marks. 'They don't look all that old,' he commented.

'That's what I said. He said they could be for anything – they make all sorts of things.'

When they returned to the office, Madame Gruye had vanished and Huppert was just replacing the old-fashioned telephone. The place looked untidy, with disordered piles of papers, bills on spikes, an ancient typewriter, and a large square out-dated reel-to-reel tape recorder connected by means of laboratory clamps to what appeared to be a home-made spring-operated wooden pedal attached to a cable. At the other end of the cable a strip of plastic with a hole in it had been slotted over the old-fashioned tumbler switch on the flat deck of the machine. Pel was staring at it, puzzled, when Huppert explained.

'Tape recorder,' he said. 'For letters.'

'What's that operating it?'

Huppert gestured. 'It's a device we made. We had the tape recorder. It was my wife's. She used to like to record music and talks from the radio but then she lost interest, and when we decided it would be easier for Connie here to do letters from a tape recorder instead of having always to take them down in shorthand first, we decided to use it. If I sit down here – ' he suited the act to the words ' – and press the foot pedal, it works this cable which is attached to this piece of plastic which slots over the switch and moves it back and forth so that it works the machine. Look.' He pressed his foot on the wooden spring-operated pedal and the small piece of plastic over the switch of the tape recorder moved to set the reels moving. Huppert's voice spoke.

'*To Messrs. A. Cariou and Company. You have the address, Connie, in the file. Dear Sirs, In answer to –* '

As he lifted his foot, the machine stopped.

'It's never let us down,' Huppert said.

Pel was staring at the old tape recorder as if he couldn't believe his eyes. It seemed to bear out Darcy's opinion that Travail des Metaux Huppert was a Mickey Mouse outfit.

Huppert seemed to feel it needed more explanation. 'We've been using it like that for twelve years,' he said. 'It's big and bulky but Connie likes it. She'd probably walk out on me if I got rid of it.'

'Is she that important?'

Huppert shrugged. 'She's worked here longer than I have. She worked for the original owner and very nearly became a director. She knows where all the contracts are and so on. I'd be lost without her.'

Pel was still examing the ancient device.

'Did your wife type?'

'Not very well. She used to work in the factory before I married her. She's – she was – clever at working metal.'

Pel's eyebrows rose.

'People took any trade they could get when things were difficult,' Huppert explained. 'But she had a bit of a gift for it. When the other girls left to get jobs they thought were more suited to them, she stayed on. Bit of an inventor, too.' Huppert gestured at the device attached to the tape recorder. 'That was her idea.'

'How many people do you employ here?'

'I told you. Twenty. I could have grown bigger but I preferred not to. We're not very important.'

'Trust them all?'

'They've all been with me a long time. All except for Garcia. He turned up six months ago and asked for a job. I'd just lost an old boy who'd retired so I took him on. Thought I might as well stick to a round figure of twenty. He's all right.' Huppert held out his hand, palm down, and moved it from side to side. 'Nothing special. But far from useless.'

'Know anything about him?'

'No. He just turned up. He lives in a caravan at Talant.'

'Full name?'

'Emmanuel Garcia. You don't think – ?'

'I don't thing anything at the moment. I'm keeping an open mind.'

71

'Why would *he* want to shoot me?'

'I didn't say he *would* want to shoot you. I haven't even spoken to him. Is there any reason why he *might* want to shoot you?'

After all, Pel thought, he could be a long-lost cousin. He could be the lover of Madame Huppert. He could be a man whose sister Huppert had seduced. He could even be a maniac. There were a thousand permutations you could think of if you tried. They didn't have to make sense. Especially judging by the rubbish you read in the papers.

9

They arrived at the Hôtel de Police late, to find Nosjean had returned from leave. Pel felt better at once. Slim, dark, looking like Napoleon on the bridge at Lodi, Nosjean was one of his best men.

'When's he come on duty?' he asked.

'Tomorrow, Patron,' Darcy said. 'How about a beer at the Bar Transvaal to celebrate?'

They were on the way out when the telephone went on the desk of the man who handled the front office. He spoke into it then turned and yelled.

'Chief Inspector! It's Cadet Martin. Hang on. He's coming down.'

As they waited by the door, Martin came down the stairs in a hurry.

'Patron, there's been a shooting!'

'Damn it, I know. What do you think we've been doing at Montenay?'

'Not that one, Patron. Another.'

'Another?' Pel's eyebrows shot up. 'Where? Same place?'

'No, Patron. This time it's at the other side of the city. Pouilly. A couple of youngsters doing a bit of courting stumbled on a stiff. They telephoned in on Emergency. A car's gone from the local sub-station to pick them up. I thought you'd want to know.'

Pel and Darcy were exchanging glances.

'You'd better stick with the one at Montenay, Daniel,' Pel said. 'I'll take this new one. You've got Bardolle. I'll take Nosjean. He'll come in, I know. We'll exchange details later. They may be connected.' He swung to Cadet Martin. 'Get in touch with Sergeant Nosjean and send him after me. Warn the Procureur, then get everybody out there. Photography. Forensic. Doc Minet. Inspector Pomereu of Traffic's going to

73

be needed with barriers. And warn Inspector Nadauld, of Uniformed Branch. We'll need extra men.'

The dead man at Pouilly lay in the undergrowth at the side of a small ride leading off the road. It was a dark place under the trees, which was doubtless why the two youngsters had been there, and the body lay among the young bracken and undergrowth, its head hidden by foliage.

'Any idea who it is?' Pel asked the police brigadier who met him.

'No idea, sir. We've touched nothing.'

'Had a look at him?'

'Yes, sir. But only to make sure he's dead.'

'And there's no doubt?'

'None at all, sir. I think he's been shot in the head. Twice. I didn't stay close in case I disturbed anything.'

'Very sensible. Right. First things first. I'll look at him in a moment. By that time Forensic and the others should be here. In the meantime I'll talk to the people who found him. Got their names?'

'Yes, sir. Yves-Pol Letour and Marie-Anne Roumiou. Both aged seventeen.'

The two youngsters were sitting in the back seat of the police car, holding hands and looking scared stiff. The girl was wearing a flowered dress and the boy jeans with his shirt tail hanging out. As Pel opened the door, they sat upright, almost at attention.

'Relax,' he said. 'Take it easy. I gather you found him?'

The boy answered nervously. 'We were walking – that's all, walking – '

'I'm not disputing it.'

'We were just talking.'

'Is that all?'

'Well, I had my arm round Marie-Anne.'

In fact they had been embracing as if the end of the world had been about to occur and the girl made no bones about it. 'He was kissing me,' she said bluntly.

The boy managed a feeble smile. 'Well, yes, I was.'

'Any reason why you shouldn't be kissing her?'

They stared at each other for a second. 'Well, no, sir. Not really. We've been going together for a long time.'

'Parents know you were here?'

There was a moment's silence as they glanced at each other. Marie-Anne's father considered that Yves-Pol's shirt wasn't the only thing he couldn't keep in his trousers and he'd heard a few stories about other girls. He didn't trust Yves-Pol and, since he'd been a bit of a goer in his youth, he had good reason to suspect others might be the same. By the same token, Yves-Pol Letour's mother didn't trust Marie-Anne Roumiou.

Yves-Pol was stretching a point. 'Well – not here,' he said. 'But they knew we were together. We're always together. I told my parents I was going to see Marie-Anne and then I went to pick her up.'

'So there's no need to be worried,' Pel pointed out. 'You were doing nothing wrong.'

They exchanged glances again. It was only due to what they had found that they hadn't been doing something wrong. They'd already reached the heavy breathing stage, as Pel had long since guessed. Young boys and girls didn't make a habit of going into chest-high undergrowth in the dusk just to look at the flowers.

'No,' Letour agreed. 'Nothing wrong. We were just walking. Well, sort of. Me with my arm round her. I was just kissing her when I tripped.'

'Over him?'

'Yes. His foot. I nearly fell. We both nearly fell.'

'And then?'

'Well, it was pretty dark. I thought it was a branch or something, then I realised it was a foot.'

They were interrupted by cars arriving, the sound of their engines rising and falling as they progressed down the uneven lane. It was Prélat, of Fingerprints, together with the men from the Forensic Laboratory. Pel watched them stop, then turned again to the two youngsters.

'Go on,' he encouraged. 'About the foot.'

'Well, we thought – ' in the weak light of the interior light Letour was wriggling ' – we thought there were two of them. A man and a woman. You know – well – '

He gave a sickly grin and the girl giggled. Pel waved him on. 'Understandable,' he said. 'So what did you do?'

'We didn't know what to do. We walked on a bit, thinking

75

that if they were – well, you know – that they wouldn't want us around. Then Marie-Anne said she thought something was wrong or they'd have jumped up. Embarrassed. That sort of thing. But nobody had moved, even when I'd fallen over the foot. So we went back and I called out. "Are you all right?" Something like that. And when he didn't answer, well – I thought he might have had a heart attack. My grandfather dropped dead with one six months ago, so naturally – '

'What made you call the police?'

'I struck a match. Then I saw his face. Or – well, what there was of it. Then I knew he was dead. So we went to the telephone in the bar back there and called the police. They told us to stay where we were and they'd join us. We were a bit scared. We thought that whoever had done it might still be around somewhere.'

'Did you see anyone?'

'No.'

'Hear anyone?'

'No.'

'Shots? Or a car moving off in a hurry? Anything like that?'

'No. It was dark and quiet. Nothing.'

Another car was arriving now and Pel guessed it was Doc Minet. Lights were being set up behind him and he saw the flash of a camera going. He turned again to the two youngsters.

'Come up here often?'

'Yes. It's quiet here.'

'Ever seen anyone hanging about up here? Anyone strange?'

Letour wriggled again. 'We don't come up here much in the daylight,' he admitted. 'It's usually after dark – because – well – '

'Ever been up here in the daylight?'

'Once or twice.'

'When was the last time?'

They glanced at each other. 'About a month ago.'

'See anyone?'

'It was a Sunday. There were a few people. But chiefly people with kids. Or dogs. Going for a walk.'

'Anybody strange? I don't suppose you knew everyone you

76

saw, but was there anyone who looked odd? Anyone who made you look twice at them?'

They stared at each other for a moment, then they shook their heads together.

'And tonight? Nobody passed you? Nothing like that?'

The answer, as before, was no.

Doc Minet was bending over the body when Pel crossed to him. He looked up as he approached.

'Any idea when?'

'Two days ago. Hard to say. I'll tell you better later when I've had a chance to examine.'

'What did it?'

Leguyader, of the Lab, interrupted. 'It was a gun,' he said. '6.35. We have a cartridge case.' He held out his hand and in the light of the car headlights Pel saw the small brass cylinder.

'How many?'

'Two,' Doc Minet said. 'There are two entrance wounds. One exit wound. There's a bullet still inside his head somewhere. There must be another cartridge case around as well.'

'We'll find it,' Leguyader said cheerfully. He liked murders. They gave him the chance not only to air his skill – which was extensive because he knew his job – but also to air his knowledge, something he never hesitated about.

'How was it done?'

'Close range,' Doc Minet said. 'There are powder burns on his cheek.'

'And inside a car,' Leguyader pointed out. 'We have wheel marks. The killer drove down the ride with him, pulled a gun on him, opened the door, and shot him so that he was flung out – or knocked out – or blown out – whatever you wish to call it. He fell there and whoever did it just drove away and left him. There's been no attempt to cover him up and nothing to indicate anybody else got out of the car.'

Nosjean had arrived by this time and, as Minet and the photographers indicated they had finished, he bent over the dead man.

'Any indication who he is?' Pel asked.

'Not so far, Patron. I think somebody's deliberately emptied his pockets. Or more likely forced *him* to empty them

77

before he was shot. It wouldn't be easy in a car to search a man, I suppose, and they didn't get out. It's a funny one, Patron. Look at this. His pockets have all been turned inside out. Every one.'

Bending down, Pel saw that every pocket lining had been pulled out and was hanging loose.

'It wasn't done after he was killed. There's no indication that anybody examined the body. It was done before. Why?'

'Something he had? Something the man who shot him wanted? Have you looked around?'

'There's nothing, Patron. Nothing at all. Everything he had has been taken away.'

When Pel returned to the two youngsters in the car, they looked at him worriedly.

'I'm going to have you taken home,' he told them. 'But I don't want you to talk about what happened.'

'My parents will want to know,' the girl said. 'We're late.'

'The policeman who drives you will explain to them. In cases like this it's best that as few people as possible know what's happened. Then sometimes the person who did it gets worried because if nothing appears in the papers he doesn't know how much the police know. And then perhaps he'll make a mistake. Do you see?'

They nodded together.

'Do you know who did it?' Letour asked.

Pel paused. Most killers were easy. You usually found them two streets away covered with blood and scared stiff. But any killer who had the nerve to remove a dead man's wallet wouldn't be like that. This one was going to be difficult.

'No,' he admitted. 'I don't.'

He just hoped Darcy's would be easier.

10

Darcy had nothing new to report. He and Bardolle had talked with all the Huppert employees.

'Particularly Garcia and Tehendu,' he said. 'Those two who might have been doubtful. No problem, Patron. Garcia was in a bar in Talant, with about twenty people to swear to it. And Tehendu was in the bosom of his family at Orles. He'd gone home for the night and they were all there.'

'Could they be covering for him?'

'*They* could. But not the neighbours. Several of them turned up to say "hello". It's that sort of village. Up in the hills. When someone goes home from the great big world outside it's as if he'd been in outer space. They all want to see if he's grown two heads. He's off drugs, too. He's taken to jogging instead. He's on to the health kick.'

Pel scowled. 'They always have to be on something, don't they? Drugs. Religion. Health. Good works. Why can't people just *live*? What did you make of him?'

'A bit of an odd-ball. But clever with his hands.'

'What's his relationship with Huppert?'

'They had him in the office to complain about his work. But that was in the early days. Nothing since.'

'Is he the type to bear a grudge?'

'How can you tell, Patron? He swears he's not on drugs now but you never really know, do you? I saw no sign.'

'Has he a gun?'

'He says not. I took him home and searched his apartment. I didn't find one. But that doesn't mean a thing. He might have chucked it in the Orche while he was out jogging.'

'What about the others?'

'Nothing, Patron. What about yours?'

'Shot through the head. He's not been identified. His pockets had been emptied.'

'Robbery?'

'Probably. Probably not. He was killed with a 6.35.'

'Another?' Darcy's eyes widened. 'Think we've got a lunatic going round?'

'We'll know better when Forensic comes up with their report.'

While they were talking, Misset entered, mysterious behind his dark glasses.

'Kid here called Jean-Pierre Petitbois,' he said. 'Says he's come about his bike. The front desk said you'd given instructions you wanted to see any kid who'd lost one.'

The boy, a square-shouldered dark youngster with a frank expression, was sitting in the sergeants' room. He stood up as Pel and Darcy appeared with Misset.

'Jean-Pierre Petitbois,' he said briskly. '17, Rue Moulins. That's on the new estate at Rosière de Bourgogne.'

Pel waved the boy down again and sat opposite him. 'You've lost your bicycle?' he asked.

The boy stood up again as he was addressed and Pel was pleased to see that he knew his manners. 'I came to see if you'd found it,' he said.

'Can you describe it?'

'Sure. Racing saddle but not racing handlebars. They're not really a help. Dark green frame with a silver line running down it. Word, *Intrépide,* on the bar down from the front fork. Straps on pedals.' The boy looked up. 'So your foot doesn't slip. Bad chip on the paint on the crossbar where I fell off it. About half-way along. Number stamped on frame just below saddle. 784326.'

Pel and Darcy exchanged glances, and Darcy grinned. 'You're very efficient,' he said. 'You ought to be a cop.'

The boy looked pleased. 'It's only second-hand but I saved up for it and it took a lot of doing. I want it back if I can get it.'

'We'll do our best,' Darcy said. 'Were you riding it two days ago anywhere near Quigny-par-la-Butte, by the way?'

'I don't even know where Quigny-par-la Butte is.'

'Were you riding it at all on that day?'

'No, I wasn't. I'd already lost it. And I think I know where it went.'

'Oh!' Darcy's eyes met Pel's. 'Where?'

'I think Philippe Lafarge pinched it.'

'Why do you think that?'

'Because it's the sort of thing Philippe Lafarge would do!'

'Is it now? You'd better tell us more about this Philippe Lafarge. Does he live near you?'

'He does now. Two streets away. Rue Dolour. He sits near me at school.'

'Which school's that?'

'The lycée. He was always on about my bike. I think he fancies it.'

'Hasn't he a bike of his own?'

'He's never had the money to buy one.'

'Father's poor, is he?'

'I don't know. They say he's been in prison.'

Darcy's eyes met Pel's again. 'Know his name?'

'Andre Lafarge. He's a plumber. At least he's supposed to be, but he never seems to do any work.'

'What was he in prison for?'

'Stealing, they say.'

'*Who* says?'

'Everybody says. My mother says. I've heard her.'

Pel turned. 'Misset, look up Andre Lafarge. See what we have on him.'

As Misset vanished, he turned to the boy. 'What's he supposed to have stolen, this Andre Lafarge?' he asked.

'I don't know. They came here from La Rochelle. They say it was there he went to prison.'

'Same people say?'

'Yes. Everybody. He's well known.'

'It seems he's not too well known to us.'

Misset reappeared. 'Andre Lafarge, Patron,' he said. '12, Rue Dolour. Found on enclosed premises. Got thirty days.'

'Any other form?'

'Plenty, Patron. Fiddling welfare payments. Pretending to be in need of help when he was in employment. Stealing lead from a builder's yard where he worked. Helping himself to a car. Breaking and entering. One assault.'

'Quite a boy, eh? Where was all this? La Rochelle?'

'Mostly, Patron. Couple of offences in Niort. One in Limoges, one in Vichy, one in Le Creusot.'

'He seems to have been working his way across the country and now he's arrived here. He'll need watching. And now he lives in the Rue Dolour, eh? I wonder if – ' Pel stopped and looked at the boy. 'Where was this bicycle of yours when it disappeared?'

'Outside the house.'

'Locked?'

'I always leave it locked. But it's a quiet road. Nobody comes there and it's only a light chain. A pair of pliers would cut through it easily.'

'That's the worst of things these days,' Darcy said seriously. 'They're not made as they used to be. Why else do you suspect Philippe Lafarge? Apart, that is, from the fact that "they" say his father's been to gaol.'

'Madame Bonhomme opposite said she saw him.'

'Did she now? Who's Madame Bonhomme?'

'She's old. About seventy. She spends all her time sitting in the window nosey-parkering. I've been in trouble more than once with my mother from things she's told her. All the same – ' Petitbois gestured, as if prepared to forgive a lot under the circumstance ' – there isn't much she misses.'

'And she saw Philippe Lafarge take your bike?'

'She thinks so.'

'Have you seen this Philippe Lafarge since you lost your bicycle?'

'Yes.'

'With the bicycle?'

'No.'

'Have you accused him of taking it?'

'Yes. He invited me to look round the garden shed. It wasn't there.'

'But you still think he took it?'

'Yes.'

'But you didn't insist?'

The boy's eyes flickered and he gave a little grin. 'He's bigger than me,' he said.

'A very good reason not to,' Darcy said. 'How about your father? Wouldn't he ask?'

'He's dead. He was killed in a car crash on the N7.'

There was a slight pause then Pel went on. 'Does this Philippe Lafarge bully you?'

82

'A bit.'

Pel could understand. People had bullied *him* at school. But not for long. 'I think we'd better see this Madame Bonhomme,' he said. He gestured at Darcy. 'I think also you'd better take Monsieur Petitbois's name and address down, Daniel,' he said. 'So we can let him have his machine back when we find it.' He tapped the boy's shoulder. 'And don't go buying a new one,' he advised. 'Because I'm sure we shall.'

Madame Bonhomme was a widow but quite different from what they'd been expecting. They'd been expecting a thin-faced, vinegary-looking woman with a keen interest in everybody else's business and a sharp dislike for boys. Instead they found a round-faced, grey-haired cheerful woman of ample proportions with swollen legs.

The estate at Rosière de Bourgogne was an area of cheap-looking dwellings with small gardens front and back and her house was in the Rue Gresset which joined the Rue Moulins and formed a T with the Rue Dolour where Lefarge lived, so that sitting in her front room she was able to see down the whole length of it.

'I sit in the window a lot,' she explained. 'I don't walk very well these days. I don't get out much, but I don't like to miss everything that goes on.'

'Such as people helping themselves to other people's bicycles?' Darcy said.

She laughed. 'Tiens, you've heard of that, have you?' She produced bottles of beer. 'I expect you could do with one, couldn't you? My grandfather was a policeman and I have the impression that a beer here and there helps keep you alert.'

'It wets the whistle,' Darcy smiled.

Madame Bonhomme gestured. 'I expect you've come about what young Petitbois said. He's a nice lad. He thinks I don't like him, but I do.' She gestured at the window. 'I pass on information to parents. Some of them think I'm a nosey-parker but most of them realise I'm trying to help. I am,' she added seriously. 'Somebody tipped me off about my son when he was seventeen. They saw him with someone who was part of a crowd who were stealing cars. Getting to know about it in good time saved him going wrong. I don't want to harm young Petitbois. He's well-behaved. Not like some I know.'

'By name Lafarge?'

'That's it.'

'This bicycle that was stolen. Did you see what happened?'

'Oh, yes. I was sitting in the window as usual and saw him go to it. He had something in his hand.'

'Pliers?'

'It might have been.'

'See him ride it away?'

'No. The telephone went just then and I had to leave the window. When I came back the bike was gone.'

'Did you tell young Petitbois?'

'Not really. Just hinted. After all, you can't accuse, can you? He knows I see most of what goes on because he's been in trouble once or twice over it himself. But only things like broken windows. He's an honest boy.'

'Did the Lafarge boy know you'd seen him?'

'They don't know me at all. They've only recently come to live here. From Vichy, they say.'

'La Rochelle, in fact. What's he look like, the Lafarge boy?'

'Big.'

'What about the father?'

'Just the opposite. Small. Slight. A moustache.'

Pel glanced at Darcy.

'Had any trouble with him?'

Madame Bonhomme shrugged. 'Not really. The boy throws things at my cat – well – you wouldn't expect fathers to do anything like that, would you?'

'Lost anything lately?'

'Lost anything?'

'Anything you left outside that's disappeared?'

She assumed an expression of deep thought. 'I lost a rake. It was in the garden.'

'Anybody else lost anything?'

'Well, there was young Petitbois's bicycle. And I heard the Legers lost their lawn mower. There've been a few things.'

'Anybody had any idea where they went?'

She looked shrewdly at them and laughed. 'I know what you're after? You think Lafarge took them.'

84

Outside, Darcy paused by the car. 'Do we bring him in, Patron?'

Pel considered. Plain clothes work wasn't just detection. Some of it involved strategy and tactics. 'No,' he said. 'Don't bring him in. Georges Ballentou lives in this area, doesn't he? Rue Louis-Levecque. Let's see if he's heard anything. In the meantime, let's just keep an eye on our friend Lafarge. Watch where he goes and whom he meets. He doesn't sound as if he's the brains behind the De Mougy heist but he might just lead us to who *is*.' He looked about him. 'Besides, it's a quiet street and you never know who might take advantage of it to turn up. It might even be Pépé le Cornet or his right-hand man.'

11

Misset's new job suited him down to the ground. He glanced at his watch and smiled as he saw that it was about time for Pel to hold his conference. Because he wasn't concerned with any of the cases involving Pel's team, he was spared the conference. Which was splendid. Since he'd always found work a bore, he also found the conferences a bore. They went on too long. Too many people said too much. And most of the time Misset had nothing to add. He was there merely to receive orders and he didn't consider it fitted the virile get-up-and-go image he felt he presented to the world.

He was feeling pleased with himself and was enjoying his independence. He was terrified of Pel and liked to keep as far away from him as possible, but he was still a little dubious about Major Chaput's story and suspected that somehow he was being used. He had no delusions about why Pel had placed him at Chaput's disposal. He even at times suspected Chaput was a fraud. But then he thought about the taxi that had picked him up with Ada Vocci from the restaurant where they'd dined. It was now in the yard at the Hôtel de Police with a bent wing to show where it had collided with the Mercedes, and its owner was not the man who had driven them away from the restaurant. Misset hadn't dreamed it. The taxi had been stolen, and he remembered uneasily how it had appeared, to pick them up the minute they had emerged. He had no doubt now that the driver was the man who'd come to the aid of Gold-thread as Misset was grabbing him. The taxi had been waiting for him. Or for Ada Vocci. Either way, he didn't like the look of it.

Stopping at the station buffet for a beer, he was accosted by the porter who had hoisted Ada Vocci's luggage on to his trolley. He was sitting on his barrow, smoking a cigarette, and he followed Misset into the bar like a harbinger of doom.

86

'Some guy was asking for you,' he pointed out. 'He was asking for that taxi driver who drove you and the dame to the hotel.'

Misset immediately thought of Chaput. 'Big type with a moustache?'

'No. Little type with a suit with a gold thread in it.'

Assailed by worry, Misset swallowed his beer hurriedly. Who in the name of the Great Lord God of Stresses and Strains was this type in the gold-threaded suit? He was always popping up and, as he'd already shown, he could be unpleasantly aggressive.

'What did he want?' he asked.

'He was asking about the other day,' the porter said. 'When the train came in. He wanted to know where you both went. I didn't know, so he tried to find the taxi that took you. But the driver's gone to Dole. His mother's ill.'

Preoccupied, Misset tossed enough money to the counter to pay for a small beer. 'Buy yourself a drink,' he said.

The porter eyed the coins. 'Thanks,' he said. 'I'll try not to get too drunk.'

Misset hurried away from the station. He didn't fancy having his throat slit. Near the Porte Guillaume, he saw Chaput sitting outside one of the bars in the spring sunshine. Chaput moved the chair next to his own in invitation and called a waiter. Misset studied him. In daylight, he looked like anything but a nutter. He seemed, in fact, to be exactly what he claimed.

'You thought I was mad that night I picked you up, didn't you?' Chaput said.

'Yes I did,' Misset admitted. 'But I've checked since. I still find it hard to believe, though.'

There seemed far too much sunshine for the murky underside of international activities to be credible and too much colour about the square from the girls in their spring dresses to be able to believe in it. 'Why did you pick *me*?' he asked.

'Because,' Chaput said simply. 'Chief Inspector Pel suggested you.'

'I'll bet he did.'

'He said you knew the woman I'm interested in.'

Misset preened himself a little. 'Elle a du chien,' he said.

'She's sexy, that one. Are you still wanting to know if she's got that file or not?'

'Yes.'

'Why can't you go in and get it?'

'Don't want to make a mistake.'

'So you let *me* do your dirty work?'

'We've got to do it right. It's got to be quick when it's done. No publicity. I don't want my face smeared across the front pages. Somebody might turn nasty.'

Misset didn't think much of the idea. After all, if somebody might turn nasty with Chaput they might well turn nasty with Misset. 'What about the other side?' he asked. 'Will they have a go too?'

Chaput shrugged. 'Expect so. They've got sources, the same as we have. We know what they're doing, the same as they know what we're doing. They're watching us as much as we're watching them. Half the time we only know when something's happening because one of the other side moves from A to B. When that happens we know that what we're after's also moved from A to B. In this game, when Father says "Turn", we all turn.'

'Don't you ever get in each other's way?'

'It's not exactly a crowded profession.' Chaput finished his beer. 'I'll be here most days about this time. If you want me, this is where you'll find me. If I want you, I'll contact your headquarters.'

Misset stared after him as he left. The interview seemed to have the mad overtones of a spy send-up. But Chaput seemed real enough, and there was a suggestion of evil beneath the farce.

Misset finished his beer hurriedly. Somehow, after listening to Chaput, he felt very conspicuous. Then he remembered Ada Vocci and felt a little better.

At the Hôtel Centrale he was about to march up to the reception desk to ask for her, determined this time to find out the truth, but someone else was there before him, a tall dark, good-looking man – younger, Misset had to admit, than he was, with better features and less of a belly.

'Mademoiselle Vocci?' the receptionist was saying.

'She's registered here,' the man said. 'I looked at your book while you were on the telephone.'

Misset's ears had pricked and, instead of remaining by the reception desk, he moved to the stairs, as if waiting for the lift, and began to examine the menu which was exhibited on a stand.

The receptionist was annoyed. 'You had no right to examine the register, Monsieur,' she was saying. 'That's for the use of the hotel and for our residents.'

The man seemed irritated by the comment and waved it aside. 'When will she be back?'

'She didn't tell me, Monsieur. People don't.'

'Did she say where she was going?'

'She didn't tell me that, either. But as it happens, I think it was into the Jura and perhaps into Switzerland. She hired a car and was asking for the road to Pontarlier and the border.'

'Pontarlier? Switzerland?' The man seemed suddenly worried. 'Did she say *where* in Switzerland?'

'No, Monsieur. Would you like to leave a message for her?'

'No.' The man hesitated.

'Are you sure you've got the right name, Monsieur?'

'No.' The man seemed suddenly doubtful. 'Where did she come from?'

'I've no idea, Monsieur.'

'What was she like? Small? Fair hair? Blue eyes?'

The receptionist smiled. 'That's not Mademoiselle Vocci, Monsieur. She's tall, with red hair and green eyes. Think of Sophia Loren and you've got Mademoiselle Vocci. I wish I'd got her looks.'

'You're sure she's not here?'

'Absolutely sure.'

'I'd better go to her room to make certain.'

'That's impossible, Monsieur.'

The man frowned. 'I'm a policeman,' he said, and Misset's eyebrows lifted because he'd never seen him before.

The receptionist was still uncertain. 'That makes it different, of course,' she admitted. 'But don't you need a warrant? Perhaps I could see your identity card? That would do.'

The dark man frowned and for a moment he looked flustered. Then he started patting his pockets. 'I seem to have left it on my desk,' he said. 'Never mind.' He was snapping his fingers irritatedly. 'I'll come back,' he said. 'I have to make sure.'

As he turned away, Misset stared after him. Who the hell was this one, he wondered. Because he was certainly no cop. Old ladies shoving their noses round doors had learned not to admit strange men into their houses – not even when they said they were cops – and any cop making enquiries would as soon go out without his trousers as without the card that established what he was.

Misset frowned. First Gold-thread. Then Briand. Then Chaput. Now this type. The damned place was filling up with mysterious strangers, all of whom seemed interested in Ada Vocci. It made what Chaput said more believable.

He became aware of the receptionist staring at him. 'Monsieur?'

Misset was still in a daze, his mind busy. Had Ada bolted? He jumped as the clerk spoke.

'Nothing,' he said hurriedly. 'Nothing. I was waiting for someone but they don't seem to be here.'

As he disappeared, the receptionist turned to the hall porter. 'The place seems to be full today of people looking for people who aren't here,' she said.

There was plenty to discuss at the conference Misset was fortunate to miss, because the car used in the hold-up at Quigny had turned up at Besançon. It was a blue Renault 9 – Number 424 HC 75 – and since the number was on the list of those cars stopped and examined near the scene of the incident, the fact that it had been abandoned had immediately led to suspicions.

Because they were handling three cases at once, it was decided to take them in the order in which they'd occurred, and the details of the car were subjected to a close scrutiny. There had been no identifiable fingerprints on it, but there were other things to interest them.

'It was one of those that passed the road block at Pontailly,' Inspector Pomereu, of Traffic, admitted. 'We have a note of its number and make. The men in it were accepted as bona fide travellers. They were dressed in suits and said they represented the firm of Constructions Gine-Romero, of Paris, and produced folders and so on to prove it. But we've checked and, though the firm's genuine, it knows nothing of the names we were given: Etienne Gambrionne, of Issy; Jean-Paul Dupont, of Viroflay; Georges Thomas, of Belleville. Their papers were false. We didn't know that, though, and there was no reason to suspect them.'

Pomereu seemed to be on the defensive. 'The car was reported missing three days before,' he went on. 'In Paris. We checked. It belongs to an industrial chemist by the name of Jacques Barnardi. Unblemished character, no record. He's identified it as his from scratches on the body and a tear in the rear seat caused by one of his dogs. We have it on the list of stolen cars but we didn't identify it at Pontailly because the number plates on it aren't Barnardi's. They'd been changed and the men in it had what appeared to be sound documentation for it. I think, after being stolen it was taken to a garage and the new plates and documentation provided.'

'In three days?' Pel said.

Pomereu nodded, accepting that he wasn't being blamed. 'And after all there are dozens of blue Renaults of this model about. There was no reason to stop it, any more than there was for the other cars that passed through.' He paused. 'Besides, the clothing the men in it were wearing doesn't match the description the De Mougys gave.'

'Perhaps there was another car waiting on the road at the other side of the forest,' Darcy suggested. 'And the loot was taken through the trees to it and disappeared with it before the road block was set up.'

'Did your men get a good look at the men in the car?' Pel asked. 'Could they have been Pat the Bang or Nick the Greek?'

'I suppose so.' Again Pomereu was on the defensive, as if he felt he was being accused of letting the side down. 'But there was no reason for my people to take more than the normal notice of them. They seemed to be what they claimed to be.'

'They could easily have had decent jackets in the car. They could have changed out of them as soon as they were out of sight of the De Mougys and thrown away the windcheaters they were wearing for the hold-up. Let's have a search made, Daniel. Anything else?'

'It was noticed that two of the men were dark and the other was fair.'

'It could have been Nick the Greek, our friend Lafarge and one other,' Pel said gently, so that Pomereu was finally satisfied no blame was being attached to him. Pel could be tough with carelessness but he didn't attach blame where circumstances didn't call for it. 'I wonder who the other one was. Was the car searched?'

'My people know their job,' Pomereu said in a huff. 'They were all searched. There was nothing in the car except two briefcases with what appeared to be genuine business documents. No jewels. No money. No extra clothing. Somebody had thought this thing through.'

'Pépé le Cornet,' Pel murmured. 'He worries a lot about details.'

'We didn't know about Nick the Greek or Pat the Bang at that time.' Even now, Pomereu was still faintly defensive. 'And my men didn't know them from Adam, anyway. They *must* have got rid of the stuff before they reached Pontailly. The whole area's covered with woods. Somebody could easily have gone across country with the loot. Even buried it and appeared at the other side of the forest as an ordinary farm worker. It's been done before.'

'That means,' Pel said, 'that there *must* have been some big organisation behind it. Only a big organisation could supply papers as fast as these were supplied. And that,' he ended, 'brings us back to where we were before. It was a gang job with a tip-off from inside.'

It was Leguyader's turn next. His boys had searched for dust to get an idea where the car had been but had found nothing helpful.

'How about Pouilly?' Pel asked, thinking of the dead man they'd found in the bracken. 'It's peaty soil there. Find any of that?'

'Nothing,' Leguyader said. 'A few scraps of gravel in the treads of the tyres, but nothing we could use to connect it to anything else we're involved with. Fingerprints are still working on it.'

'What about De Mougy?' Pel asked. 'Was he insured anywhere else apart from the firms we know of?'

Lagé sat up. He was growing slow as he approached

retirement but, though he was never in the habit of coming up with brilliant deductions, he could be relied on to work carefully. He made no mistakes.

'I checked, Patron,' he said. 'I was at it all yesterday. I worked through every known insurance company in the country. And I made them go back to their head offices just in case. Apart from the ones we know, no extra insurances have been taken out in the name of either of the De Mougys. There may be a few small ones I've missed but I'm still checking and so far I've found no insurances on the jewellery beyond the one we know about. It doesn't mean there weren't any, of course. They may have used a false name or gone abroad. Belgium, for instance. Or Holland. It's easy to get there and they have big insurance companies, some of them connected with English companies. It may have been hidden. I'll keep checking.'

Nosjean appeared. He'd been called to the telephone and he slipped into his seat quietly. Pel glanced at him. Nosjean had become the expert on stolen jewellery and silver. He'd got to know all the antique dealers during a recent case and in addition had a girlfriend in the antique trade who was never against giving a little help.

'Nothing, Patron,' he reported. 'I've asked. Nothing's appeared.'

'What about the footprint that was found?'

'Nothing unusual, Patron,' Nosjean said. 'Except that it was small.'

'As if made by a small man?'

'It wasn't deep so he wasn't heavy.'

'Which again could mean our friend, Lafarge.' Pel swung to Darcy. 'What about him, Daniel? Are we watching him?'

'Aimedieu's there now,' Darcy said. 'He's got the use of a telephone to call in with if he sees anything odd.'

'Where is he?'

Darcy smiled. 'Madame Bonhomme's letting him use her front bedroom. I think she's thoroughly enjoying herself.'

'Have we dug up anything more about Lafarge?'

Darcy gestured. 'Ballentou's come up with something interesting, Patron. Lafarge was in jail at the same time as he was, and he was friendly with Nick the Greek.'

'So it *could* be a Paris mob job.'

'It very well could. With Lafarge as the stooge.'

'I wonder how they got to know about it? Who's the contact who gave them the tip-off?'

'I can only think of the chauffeur, Patron.'

'I'd rather look for a woman,' Pel said. 'Nick's good-looking.'

As they were moving on to the next case, Prélat from Fingerprints arrived. His department had just finished working on the car found at Besançon and he couldn't wait to tell them his news.

'Clean, Patron,' he reported 'Somebody had been over it. Every inch. Professional job. Someone who knew what they were doing.'

'Which also encourages the belief that it was a gang.'

Pel frowned and Prélat grinned. 'On the other hand, Patron,' he said, 'we do have *some* good news. The guy at Pouilly. We've got an identification. His dabs are in the file. It's Richard Selva. You'll know him.'

Pel rubbed his nose thoughtfully. 'Richard Selva? Is it now? Well, we won't be wearing black armbands for *him*.'

'He's only just out of gaol,' Darcy put in. 'He didn't last long, did he? I suppose there's no doubt?'

'No doubt at all.'

Pel frowned. 'When exactly did he come out of gaol?'

'Just over three weeks ago,' Darcy said. 'Drugs. He belongs to the Paris mob. One of Pépé le Cornet's men. Handles that side of the business for him.'

'There's another thing, Patron,' Nosjean added. 'Although his pockets had been emptied, on the lining of the right jacket pocket there were traces of heroin. He was obviously back in the game.'

'It doesn't take them long, does it? And the gun that killed him?'

The man from Ballistics came to life. 'As we thought. Another 6.35.'

'And *when* did it happen?'

Doc Minet looked up. 'When I thought,' he said. 'He'd been dead about forty-eight hours. The post mortem made it quite clear.'

'Are you sure?'

'As sure as I can be.'

Pel frowned. 'That puts it just about the time Madame Huppert was shot. Is it some type who's going round shooting people with a 6.35 for some reason?'

'And what's the connection between Selva and the Huppert shooting?' Darcy asked. 'Have the Paris mob been falling out or something?'

'Perhaps he was killed for cash,' Nosjean suggested. 'Perhaps the killer was looking for heroin, but Selva had just got rid of it, in which case his wallet was full of cash and the killer took that instead.'

'Has his wallet been found?'

'No, Patron. Not yet. We've made a search where the body was found, and along the verges of the bridle path and the road. If the type who killed him examined the wallet there, he didn't throw it away there. There were also no footprints where he was found. Tyre marks, but nothing very clear. I think it was just as Forensics say. Selva was in a car with the type who had the 6.35. They stopped, and the type with the gun opened the door, shoved the gun against Selva's head and pulled the trigger, so that he was literally blown out of the car. The door was slammed and the car was driven away. He *must* have got the wallet or the drugs off him before he shot him.'

'If the Paris mob did it,' Pel said slowly, 'then why? Was Selva double-crossing them? And Huppert – could Selva have been using Huppert's place as a drop for something? Drugs, for example. Without Huppert's knowledge, even. That would explain the first intruder. Perhaps he was trying to pick up what was hidden there. He couldn't find it the first time and had to go back.'

'If it was drugs,' Darcy put in, 'it would explain the shooting. Those boys don't take chances. They've a lot to gain and a lot to loose.'

'It wasn't drugs, Patron,' Bardolle interrupted. 'I thought of that and I had the sniffer dogs in. They found no trace.'

'So what was it? There must be *some* connection between Madame Huppert and Selva.'

'Not just Madame Huppert and Selva,' the man from Ballistics said. '*All* of them.'

Pel's head jerked round. '*All* of them?'

'All of them, Patron. Selva, Madame Huppert, Huppert,

95

the man who fired at Huppert. *He* was shot with a 6.35 too. We're dealing with *four* guns. All 6.35s.'

There was a long silence before anyone spoke.

'*Four?*' Pel said. 'In the name of God, has the man an armoury?'

The Ballistics man shifted uncomfortably in his seat but he didn't change his opinion. '*There were four guns,* Patron. The one that killed Selva at Pouilly. Huppert's, which we've got and identified. And two others, one of which killed Madame Huppert.'

'*Two* others? At Montenay?'

'Yes, Patron.'

'So there were *two* intruders?'

The Ballistics man looked puzzled. 'Don't ask me, Patron. I just supply the details, not the guesswork. But there were four altogether and they were all the same calibre and we think the same type of gun. All FAS Apex 6.35s. Eight-shot single-magazine guns like Huppert's. Made by Fabrique d'Armes Automatiques de St. Etienne. They're cheap and not difficult to get hold of and people buy them for self-protection. But they're small and not much use at long distance. They're not a hit-man's weapon.'

'Go on,' Pel said.

The Ballistics man looked at his notes. 'Two shots were fired at Pouilly. From a 6.35. Ten shots were fired at Montenay. Six in the yard, from two different guns but *both* 6.35s. Three from Huppert's gun which we've got and identified, because we've found both bullets and cartridge cases. The 6.35 has magazine-fed cartridges and the *spent* cases are ejected automatically. At the same time a fresh round's pushed into the breech and the weapon's recocked. We fired shots from Huppert's gun with his ammunition. We identified the bullets he fired without difficulty.'

'And the others?'

'As I said, six shots in the yard, three from Huppert's gun. Madame Huppert was shot by a different 6.35, which also fired three shots in the yard, one of which hit her. The other two hit the wall. In the forge two shots were fired by Huppert. We found them embedded in the plaster in the wall opposite the door where he says he was standing. Two other shots were fired in there, too – presumably at him by the intruder because one was in the wall by the door and one was in the beam alongside. They were also 6.35s. *But those were fired by a different gun.*'

'Different from what?'

'Different from the gun that was fired in the yard and killed Madame Huppert. In my opinion it was an FAS Apex, like the others, but a different gun all the same. Three guns in all – one at Pouilly, two at Montenay – four, if you count Huppert's. And all, I'd say from the same batch, except Huppert's which was older.'

They all looked puzzled.

'Let's get this straight,' Pel said. 'Ten shots were fired at Montenay, but none of them by the gun that did the shooting at Pouilly, even though it was the same type.'

'That's right.'

'And six of those shots were fired in the yard, three at Huppert, one of them killing Madame Huppert, and three by Huppert's gun at the intruder.'

'That's correct.'

'Then, as Huppert went into the forge, he fired two shots with his own gun, and two shots were fired back at him – one of them wounding him – but with a different gun from the one that was fired in the yard and hit Madame Huppert.'

The Ballistics man shrugged. 'That's how we work it out, Patron.'

They looked even more bewildered.

'So there *were* two intruders.' Pel said. 'This is the first we've heard about a second burglar. Huppert thought there was only one.'

'*I* think there was only one too, Patron,' Bardolle added.

'In that case, he had two guns. *One intruder with two guns.*' Pel's frown deepened. 'But if one intruder, why *two* guns? Why carry two? And why fire with a different one. He'd only fired three shots in the yard from an eight-shot weapon so he had five shots left. So why change weapons? There *must* have been two intruders.'

'He might have been an amateur,' the Ballistics man said. 'We've found that some people who don't know much about guns think that only the ammunition supplied *with* the weapon will fit it properly. Or perhaps he was short of ammunition and the gun fired in the yard wasn't fully loaded, so he had to change weapons.'

They discussed it back and forth for some time without coming to any satisfactory conclusions, before passing on to the shooting at Pouilly.

'What about the gun that shot Selva?' Darcy asked. 'That was an FAS Apex 6.35, too?'

The Ballistics man agreed. 'Without doubt. But a different gun again. Same calibre, same type, but definitely a different weapon. That's clear from the markings on the bullets and the spent cartridges we examined. We know Huppert's gun was an Apex and I'd bet my pension all the other three were, too.'

12

Pel stood in the shower, cursing as he failed to adjust the water temperature to his satisfaction.

He liked two taps and a single pipe to the shower and in his new house he had a device like the wheel of a drainage system, dreamed up by some bright little man to make showering as difficult as possible. Pel hated bright little men. They invariably complicated the simple procedures of what was already the difficult business of being alive. The industrial world, he felt, was full of bright little men all busily thinking up ways of making it more burdensome. His latest hate was for the man who put new toothbrushes in plastic-covered cases for which you needed a hammer and chisel to get them out.

He got the temperature right at last and stood deep in thought, enjoying the warmth. Four pistols, he thought. All the same type. All the same calibre. One of them used to kill Richard Selva at Pouilly. Three in the gun battle at Montenay. The old trade of killing was becoming infectious. Still – his wet shoulders moved in a shrug – perhaps it was hardly surprising in a nation whose national anthem constantly urged people to set about each other. It's whole theme was insurrection. 'Aux armes, citoyens!' It was there in the *Marseillaise* for everybody to hear.

He emerged from the shower pink and shining, and studied his frame in the mirror. Not what you'd call impressive, he decided. Hardly Superman, and with an incipient pot belly, too. Fortunately Madame, thank God, seemed quite satisfied. Dressing in a hurry – he was never one to linger over his clothes or to dally over the choosing of a tie – he appeared downstairs for breakfast.

'Yesterday's croissants?' he asked as Madame Routy appeared.

99

'No,' she snapped. 'The day before's.'

The usual hostile exchanges sorted out for the day, Pel sat down as Madame Routy disappeared to the kitchen. Both were satisfied. They had lived in the same house so long, snarling at each other, that they had discovered that when they'd stopped for the sake of Madame Pel they were suffering traumas, so they'd started again.

Madame confined herself to a mild reproof.

'You mustn't bully her.'

'Why not? I expect she's been at the whisky again.'

'It's one of the perks of working here,' Madame said gently. 'Everybody has perks. I don't fool myself that my assistants don't help themselves to shampoo. In the same way people who work in printers' shops are never short of paper.'

It made sense but to Pel it was shocking. Whisky was as expensive as uranium and sometimes as difficult to obtain. In his Rue Martin-de-Noinville days he had often been tempted to draw a pencil line on the label of the bottle so he'd know what Madame Routy had guzzled. However, he bowed to his wife's greater wisdom. If nothing else, being pleasant made life less crowded with aggressive incident.

Nevertheless, when he reached the Hôtel de Police, he had once more worked himself up into a state when he was quite ready to have a fight with someone and was almost pleased to learn from Darcy that a search of the woods had been made between where the De Mougys had been held up and the road block at Pontailly, and there had been no sign of the discarded windcheaters they had been half-expecting to find.

However, there was no need to cry 'All is lost' because the ship hadn't quite sunk yet. Brochard and Debray, the Heavenly Twins, had been running a check on guns and had been very thorough.

'Huppert had a licence for that gun of his,' Debray reported. 'No problem there, Patron. And we've checked every other gun in the area we know about. We insisted on seeing them, too, and there was no question of them having been recently fired. They hadn't even been recently cleaned. Mostly they were full of spiders and cobwebs. They hadn't been handled for months.'

'So where did these three different 6.35s come from?'

Brochard had the answer to that, too. 'That consignment that was stolen en route from St. Etienne to Paris,' he reported. 'We've been in touch with Paris and they gave us the full story. There were various kinds. Nickel-plated for ladies' handbags. Ordinary gun-metal for men. Just the job for polishing off your neighbour or your lover.' Brochard liked to think of himself as a humourist. 'But all FAS Apex 6.35s. And with consecutive numbers, too. They were headed for a gunsmith's in the Ile de la Cité. Paris thinks Pépé le Cornet's mob were behind it.'

'I'll bet they were too,' Pel said. 'Have we the numbers?'

'We have, Patron.' Debray's pale face was excited. 'Huppert's gun wasn't one. It was older, but the others might well have been.'

'And now they've turned up here? Two at Montenay. One at Pouilly. And it's my bet all three have been got rid of by this time, too. Where?' Pel looked at Brochard. 'If you wanted to get rid of a pistol, what would you do with it?'

'Throw it away, Patron.'

'Where?'

'In the canal.'

'Where in the canal?'

'From the bridge that goes over it at the Chemin de Chevre Morte. I could also chuck it in the dustbin, of course, and it would disappear that way. I could find a thicket of undergrowth and throw it down there. I could even bury it. I could do a lot of things with it.'

'If you were in a hurry, though, and a bit scared of being found with it you'd probably just toss it in the canal, wouldn't you? Because it's easiest.' Pel turned to Darcy. 'Let's have it searched, Daniel. Get hold of someone with a frogman's suit and see what he brings up.'

As Darcy reached for the telephone, Pel frowned. 'And what's the connection?' he asked. 'Richard Selva. Nick the Greek. Pat Boum. They've all worked at one time or another for Pépé le Cornet. Let's have photographs of them all. Have them printed and handed round. To Uniform. To Traffic. Everybody. Somebody might have noticed them together at some time.'

As Darcy made a note on a slip of paper, Nosjean joined in. 'I hear Nick has a girlfriend, Patron,' he said.

'It's more than likely,' Pel agreed. 'Do we know who she is?'

'I'll try to find out, Patron.'

'He likes the good life, too,' Pel added. 'He latches on to women with money. The Hôtel Centrale's the sort of place he frequents. Have a word with Misset. He's watching it. He might have noticed him around. He's hard to miss. You could also ask Ballentou again. He might have heard which hole in the woodwork he's disappeared into.'

They decided to try Montenay again. When they arrived, there was a small crowd on the patch of land outside the little factory. At first they thought there'd been another shooting but, in fact, they were watching a dog trying to mount a bitch. Pel stared at them with cold eyes. People, he thought, were stupider than you could believe. A crowd would gather for anything. If a man discovered his car had a puncture and stopped to stare at it, within minutes there'd be a dozen round him all doing the same thing. As a small boy he'd once stood in the village street at Vieilly and pointed at the sky. Within seconds there had been a dozen people round him all staring at the same empty spot in the heavens.

He approached the factory yard warily, ready to defend life and limb against the dog. But there was no sound and the chain lay coiled across the yard without the dog. The policeman on duty explained.

'They got rid of it,' he said.

'Who did?'

'Huppert, sir. Well, actually, I gather it was old Connie. She never liked it much. She made him get rid of it.'

Pel's eyebrows rose. 'She has that much influence?

The policeman shrugged. 'She's been here a long time.'

As they stood by the kitchen door staring at the yard, Bardolle appeared from the forge. He seemed baffled. 'It beats me, Patron,' he said. 'We've turned nothing up. I can't imagine what he was after. Pay day wasn't until the following day so there's no point in chasing that angle.'

'Could someone have thought it *was* pay day.'

'Not if he lived in Montenay. Everybody here knows when pay-day is.'

Huppert appeared. He seemed to be using his arm normally

again and Pel indicated it with a gesture. Huppert flexed it. 'Coming along,' he said. 'But I've had to get Connie to drive me.'

Pel tried the idea of someone using Huppert's premises as a drop. 'They get up to a few tricks, you know,' he said.

Huppert didn't think it possible. He was also in no doubt that there was only one intruder.

'And you've no idea what he could have been after?'

'None at all. Unless . . . unless it's some employee we sacked in the past who's trying to do for me.'

'Got any names?'

Huppert fished in his pocket and produced a piece of paper. 'Yes, I have,' he said. 'It set me thinking and I wrote them down. I can only think of four since I took the place over.'

'When was that?'

'Eighteen years ago. Mostly we were on good terms with everybody. A few left of their own accord but these four left in bad odour. They thought I had no right to sack them.'

'Etienne Douaud. Michel Redaudineau. Yvon Muller. Robert Carruolo.' Pel read the names aloud. 'All French?'

Huppert shrugged. 'Two of them live here in Montenay. Douaud and Muller. Redaudineau came from the south. Lyons, I think. I think Carruolo was a Portuguese, but I'm not sure.'

'Why did they leave?'

'Carruolo stole tools. I sacked him.'

'And the others?'

'Bad timekeeping. Douaud and Muller just couldn't get here in the morning. I warned them several times.'

'And Redeaudineau?'

'He always went out for his lunch and he could never get back on time. I think he had a drink problem.'

'Better check on them, Bardolle,' Pel said, passing the list across. He turned back to Huppert. 'Nobody else who'd want to see you dead?'

'None that I know of. What do *you* think he was after?'

'Apart from you, I don't yet know.'

They were moving now through the forge. It was empty of workpeople and Pel moved round the benches and past the cold furnace. Eventually, he came to the chalk marks on the

103

bench and the dirty floor. They looked fainter – as though someone had tried to clean them off.

'Those marks,' Pel said. 'Remembered what they were for?'

Huppert stared at the marks. 'No. We make all sorts here. They could be for anything. They've been there a long time. I've asked but nobody can remember.'

'Somebody's tried to erase them.'

'Me,' Huppert admitted. He gestured. 'The place looked scruffy.'

Pel paused. 'When you came out looking for the intruder,' he said, 'you didn't turn the light on?'

'No.'

'Wasn't that dangerous? And you might have seen who it was.'

'He might have seen me, too.' Huppert shrugged. 'I just didn't think, I suppose. And I had a torch, of course. As I went into the forge I heard a door opening and closing, then the bullet hit me in the left arm and I dropped the torch. I decided it was too dangerous, so I bolted for the house to see if my wife had got hold of the police. It was then I found her.'

As they continued to study the forge, Huppert drifted away. Pel was frowning heavily, lost in thought. Bardolle nudged him back to the present.

'The chap next door's returned from Paris, Patron,' he said. 'I gather he's off again soon. Don't you think we ought to see him?'

The next door house abutted on to Huppert's property but it was impossible to see on to Huppert's land except from one window upstairs. The owner of the house was the man called Alexandre Démy. He worked for Electroniques Bourguignonnes and he was a strong-jawed, sour-visaged, hard-voiced man, who clearly didn't like the Hupperts much.

'The noise that comes from that place is damnable,' he said. 'I've been trying to have it stopped.'

'How?' Pel asked. 'Through the Mairie?'

'No.' Démy frowned. 'I couldn't get any joy at all through them. So I tried to get signatures from as many people as would sign so I could get some action. With that, they'd have *had* to do something.'

'How many did you get?'

'About four.'

'Is that all?'

'People round here have no civic feeling,' Démy snorted. 'You'd think they'd be concerned about what was happening in their village.'

'What *is* happening? Inform me.'

'The damn place's becoming industrialised. Montenay's a village, not an industrial estate. Forges belong on industrial estates. Not in the middle of a rural area.'

'How long have you lived here, Monsieur Démy?'

'Eight years.'

'But the forge's been here three times that length of time. Monsieur Huppert himself has been running it for eighteen years.'

'It should never have been allowed in the first place.'

'But, since it was, when you were looking for a house wouldn't you have been wiser to choose one somewhere else?'

'I try to keep France as she should be.'

Démy obviously considered everybody out of step but himself. Pel forced himself to divorce himself from what he realised was a growing dislike for a man he'd decided was a self-centred bully.

'Where did you come from, Monsieur?' he asked.

'Paris. And let me tell you, in Paris, they make sure you behave properly to your neighbours. No noise, no burning of garden rubbish until evening, no – '

'This isn't Paris, Monsieur!' Pel pointed out sharply. 'It's Montenay. In the country. In Burgundy. People have more land here than they normally do in Paris, and garden rubbish here isn't measured in kilos or barrowloads. Things are different. Have you not also noticed the birds – ?'

'I've noticed the cockerels. *And* that damned dog the Hupperts have. It's always barking.'

'It won't any more. It's gone.'

Démy looked surprised. 'Gone? Where?'

'They've got rid of it.'

'Who has?'

'Madame Gruye, I understand.'

Démy smiled. 'Throwing her weight about, I suppose, as

105

usual. You want to watch her, you know. She's after Huppert.'

'Is that so? Why do you say that?'

'It's obvious. Frustrated widow. She's after everyone. Any man she can get hold of.'

Pel eyed him sideways. 'Was she after you, too?'

'Of course she was. They all were.'

'All of them?'

'This village is full of women like that.'

Pel said nothing for a while. He glanced at Bardolle who was staring at the ceiling as if he'd found something tremendously interesting up there.

'You'd better tell me about it,' Pel said.

Démy was only too willing and in the end Pel had to hold up his hand. He was becoming involved in the antics of a self-important and not very pleasant man. 'Let's talk about what happened next door the other night,' he said. 'Did you see anything?'

'I looked.'

'You did?'

'With binoculars. They're good ones, too. Powerful.'

'Do you usually examine your neighbours' behaviour with powerful binoculars?'

'Why not? I expect people examine me.'

'Have you seen them?'

'Well, no. But I suppose they do.'

Pel studied Démy with narrowed eyes. This one, he thought, is a funny one.

'Let's go on,' he said. 'Did you hear anything?'

'No.'

'Not even the dog?'

Démy stopped, and considered. 'I must have been asleep,' he said. 'The first I heard was that lunatic next door shouting. Then all the shooting. Or perhaps it was the other way round. Then people opening windows. That sort of thing. *Then* I noticed the dog. It seemed to be going mad. All the yelling, I suppose. It did it last time.'

'Last time?'

'When he said he was shot at before. About a month ago.'

'Are you familiar with firearms, Monsieur?'

'Of course. Dead shot. I did my time in the army.'

106

'Automatic pistols?'

'Of course. I – ' Démy stopped dead. 'Here, you're not thinking – '

'I'm not thinking anything,' Pel said. It was a lie because Pel was thinking a lot. 'Do you meet Monsieur Huppert much?' he asked.

'Not if I can help it.'

'What about Madame Gruye?'

'She's jealous as hell.'

'Of whom?'

'Madame Huppert.'

'How do you know? Did *you* get on all right with Madame Huppert?'

'No reason not to.'

'But you don't meet Huppert himself?'

Démy made a sweeping gesture. 'He hates me.'

Pel's eyebrows lifted, and Démy hurried on. 'He tried to kill me, you know?'

'He did? When?'

'Last year.'

'Why?'

Démy gestured. 'Because he's unbalanced. Full of obsessions. Full of funny ideas. He thought all the women in the village were after him.'

Bardolle's study of the ceiling became more intense.

'Why did Huppert hate you?' Pel asked.

'Because his wife had fallen for me?'

'She had? How do you know?'

'The way she looked at me when I offered to lend her my gun. She was scared of being alone. So I offered it. I have one. These days you don't know who your neighbours are.'

'What is this gun of yours?'

'6.35.'

'Type?'

'FAS Apex.'

Pel glanced at Bardolle.

'They're cheap,' Démy said.

'And you lent it to her?'

'No. She said she'd got one. Huppert's. She showed it to me. He kept it in the safe in the office.'

'I think I'd like to see this pistol of yours. *And* the licence.'

Démy produced the licence and the pistol.

Pel showed it to Bardolle. '6.35,' he said. 'Just as he said. Let's have it down to Ballistics.'

'Look here –' Démy began to protest but Pel interrupted. 'You'll get it back,' he said. 'In the meantime, there are a few more questions. The night of the shooting – the second shooting when Madame Huppert was killed – did you see clearly what happened with those binoculars of yours?'

'No. I'd gone to bed early. I'd had a long day driving and I had another one the next day. I heard the shouting. I told you. *Then* I got up.'

'And went to the window? With the binoculars?'

'Yes.'

'What did you see?'

'I saw Huppert with the gun in his hand. He was yelling.'

'What was he yelling?'

' "Come down. Somebody wants you." '

'Not "Come down. Ring the Police"?'

Démy shrugged. 'Well, I don't think so but it might have been.'

'Can you describe what you saw?'

'What I told you. Huppert. He had a towel over his shoulders.'

'Round his neck?'

'Yes, but the ends were dangling. He was shouting. I saw him fire several times. Then he went into the forge – the one where all the noise comes from. There were more shots.'

'How many?'

'I didn't count. One or two, I think.'

'Was it one or *two?*'

'I'm not sure. Then I heard him yell and he came out with the towel round his arm. There seemed to be blood on it.'

'What did you do?'

'Well, when he went inside, it seemed to be all over, so I went back to bed.'

Pel's eyes widened. '*You went back to bed?*'

'Well, it was none of my business, was it?'

'And you went away the next day?'

'Why not?'

'A woman had been shot. She was dying.'

'Well, I didn't know that, did I? All I knew was that there'd been the usual row I'd always been complaining about, so I thanked God it had stopped. I don't take much notice of what goes on in the village. I don't get on with the people here.'

'Do they get on with you?'

'They don't try.'

'No,' Pel said. 'I suppose not.'

13

The trouble with criminals, Pel decided, was that they were selfish, impatient and in too big a hurry. Never for one moment did they think of waiting their turn. If only one lot could manage to wait for the police to clear up the misdemeanours of the lot before them, life would have been so much easier. But it never worked out that way and someone always started jumping the queue and getting up to his tricks before they'd cleared up the mess left by his predecessor. Here they were, with the De Mougy robbery on their hands when someone had had the indelicacy to start letting off a gun at Montenay; and they'd no sooner got that investigation under way when someone had shot Richard Selva at Pouilly. Selva's death didn't worry Pel overmuch. He was another drug pusher who wouldn't be missed. But his murder had to be cleared up. In the meantime, there were all the other things that plagued the Brigade Criminelle – the muggings, the burglaries, the indecent assaults, the thefts, the swindles, the frauds – so that the police were always stretched to the limit. Especially when you also included demonstrations by lorry drivers insisting on free entry to Switzerland and Italy, and wine growers who liked occasionally to blow up with plastic explosive the vats of imported wine which they considered was ruining their businesses.

Nosjean was handling the shooting at Pouilly; De Troq' the De Mougy theft; and Bardolle, with the backing of Darcy, the shooting at Montenay. Pel was presiding over the lot – with the exception, thank the good Lord God, of Misset who was watching Briand's counterfeit notes and Chaput's supposed spy, in whom Pel just couldn't bring himself to believe. Aimedieu was still growing fat on Madame Bonhomme's cakes as he watched Lafarge's house from her front bedroom; and they were still awaiting a report on Pépé le Cornet from Paris because the events they were involved in seemed also to touch on *their* diocese. Pel didn't expect much from the report. He'd been involved with the Paris mob before and he knew there were always too many people between the event and Pépé le Cornet himself, who nowadays cultivated the image of a successful entrepreneur with no interest in crime. Every policeman in the country knew he wasn't a businessman but it was a different matter proving the fact, and Pépé went on living a life of luxury with houses as big as the Elysée Palace, expensive foreign cars and dancing attendance on him little dolly girls blessed with the sort of beauty that reduced strong men to tears. Life, Pel sometimes thought, was decidedly unfair. God was doubtless all-powerful but He seemed at times to have overlooked the details, and it was strange that the good often went to the wall while the wicked survived in luxury.

Now, to complete the picture, the Baron De Mougy had talked to a friend of his and someone had pulled strings and a detective was due from Paris to look into the theft of his valuables. The place was becoming knee-deep in people from Paris, none of whom seemed to know what was going on or where to search, so that they were constantly in the local boys' hair. Since all their information came from the local people, anyway, they might just as well have all stayed where they were and left it to them, because it was a well-known fact that so long as the local boys were intelligent they always had the best chance, for the simple reason that they knew their locality and the people in it. And Pel's people *were* intelligent. With the exception, he had to concede, of Misset, who was probably a congenital idiot.

Even Madame Pel had not been able to help. She had heard nothing of any shady deals which involved the Baronne de Mougy, but she *had* heard that the Baron was not the only man in her life.

'Who is?' Pel asked.

'The one she had before,' Madame said. 'Paul-Edouard Piot. The man who has that estate at Butte-Avelan.'

'Did she go back to him?'

'She probably never left him.'

'I hope to God the Baron doesn't find out or we'll have

another murder on our hands.' Pel looked at his wife affection-ately. 'How do you find out these things?'

She smiled a secretive smile. 'It's amazing what women talk about under the dryers.'

'Even about their lovers?'

'Not their own as a rule. Usually other people's. Someone hears a rumour. Someone's given a confidence.' Madame smiled. 'And, having been given a confidence and told not to repeat it, she immediately has to find someone to repeat it to. We usually get the rumours third or fourth hand, heard as they're passed on to friends under the next dryer by people who've been begged not to say anything.'

As they talked, the telephone went. It was Darcy. He sounded excited.

'I've just heard they've found something in the canal by the bridge,' he said. 'I'm going there now!'

When Pel arrived, he found to his surprise that the frogmen, who'd arrived from the Navy at St. Nazaire, had come up with not *one* 6.35 but *two*. In addition, they had produced a revolver, very rusty, old and useless, and what appeared to be a dagger, also very old and rusty. But the two 6.35s were undamaged by the immersion, the film of oil on them still giving them protection. And they had consecutive numbers, which matched the numbers in the stolen consignment from St. Etienne.

Darcy had them lying on a sheet of plastic in the boot of his car.

'There's something a bit odd about one of them, Patron,' he said as he opened it. 'Somebody's sawn the trigger guard off.'

The cut was still clear, the metal still bright despite the immersion in the canal.

'That seems a damn silly thing to do,' Darcy said. 'Especially with the Apex. It doesn't have the solid block trigger, just the curved spindle type and without the guard, you could catch it in your pocket lining and shoot yourself in the balls. Why would anyone want to do that?'

'I expect,' Pel said, 'that there was a very good reason and when we find out why, we'll probably know why Madame Huppert was shot. Or vice versa. Our friend who did the shooting at Montenay tossed them away together. Anybody see anything?'

'We're asking,' Darcy said. 'But I don't suppose we'll find anybody. He could just toss them through the window of his car. Simplest thing in the world.'

'Not always,' Pel said. 'There was that case of the type who killed that farmer near Le Havre and tossed the gun over the parapet as he was crossing the Pont de Tancarville. Unfortunately, it hit one of the uprights and bounced back into the road and was spotted by a police car ten minutes later. It even had his name on it. He could never understand how it was fished out of the water so quickly.'

It didn't take the press long to learn of the police activity at the canal and they were round in no time, like vultures after a carcass.

Pel shrugged. 'Give them their ration of excitement for tomorrow's readers, Daniel,' he advised.

'How much do we tell them, Patron? They're on to both the shootings.'

'What about Misset's case?'

Darcy grinned. 'They've not heard of that.'

'Misset *will* be disappointed. Right. Give them the bare details. No more. We've been looking for a gun. That's all. Don't tell them we've found one.'

'And the De Mougy business? They'll want the latest on that.'

'As much as you like on that. And if you can make De Mougy look an ass,' Pel added maliciously, 'so much the better. But nothing about Nick the Greek or Pat the Bang. And nothing about Lafarge. I want Lafarge in particular kept quiet. I don't want him to know we're interested in case he leads us to whoever was in it with him.'

Ballistics were quick with their report on the guns fished from the canal. One of them was the gun that had killed Madame Huppert. The other was the one that had wounded her husband. The striations coincided with the bullets they'd found. There was more news, too, from Inspector Pomereu of Traffic, who met them when they returned to the office.

'Nick the Greek, Patron,' he said.

113

'What about him?'

'He's been spotted. Near Montenay. He was in a car.'

'On his own?'

'He had a girl with him.'

'He would have.' Pel had been hoping, maybe, for Pépé le Cornet. 'What was the car?'

'Citroën. A big one.'

'His own?'

'Of course.'

Pel frowned and looked at Darcy. 'Where in God's name do they get the money?' he asked. 'He's only been out of gaol a month, yet he already has a car and money in his pocket. What was he doing in Montenay?'

Pomereu shrugged. 'He seemed to be trying to look as if he was just passing through.'

'And was he?'

'At the speed he was going, I doubt it.'

'Perhaps that's where his girl lives. Did you get the number of the car?'

Pomereu looked smug. 'We did.'

'Right, check the records, find where he's living and bring him in.'

Arion Nicopoloulos was a handsome young man, tall, grey-eyed and dark-haired, with a splendid profile which he knew how to use to advantage.

He smiled at Pel. 'Can't you leave a guy alone?' he asked. 'I've only just got out. I haven't had time to get up to anything yet, even if I wanted to, which I don't. Not again. I've had enough of that place. I'm not going back.'

'That's what they all say,' Pel said dryly.

'I mean it.'

'You did last time.' Pel smiled silkily. 'You're living in the Rue Clochemarc, Nick. It's a nice area. Are you on your own?'

Nick's handsome face twisted in a sneer. It was obvious that he thought that, while there were women in the world, living alone was for fools.

'What's her name?'

'Loïs Dubois.'

'Does she know about you?'

'No.'

'Not told her?'

'Would *you?*'

'Who're your friends these days, Nick?'

'Come again?'

'You used to be friendly with Dick Selva. He was in the nick with you. Still friendly?'

'No. We – well, we – er – had a disagreement.'

'Go for him, did you?'

'Not me.'

'Someone else? Who?'

'It happens all the time.' Nick's handsome teeth showed as he smiled.

'What about the Paris mob, Nick?'

'What's the Paris mob?'

'Pépé le Cornet's lot.'

'Never heard of them.'

'Come off it. You were mixed up with them more than once. You used to work for Pépé.'

'Oh, *him!*' A great light seemed to dawn, then Nick shook his head. 'Not heard of him for years.'

'Pépé used to be keen on jewels,' Darcy put in.

'He likes to flash them around,' Nick agreed.

'He likes to get his mitts on them, too. Especially other people's. Did he have anything to do with the De Mougy robbery?'

'What's the De Mougy robbery?'

'You won't have heard, of course?'

'Not a word.'

'Someone held up the Baron de Mougy and removed his wallet and his wife's jewels. On the 30th of last month. Three types. Stocking masks. Guns. The lot. Know anything about it?'

'I don't go in for that sort of thing.'

'You did last time.'

Nick looked pained.

'Where were you on the 30th?'

'I was in Dole.'

'See anybody who'd verify it?'

Nick scowled. 'Do I have to have people to verify where

115

I've been?' he said. 'I've come out. I've done my lot. I'm free. Even from the flics.'

They got very little from him and they had to let him go. From the window they watched him stroll out of the Hôtel de Police. The big Citroën was waiting for him, a girl in the driving seat. As he appeared, she moved over and Nick took the wheel.

'He's in with the Paris mob again,' Pel said. 'That's were that car came from. I dare bet Pépé provided it. On terms, of course.'

'Such as "I've got a little job I'd like you to look at." '

'Exactly. Keep an eye on him, Daniel. And on the girl. She might not be as innocent as he pretends.'

'Do I talk to her, Patron?'

'No,' Pel said. 'Leave her for the moment. Leave Nick, too. Let him think we've lost interest. He might get over-confident. He *was* in the De Mougy business. I know it. It's typical Pépé le Cornet style to get someone small and not connected to the mob like Lafarge for the dirty work, with Nick as the go-between. That way Pépé's not involved.' He picked up the telephone and dialled Madame Bonhomme's number. Madame Bonhomme answered.

'Have you found out anything yet?' she asked.

'Not yet, Madame. But we will.'

When Aimedieu came to the telephone, Pel asked if he'd seen anything.

'Nothing, Patron,' Aimedieu said. 'It's as quiet as the grave. And about as exciting.'

'Nobody visiting Lafarge?'

'Just a woman and a boy, who go in and out. Madame Bonhomme says they're his wife and son. I've seen Lafarge in the doorway but he never moves outside.'

'You couldn't miss him?'

'Not possible, Patron. When I'm not watching, Madame Bonhomme is.'

'And when she's watching, what are you doing?'

'Making the coffee. Cutting the bread. Cooking the lunch.'

'And doubtless vacuuming the sitting room and making the beds?'

Aimedieu chuckled. 'Not exactly, Patron. But I help a bit. And you've no need to worry. Madame Bonhomme's better at it than I am. She knows everybody who ever visits these houses. And she's probably got more patience. She's been sitting in the window for so long because of her legs it's become second nature. What's more, she doesn't have to hide. Everybody's used to seeing her.'

'I want to know at once if anybody unusual calls.'

'It's as good as done, Patron.'

'I think Aimedieu's enjoying himself too much,' Pel said as he replaced the telephone. 'I think we'll have to relieve him before long, or give him someone to share it with. For the meantime, let's keep a low profile. It might worry them if we make no move.'

Darcy nodded. 'What about Pat the Bang?' he asked. 'I'd bet my wages he was the third guy – the one who brought the car up. He's done the driving on jobs before.'

'Have we picked up anything on him?'

'Not a thing.'

'Nothing from Ballentou?'

'Nothing at all. He seems to have sunk without trace.'

'Not sunk,' Pel said. 'Just submerged for the time being.'

14

Sergeant Misset was worried. He'd been worried ever since he'd heard the dark man asking for Ada Vocci at the Hôtel Centrale. She'd been out then and Misset wondered if she'd returned, and what she'd been up to in Switzerland.

Inspector Briand, of Counterfeit Currency, had vanished from Misset's mind. It wasn't a mind that you could fill with facts and expect to draw on at any time like a computer, and with the arrival of Ada Vocci and now Major Chaput's ominous rumblings about spies, it had completely lost Briand among the junk. Briand had never reappeared since his first interview and Misset had long since decided that, his quest having proved fruitless, he had disappeared back to Paris. Misset's mind was never very elastic.

Chiefly he was wondering if Ada were ever coming back and whether, in fact, being what Chaput said she was, she was at that moment somewhere negotiating the sale of the file Chaput said she possessed. Had Misset missed a chance to capture an international spy? Had he missed the chance he'd been longing for, for years?

He decided to check.

Reaching the Hôtel Centrale, he didn't bother with the desk but headed straight for the stairs as if he were staying there. No one stopped him as he made his way to Ada Vocci's room. The key had been missing from the hook above the reception desk, he'd noticed, and when he arrived, the chambermaid was there, turning down the bed.

'I'll wait inside,' he said. 'Mademoiselle's on her way up. She's just changing some money at the desk.'

A ten-franc note clinched the deal, and for some time he sat on the settee. The heavy box he'd rescued from the railway track stood in a corner of the room. Alongside it was a valise and the two white suitcases. For a while he gazed at the wooden box. The hole in the lock seemed to stare back at him with malignant intensity. Everything Chaput had said came back into his mind as it held his eyes, and reluctantly he crossed the room towards it.

He moved slowly round it, staring at it, the dark glasses down his nose, then he prodded the valise with his toe. It was empty. Almost as if his actions were governed by some will other than his own, he tried to open the suitcases but they were locked.

Casually, he began to examine the brass-bound box. It was unlocked and the marble chippings where the urn had rested were still inside. Curious, he glanced round and noticed that the urn had gone from beside the bed where he'd last seen it and he wondered if Ada Vocci carried it round with her for safety. The brass-bound box caught his attention again, obsessive and compulsive, and he tapped it. Then, remembering a long-handled umbrella he'd seen in the wardrobe, he fished it out, and pushed it down through the marble chippings until he felt it strike against the bottom of the box. He tapped it once or twice more, then, making a note of where the upper edge of the box lay against the umbrella, he took it out again and measured it against the outside. There was a difference of around ten centimetres.

He put the umbrella down and stared at the box. No box of that size would have a base ten centimetres thick. It didn't make sense.

For a long time, he sat on the bed, staring at it, then, on a sudden impulse he fished a couple of newspapers from the wastepaper basket and tipped the marble chippings on to them and stirred them up. There was nothing ominous about them. They were simply marble chippings and nothing else.

He measured the inside of the box against the outside and tapped the base. It sounded hollow. Replacing the chippings, he stared at it, frowning. Chaput had been right. It *had* a false bottom.

He was still kneeling by the box, wondering how to find the secret compartment, when the door clicked and he whirled to find himself face to face with Ada Vocci herself. She was wearing a bronze-coloured dress and on her arm was a large straw bag in which he could see magazines and the top of the urn.

Her gaze flew at once to the box, then to the umbrella lying alongside, and finally to Misset's face. Her eyes seemed cool pinpoints of jade.

For a moment there was silence as they stared at each other then she sat down abruptly on the bed, her mouth taut, her eyes hard.

'You've found out,' she said. 'You've found out about me.'

For some time, Misset said nothing. He wasn't sure whether to be afraid or put on a show of masterful dignity, or even, if she pulled a gun, to duck.

'Well,' he said at last, 'I've found out something but I'm not sure what.'

She dabbed her eyes with a handkerchief but he knew she wasn't crying. Underneath that highly desirable exterior, he suspected she was as tough as Old Nick's nag nails and nothing about her had ever led him to believe she was the type to sob out her troubles on a stern male breast. When he didn't rush to her assistance, she stopped abruptly and, fishing into the bag she'd been carrying, she dug out the urn and placed it on the table beside the bed.

Misset stared at it fascinated. 'What *is* in that thing?' he asked.

She looked up, calm again and with no sign of tears. 'Serafino,' she said sharply. 'I told you.'

'You told me a lot of things but I'm not sure they were all true. Is it really Serafino?'

She nodded silently and he rubbed his nose, bewildered, wondering how much she knew about Chaput.

'Then why did you put him in a box with a false bottom?' he asked. 'Don't tell me *that* was part of the undertaker's plan, like the marble chippings and the perfumed crystals.'

She said nothing for a moment then she looked up at him. 'Why did you *expect* a false bottom?' she asked.

'The size of it.' He decided not to tell her about Chaput. 'After all – to bring out a little urn you could carry in your bag. It *is* a false bottom, isn't it?'

She nodded.

'What was in it? What were you trying to get out of Poland? You must have been trying to get *something* out.'

She sniffed. 'You think I'm a spy? You think I'm this agent who's escaped with a list of other spies?' Briefly the cold look appeared in her eyes then it was gone again. 'Where did you get *that* idea?'

Suddenly Misset felt a fool and once more that he was being used.

'You know how it is,' he said lamely. 'All this story about Serafino. And then finding the box had a false bottom. After all, why didn't you bring the old boy out in your bag? You had him there today.'

'I like to have him safe.'

'Because you loved him?'

She made a noise that came remarkably close to spitting. 'Pchah! Of course not! But with the ashes and the documents from the crematorium I have proof that he's dead and that all he owned is mine.'

'And what *was* in that false bottom?'

She lay back on the pillows and, putting her feet on the bed, suddenly in control of the situation, she looked up at Misset under her lashes, so that he had to breathe deeply. 'Serafino's money,' she said.

'From Poland?'

'Perhaps you don't know the regulations that exist at the other side of the Iron Curtain? Western businessmen who make money there have to spend it there. Actors who act there have to draw their salaries there and spend them before they leave. Authors whose books draw royalties there have to take a holiday there to spend them, otherwise they lose them. And, since most people can't manage to spend all they earn in the short time they stay, the system benefits a great deal. *I* decided that the money Serafino had earned was coming home. I need money. I am a type who can't do without it.'

This was something Misset could understand. He was, too. He put his feet up on the bed and leaned back on the pillows alongside her, Misset again – Napoleon Misset, Alexander the Great Misset, Louis XIV Misset, Charles de Gaulle Misset – he stared down at her in admiration, making the most of the view down the top of her dress.

'Go on,' he said. 'What else?'

121

'I was there before he died,' she said. 'And when he did, for a long time I managed to conceal the fact that he'd gone. I had the body cremated but I didn't mention it to the authorities. I managed to go on drawing cheques on his bank as though they were going into his business there. The banks paid and gradually I accumulated most of what he owned. When I had it all I set about forming a plan to get it home. I used Serafino. It wasn't difficult. Through my friend at the American Embassy I managed to get it all changed into dollars so that it would be easier to get rid of on this side. I wanted dollars; the Americans wanted zlotys. For their CIA to use, I suppose.' She jumped off the bed and, crossing to the wardrobe, dragged out one of the white suitcases. Taking a key from her handbag she unlocked it and threw the lid back. It contained dollar bills. Misset shot upright on the bed, his eyes bulging behind his glasses.

'Holy Mother of God!' he said. 'Are they real?'

'Of course they are? Do you want to check them?'

'Why dollars?'

'Best currency in the world. I transferred them from the box.'

'Is that what's in the other suitcases, too?' he asked.

'That's empty. I've been changing them into francs and putting them into a Swiss account. Now are you satisfied?' She re-locked the case and returned to where Misset was still sitting on the bed. Pushing him back on to the pillows, she took her place alongside him, leaning on his chest. The softness of her bosom made his heart pump abruptly and his hands were suddenly moist. Her face was close to his and he suddenly noticed how blurred his glasses had become.

'And the friend?' he asked thickly. 'The friend who helped you?'

She sighed. 'Poor Dexter. They found out. The CIA informed on him. He got sent home.'

Misset promptly saw Dexter tramping round Times Square in New York without a job and in danger of being arraigned on a charge of high treason.

'He was transferred,' she explained. 'I shall send him a nice present.'

She lay back on the pillows and Misset leaned on one elbow

122

to look at her. Her story had carried conviction but he still had his doubts.

'As a matter of interest,' he asked, 'just how much did you get out?'

She beamed up at him. 'Four hundred thousand dollars,' she said. 'I've already changed half of it.'

'And the rest?'

'You've been looking at it. I am making little trips about the country and changing it in small sums. I'm going off again tomorrow. When it's all gone, I shall go, too, and spend it.'

He looked startled and she lifted her arms and pulled him down to her.

'I am going to spend and spend,' she said gaily. 'I shall never go back to Milan. Why should I? Why should I worry about Serafino's family. They never liked me anyway.'

'And what about Serafino? Shall you always cart him about with you?'

She shook her head. 'When I have finished with him I shall throw him in the lake at Zurich.'

Misset was shocked. 'Poor con,' he said.

'Yes.' She kissed him cheerfully. 'Poor con. Now are you satisfied I'm not a spy?'

Misset nodded. He noticed it was growing warm and his glasses had steamed up once more. Chaput had got it wrong again.

'Let's have a drink on it,' he said.

She shook her head.

He felt his arteries swell. He was a man of powerful enthusiasm but, faced with a moral problem of this kind, the feeling of guilt put him off a little.

'Aren't you thirsty?' he asked.

'No,' she said quietly.

The heat seemed to be growing intense. Without taking her eyes off him, she kicked off her shoes and bounced gaily on the bed. 'It's too warm for clothes,' she said, unzipping the bronze dress.

Misset fought with himself a little longer, watching with the fascinated stare of a rabbit ambushed by a snake. 'Yes,' he agreed as she tossed the dress on to a chair. 'It is.'

He took off his glasses and placed them down carefully.

'The door is locked,' she pointed out.

'There's just one thing.'

She looked up.

'Serafino.'

She smiled and pushed the urn under the bed. 'Of course,' she said. 'He makes you think you are being watched.'

It was late when Misset left the Hôtel Centrale and the streets were empty. He knew he ought to be hanged, drawn and quartered, probably even canned and sold as dogmeat in the supermarket at Talant. But he was feeling on top of the world, despite the fact that he knew that Ada had played on his urges like a gypsy minstrel on a violin. He felt almost willing to do some work. The next day, Ada had said, she had to go to Zurich again on business in connection with the late lamented Serafino's estate, but that she'd be back by evening.

'Tally ho,' he murmured. 'La dolce vita. La grandissima fornicazione. Josephe Misset, what a thorough-going, dyed-in-the-wool, copper-bottomed bastard you are!'

It was about then that he remembered Briand and the fact that, in addition to working for Chaput on the security of the French Republic, he was also supposed to be working with Counterfeit Currency. In his eagerness to find Chaput's defecting Russian and his delight in Ada Vocci, he had allowed to slip his mind entirely the fact that he was also supposed to be on the look-out for counterfeit dollars.

15

Misset frowned. He'd been frowning a lot in the last forty-eight hours as the memory of the box in Ada Vocci's room came back to him. He accepted now that the rosy glow he'd felt in the session that had followed its examination had helped to obscure certain important facts of which he ought to have made a note. In the cold light of day he wasn't satisfied.

Misset frowned as the thought set a whole train of ideas in motion. If Ada wasn't all she seemed to be, he realised uneasily, then it wouldn't be unreasonable to suppose that Chaput might be right. He had certainly known plenty about her. And Briand? Was *he* right? One of them must be. Perhaps both. Ada Vocci was a remarkably resourceful young woman.

Misset's expression changed again and this time it was closely bordering on alarm. A whole string of events he hadn't even thought of before began to come back to him. Something, he decided, was rotten in the state of Denmark, as that English chap he'd read at school had said. There were a great many questions that still required answering. Too many inexplicable things seemed to be happening at once. Aware of a prickling down his spine, he decided he wasn't really cut out for the sort of work Chaput was doing.

The city, teeming with people, wore a smug look of normality. But there were all sorts of currents of suspicion and violence under the surface that only he knew about. At that moment even the doorways seemed to hide assassins.

He located Chaput at the bar near the Porte Guillaume. He was sitting at his usual place, studying a small notebook which he hurriedly put away as he saw Misset. His face seemed harder than Misset remembered and there was an icy look about his small eyes.

'Ah, Misset,' he said. 'Thought you'd turn up eventually.'

Misset offered him a cigarette. 'I think we need to talk,' he said.

Chaput ordered drinks. It was hot in the sunshine and there were damp marks under Misset's armpits. Suddenly Chaput looked seedy and unreliable and his eyes were as hard and unblinking as a barracuda's. Not by any means did he look like a man who would do any dirty work when there was someone else to do it for him.

'Look,' Misset said, 'some funny things have been happening lately.'

'Better tell me, mon vieux.'

'Well, first there was this type in the suit with gold thread in it at the station. He came out looking as if he'd lost a fortune.'

'Perhaps he had. Got any names? Any descriptions?'

'I think someone tried to kidnap us the other night when I met you. Me and Ada Vocci. You know – the girl who – '

'I know who Ada Vocci is,' Chaput said sharply.

'They had a taxi laid on. It was stolen. There was this other type, too. Tall chap. Good-looking. Asking for her at the hotel.'

Chaput shuffled to a more comfortable position. 'Perhaps the other side's arrived.'

'What other side?'

'There's always more than one, mon vieux. They'll go to any length.'

'Who will?'

'The Russians.'

'Will they be here?'

'I expect so. Americans, too. Perhaps even the West Germans and the British. Be careful. They're not against making a concrete pudding of a man and dropping him in the sea at Le Havre to make a new breakwater. I could get you a gun if you wanted one.'

'I've got a gun. All cops have guns. Why is this Gold-thread type interested in me?'

'I told you. The file.'

'I've got nothing to do with the file.'

'You have now. The girl. That's why they're following you. You're the man in the middle.'

'Ada's no agent,' Misset said. 'All she's after is security.'

126

Chaput was unimpressed. 'Security's a habit,' he said coldly. 'Like insecurity. People'll do any kind of dirt for security. Kill. Thieve. Even pinch plans. Why do you think she's not in it?'

'I looked at the box. It *had* a false bottom.'

'It *did?*'

'But not for what you thought. She explained.'

'They all do. Even when you find their pockets stuffed with hidden microphones.'

'Well, I've heard more than one version of her story and none of them seems to indicate she's a spy. She's just bringing out the ashes of her husband.' Misset paused. 'I think,' he added.

'And in the false bottom of the wooden box?'

'Money. That's all.'

'Money. Are you sure?'

'Of course I'm sure.'

'What sort of money?'

'Four hundred thousand francs in dollars sort of money.'

Chaput looked interested. 'That's a lot of money,' he said. 'Is it illegal to bring that much in?'

Chaput smiled. 'It is, to take it out, but I can't imagine any government objecting to nearly half a million dollars being pushed into the economy.'

Misset didn't mention that Ada had been busy as hell taking it right out again and stuffing it into a numbered Swiss account.

'I'll have to enquire,' Chaput went on. 'Where did it come from?'

'Poland. It was her husband's. They wouldn't let her bring it out so she got the idea of smuggling it out with his ashes.' Misset went into detail, his words tumbling over themselves.

'Where is it now?'

'In a bank. What's left's in the suitcase. Locked. In her wardrobe. Those suitcases had me baffled for a bit.'

'You and I, mon vieux,' Chaput said soberly, 'are in the wrong job. You actually saw this money?'

'Of course I did.'

'And you're sure there's no file?'

'Yes. Call your dogs off. Call everybody's dogs off.'

Chaput sat back, his fingers together like a steeple. 'They'd never believe it,' he said.

'Why not?'

'Same reason I don't. There's no Serafino Vocci. There never was.'

Misset's jaw dropped and Chaput smiled.

'I made a few enquiries, you see,' he said. 'There never was a type called Serafino Vocci who carried on business behind the Iron Curtain.'

Misset stared at him for a second then he swallowed what was left of his drink. 'You sure? You couldn't be wrong?'

Chaput gestured. 'I've told you. The route: Poland and East Germany to France. Lüneburg; Enschede in Holland; Maastricht in Belgium; Luxembourg; into France at Dude-lange; then Metz; and finally here. She was followed all the way after crossing over in Berlin. If I say there's no Serafino Vocci, there's no Serafino Vocci. Everybody else thinks the same, or they wouldn't be here, would they?'

'I think,' Misset said slowly, 'that this thing is getting dangerous.'

'Always was a bit,' Chaput admitted. 'What we want to do is get the woman and the file away from here – fast. Paris. Or New York. It doesn't matter. Anywhere in the West. The Americans would help. They'd foot the bill even. What are you going to do about it? You've got to pee or get off the pot.'

For a long time, Misset sat still, then he put down his empty glass and rose.

'Where are you going?'

'To see Ada Vocci. Name of God, I'll get the truth out of her this time or die in the attempt. Are you coming?'

'No. You get her out of the hotel. I'll be waiting.'

Misset went up the steps of the Hôtel Centrale two at a time. The affair seemed to be reaching some sort of climax and he felt a vague sense of relief that it would soon be over. Underneath his determination, too, there was a vague uneasy feeling about the money he'd seen. Was Ada Vocci passing counterfeit money *as well as* smuggling files? And if she was, where had it come from? For a moment – a very brief moment – Misset was thinking like a cop.

As before, he didn't ask permission and he didn't use the lift but headed straight for the stairs. No one stopped him. Ada's door was unlocked and Ada was sitting up in bed drinking champagne and eating a sandwich, her face still flushed from sleep. Her clothes were on the floor with her nightdress and the sight of her made Misset take off his glasses and polish them abruptly. For a moment she stared at him, startled, then she relaxed.

'I just got back from Basle,' she said. 'I hired a car and stayed there the night. I was hot and tired and I thought I'd rest. For a moment I thought you were the burglar come back.'

Misset gaped at her. 'What burglar?'

'Somebody had been here when I got back. He'd been through the drawers.'

'And the suitcase?'

She smiled. 'After I found you making investigations, I had it locked away. It goes to the basement when I'm away. I pick it up when I return. It's in the wardrobe now.'

For a moment Misset wondered if Chaput had decided to opt out of the secret service and go in for crime. Then he remembered the man in the gold-thread suit. 'Anybody see him?'

'No.'

'Did you report it?'

'Of course not. They'd have asked questions. Besides – ' she smiled ' – I have my own private policeman. You, Josephe.' She made herself more comfortable in the bed. 'I didn't expect you until this evening.'

He eyed the champagne. 'I suppose you couldn't spare a glass of that?' he asked.

'Of course. Have you locked the door?'

He was on the point of saying: No, and I don't intend to, but the amount of naked flesh made him decide that it would be as well, just in case. Misset was a weak vessel. Without a word, he turned round and slipped the bolt.

She handed him a glass. 'I'm hardly awake yet,' she said.

He swallowed the champagne at a gulp then, putting the glass down, he stood at the end of the bed and leaned over her, angry.

'Just as well you're hardly awake,' he said sharply, though

129

when he looked at her he found his resolution melting with every word. The sight of her there on the pillow with her long cool throat and the deep cleft between her breasts and her eyes still drowsy, was enough to melt the marrow of a murderer. Misset thought of his wife. He'd once looked at her, too, like that.

He continued more slowly, his anger draining away rapidly. He was a policeman. He needed to know because he was on duty – always. On the other hand, he felt, there was no immediate hurry.

'Perhaps if you're not quite compos mentis,' he said, 'I might get the truth out of you.'

She reached quickly for what looked like a strip of chiffon and slipped her arm into it. 'What do you mean?'

'There never was a damned Serafino Vocci,' Misset said heavily. 'Never. You've been stringing me along all the time with a whole parcel of lies. This time I want to know.'

Her mouth tightened.

'How did you find out?'

'Chap I know. Enquired in Milan.'

'You didn't trust me.'

Misset put on his tough cop face. 'I'm a policeman.'

She slipped from the bed and moved to the window. 'Who is this man?' she asked quietly.

'Another cop,' Misset said. 'He looked it up for me.'

There was a long silence then she looked round at him. 'And now you are angry with me?'

'Yes.' Misset felt large and hot and clumsy as she stared coldly at him. 'You made me look a fool.'

Her eyes rested on him for a long time, then she refilled the glass and passed it to him. He swallowed it quickly.

'Very well,' she said in a manner that was suddenly brisk. 'So you found me out.'

'You'd better get dressed.'

'You're going to arrest me?'

Misset didn't want to. Up to now he'd always managed to avoid arresting attractive women. She eyed him with an amused smile.

'Your friend is right, of course,' she said calmly. 'There *is* no Serafino Vocci in Milan.'

'Then who – ?' Misset indicated the urn alongside the bed.

'Serafino Vocci,' she said. 'But he wasn't a Milan businessman. Nor was he a Neapolitan businessman. Nor a Roman. Nor a Florentine. So you can tell your clever policeman friend he needn't look him up again. He was a Pole.'

'A what?' Misset stepped back from the urn as if it might bite.

'A Pole. He was my father.'

'Holy Mother of God!' Misset sat on the bed, his head whirling. She sat alongside him and, filling his glass again, put her arm round his shoulders and ran her fingers lightly through his hair.

'Poor Josephe,' she said.

'Let's have it,' he said wearily.

'It's a long story.'

'It was last time.'

She kissed his ear. His inclination was to push her away but he could feel her warm flesh and smell the perfume on her skin, and the inclination gave way to another feeling which never failed to be strong in Misset. He let her stay.

'For God's sake,' he begged. 'Tell the truth this time!'

'I'll tell the truth,' she said. 'But first take off your coat. It's become very hot suddenly.'

He allowed her to remove his jacket. 'Come on now, the truth,' he insisted.

Disconcertingly she pulled the scrap of chiffon round her and sat on the bed alongside him, her legs tucked underneath her.

'Put your arms round me,' she commanded.

Misset didn't argue. There was plenty of time to arrest her later, he decided.

'I am a Pole, too,' she said. 'But not entirely. My mother was French – '

'Which is why you speak such good French?'

'Of course.' She moved closer to him and put her hand inside his shirt.

'It's no good doing that,' he said. 'I want to hear the story.'

'Very well,' she agreed, but she didn't remove her hand. 'My father escaped to France in 1940. He married my mother in Paris. I was born there after the war. They went back to

Poland during the amnesty the Communists allowed and I went with them.'

She leaned over him and he had to fight hard to keep his hands off her.

'The story,' he repeated.

'My father went back because he was a Pole. He had won many medals with the French army and was a hero, and he was a master-printer and hoped to do well. He worked for the Polish government. He printed their bank notes. My mother died. Then he was taken ill too.'

Misset's head was whirling and he wasn't sure he was following the story properly.

'Before he died, he let me into a secret.'

'He'd robbed the till?'

She looked puzzled, and he waved her on.

'He had managed to overprint many of the issues and had put the notes aside. He had two suitcases full of them.'

'And that's what you brought out? Not Serafino's money.'

'It *was* Serafino's money. He was my father. Except that his name wasn't Serafino. I decided to come here. France is always hospitable and sympathetic to political refugees.' She giggled and kissed him. 'They also have good banks,' she added. '*And* they don't ask questions. And it is handy for the Gnomes of Zurich. I wanted to escape. You have never lived in Poland, so you could never understand why. I got the money into Austria and put it into an account with the Creditanstaltbank then I used the savings book and code word system to draw it out again. In dollars.'

Misset hadn't the foggiest idea what she was talking about but Ada obviously did.

'All you do,' she explained, 'is offer your savings book and write the code word on a piece of paper and you've got your money – fast. I was away before they'd noticed I'd arrived.'

Misset had long since given up trying to concentrate. There was too much of Ada Vocci in close proximity and not enough of it was covered.

'Why didn't you tell me this the first time?' he managed.

'Because it was dishonest.'

'Well, the second time then.'

'I didn't want you to think badly of me.'

'I might have, mightn't I?'

She shrugged and settled herself inside the curve of his arm. 'If you look at it in some ways,' she agreed. 'If you look at it in other ways, you might not. My father had his own business before the war, but it was destroyed and they wouldn't let him build it up again. The Communists said he had fought for the Fascist-capitalist nations. They said he had no status because he'd fled when the Germans came, instead of staying behind to defend his country.'

'Why don't you apply for political asylum?'

'No.'

'I could tell you how to go about it.'

'No.'

'Why not?'

'I don't want to!'

'But – '

'I tell you, no! I'm doing exactly as my father wished.'

'Surely he wouldn't object.'

'No!'

Misset was feeling a little drunk now and was stroking her shoulder, trying desperately to keep a grip on events which still seemed in danger of whirling away out of control.

'He was determined I should get what he was entitled to,' she went on. 'He told me on his deathbed what I must do. He was to be cremated – '

'And put in an urn?'

'And the urn had to be in a funeral casket.'

'With the money in the false bottom.'

She smiled, and nodded as he finished her story with a rush. 'And you were to say you were taking him home to your native land because officially you were born in France and had the passport to prove it?'

Misset sat up but she pulled him down again so that his glasses were knocked askew. 'My God,' he said, coming up for air once more, 'what an idea!'

She reached purposefully for him. The contact made him giddy. Misset was a man without many scruples and, always short of funds, he was even beginning to think of ways of getting his hands on some of the money. At that moment he wasn't even bothered if it *was* Briand's counterfeit stock, so long as he could share it.

'You don't think too badly of me?'

The soft voice in his ear brought him back to life. 'I think you've been damned clever,' he said in a thick voice that didn't sound like his own.

'And what are you going to do with me?'

Misset stared at her. His head was full of ideas and they all seemed to crystallise into the same thing.

'Do you want to go now?' she asked.

Misset's head seemed to shake of its own accord. 'I'm in no hurry. Plenty of time.'

She smiled and patted the bed alongside her. 'Then let us stay here for a while. As if we were an old married couple – ' She paused. 'Well,' she ended, 'not *too* old.'

She stretched luxuriously and Misset took off his glasses and laid them on the tray on the table beside the bed. Then his eyes fell on the urn.

'What about Papa?'

She smiled. 'He always liked to see me enjoying myself.'

16

It's no good, Misset thought weakly as he lay in bed alongside his wife. Once a rat, always a rat. You couldn't make a silk purse out of a sow's ear.

It was the drink, he told himself. He'd had too much. It had melted his resolve. It always had done. By his usual devious process of reasoning, he was trying hard to convince himself that he couldn't be blamed for what had happened.

But what a girl! What a story! He was swept by admiration.

Then abruptly, as if a bucket of cold water had been thrown over him, he remembered it was the *third* story he'd heard. And they'd all been equally clever.

His mind was clearing rapidly. According to Chaput, half the secret agents in Europe were at that moment pouring into the city by every train and bus and plane. The place was becoming jammed with them, and the sort of in-between-the-sheets behaviour he'd indulged in was hardly the pastime for a man in imminent danger of being dropped in the sea inside a block of concrete.

He sat up in bed, staring in front of him, his mind sharpening rapidly as he fought off the effects of the drink. 'Ada,' he croaked. 'For God's sake!'

There was a heave in the bed alongside him and his wife sat bolt upright alongside him.

'What?' she said.

He came to his senses abruptly and passed a hand across his face. Whatever the truth of Ada's story – *any of her stories!* – things would be unpleasant for her if she were dragged back behind the Iron Curtain.

'Who's Ada?' Madame Misset demanded.

Misset came down to earth. He stared at his wife. She looked blurred so he scooped up his glasses from the bedside table and slammed them on his nose.

'Ada?' he said.

'Yes,' she snapped. 'Ada. Who is she?'

He struggled to get his mind working. 'A woman I've been following,' he said. 'At the Hôtel Centrale.'

'That'll be why your clothes smell of perfume, I suppose.'

'I don't smell of perfume.'

'Yes, you do. You've been smelling like a brothel.' Madame Misset snorted. 'She must be a cheap type to use such stuff.'

Misset struggled to sort out his thoughts. Ada Vocci, he felt, could give half the length of the track to his wife and still beat her by the other half.

'I've been keeping an eye on her,' he said. 'Hôtel Centrale. I told you.'

'Does keeping an eye on her mean clutching her tightly enough for her perfume to be all over your clothes and for you to leap up in bed yelling, "Ada, for God's sake!"? For God's sake, what? What did she do?'

'Nothing. Nothing. I was dreaming.'

'I'll bet you were. And not about me either. Who is this Ada woman?'

Misset answered without thinking. Normally he answered warily and tried to give his wife the impression that any woman he was connected with during his work had a face like the back end of a bus. He just wasn't alert.

'Looks like Sophia Loren,' he said. 'You'd never believe – '

Madame Misset yanked the pillow from behind her and swung it with all her force. It hit Misset in the face and slammed him back against the bedhead with a jolt that cracked his head and made him see stars.

Stunned, he lay there for a moment then he scrambled from the bed. The carafe of water that always stood by his wife's side of the bed smashed against the wall. The glass followed. Then a hairbrush and the Bible his wife liked to read from time to time. He decided it was time he disappeared.

As he snatched up his clothes he was under a hail of everything Madame Misset could lay her hands on, and as he slammed the door behind him it shuddered under the impact of the glass tray she kept on the dressing table for her lipstick, face powder and curlers. He bolted, hopping down the stairs on one leg as he tried to put his shoes on as he went.

Outside, finally dressed, Misset lit a cigarette and took a deep drag at it. He was scared. The time had come to stop. It was the point of no return. Much more of this, he thought, and he'd never be able to back off. He'd lose his job and his wife – though *that* didn't worry him too much – and he'd be finished. It was all right daydreaming about a golden future and a world of beautiful women, but it seemed a damned sight wiser to turn his back on them and go in for a dull grey present. Come home. All is forgiven. That was what he wanted to hear. The safest thing, he decided, would probably be to be a hermit – but, name of God, that would be a damned spartan existence! Safer to plump for a bit of for-richer-for-poorer.

He crushed out the cigarette half-smoked, suddenly stone-cold sober. He looked at his watch. It was late but he'd got to talk to Ada. He'd got to clear the thing up. He'd got to arrest her or back off. As Chaput had said, he'd either got to pee or get off the pot.

In the cold clear light of day, it was obvious what Ada Vocci had been up to, even if she wasn't the agent with the file everybody was looking for. She was handling counterfeit dollars. She had to be.

He'd let it slide, he realised, because every time he got around to discussing it she got him on the bed with all the wicks turned up to boiling point. He should be sold into slavery for the things he'd done. On the other hand, he couldn't hand over someone who looked like Ada to Number 72, Rue d'Auxonne, which was the name by which the local clink went. She'd die in a place like that. He'd *got* to get her away. Get her to demand political asylum. And then get her out of France. To America for instance. There was only one thing to do. March round to the Hôtel Centrale and grab her straight away.

Despite the hour, there were signs of agitation at the Hôtel Centrale when he arrived and the receptionist gave him a glare. None of them trusted him, the way he was always hanging around.

He became aware that people were moving about in surprisingly large numbers considering the hour, and that a

137

policeman from Inspector Nadauld's Uniformed branch was standing by the desk.

'What's going on?' he asked.

'God only knows,' the cop said. 'Somebody dashed out and fetched me off the street. I think it's all cleared up now. Some fight between a man and a dame.'

'Which dame?'

'I don't know. I didn't see her. Some Italian, I gather.'

Misset pushed him aside and dived for the desk. 'Mademoiselle Vocci?' he demanded.

The clerk gave him a pained look. 'Not another one?' he said.

'Listen.' Misset was quick to fall back on his proper rôle. 'I'm a cop. I've been keeping an eye on her for some time.'

'We wondered why you were always hanging around.'

'What's happened?'

'Some type came asking for her.'

'Which one? That one who was here the other day? Tall chap. Good-looking. Bit film-star-ish.'

'No. Not him. A little man.'

'Did he give a name?'

'No.'

'What was he like?'

'Cheap and nasty. Brown suit with shiny bits running through it.'

Misset fished out his identity card with its tricolour strip. 'I'm going up to her room,' he said.

The clerk shrugged. 'Well, everybody else's been up,' he said. 'I don't see why you shouldn't.'

Misset turned and tapped the uniformed man on the shoulder. 'You,' he said in his most magisterial voice. 'Come with me.'

Ada Vocci's room was a shambles. Drawers hung open and clothes were draped untidily from them. The bedclothes, the pillows, even the mattress, were on the floor. The box containing the chippings was open, the chippings scattered, and a white suitcase had been flung in one corner. It was open and was full of dirty clothes. The hotel's housekeeper was staring at it, bewildered.

'Who're you?' she snapped.

138

'Police.' Misset fished out his identity card again and flashed it. 'What happened?'

'God knows?' The housekeeper looked bewildered. 'I heard all this din and when I appeared they were throwing things.'

'Who were?'

'The woman. And a man in a brown suit. She ran off. He went after her, but then he came back and grabbed one of her suitcases. Who was he? Her husband?'

'I don't know who the hell he was,' Misset admitted.

He stared around. The urn containing Serafino was still by the bed, undamaged. He gestured at the cop.

'Money,' he said. 'Look for money.'

'Money?'

'Counterfeit money! The damn woman was carrying a fortune in counterfeit notes.' By this time Misset was certain.

It didn't take long to get the thing sorted out. It seemed that Gold-thread, whoever he was, had turned up with a gun and, at the sight of it, Ada Vocci had vanished at full speed, pausing only to snatch her handbag. There had been a brief wrestling match then she'd bolted down the corridor wearing only one shoe, and snatched a taxi which had happened to stop outside the main entrance with a couple of late-night revellers. Gold-thread had torn the bedroom apart while the horrified upstairs staff had been telephoning to the management downstairs who, in their turn, had telephoned the police. By the time Nadauld's men had arrived, Gold-thread had also disappeared and so had one of the white suitcases. Misset knew which one, too. The one with the money in it.

At the Hotêl de Police, Misset placed the urn containing Serafino, now clearly marked with a sticky label, 'Serafino Vocci. Ashes of', on his desk and sat down to the laborious task of writing out the report.

Briand turned up as soon as he could be contacted and was quickly on the telephone to the frontier police demanding the arrest of a man in a gold-threaded suit who was expected to try to cross. Then Chaput turned up, all his bounce gone, wanting to know what had gone wrong.

Misset sighed. All that remained of a beautiful friendship was the urn containing Serafino, now locked in Pel's safe until somebody claimed him.

Misset's report was written with care and the Chief had him in and praised him for his skill in halting the issue of counterfeit money. Pel was disgusted. Misset, of all people! The man who was never known to do anything extra – not even the normal amount if he could help it.

But the counterfeiters had fled. Nobody could deny that. But Ada Vocci had been clever enough to change half her notes into French francs and had disappeared with them safely locked in a numbered Swiss account. And the other half of the money was swanning about somewhere to the south as US dollars in the possession of what must be a very frightened little man in a gold-threaded suit.

'Name of Horstmann,' Pel said after a talk to Paris. 'Heinz Horstmann. German crook. Demi-sel. Small time. He was her henchman. The trouble was she'd outwitted him and was in danger of getting away with the loot. He objected. Naturally.'

Misset nodded, trying to look as if it had all been due to his intelligence and daring.

'You can forget your spy nonsense, now,' Pel said. 'She wasn't the one. I'm sure Inspector Darcy can find something for you to do.'

So Misset was back to answering the telephone, with little else but the memories of Ada Vocci.

'What about the urn?' he asked, feeling somehow that somebody should surely put poor old Serafino away safely with a modicum of decorum.

'He stays where he is,' Pel said firmly. 'In the safe. Until the thing's properly cleared up. Paris will probably want him in the end. They might even empty him down the sink and use the pot to put a geranium in.'

17

The Paris panic was over. Briand was chasing up and down the frontier posts between Switzerland, Italy, Belgium and Holland. Somewhere, presumably, Heinz Horstmann in his gold-threaded suit was trying to get the suitcase of counterfeit notes to safety. Chaput had disappeared back to Paris, disillusioned and despairing. The great spy chase was finished. As Pel had suspected, it had all been for nothing.

The story was round the office in no time. Briand's praise for Misset's brilliance came over loud and clear. Everybody gathered round Misset, clapping him on the back and demanding once more to look at the photographs of Ada Vocci.

'No wonder you never let her out of your sight,' Brochard said enviously. 'I bet you enjoyed that case. Did you – ' he paused ' – you know?'

Misset put on his James Bond look. 'I've never been known to argue,' he said with what was supposed to be a modest smile.

Pel was watching Misset. There'd be no getting rid of him this time. It was the way things went, though. While everybody else used their brains and worked their guts out, Misset, who probably didn't have a brain at all – just a hole inside his head – and who never lifted a finger if he could avoid it, had cracked the counterfeit money racket – even if only by accident. There'd be no holding him now. He'd be putting in a request to be considered for an inspectorship at any moment.

All the same, Pel thought, now that they'd got rid of Chaput and were about to get rid of Briand they might be allowed to get on with their work, clean up their own patch, and get back to normality. That was, of course, the normality allowed by two murders and a pretty hefty robbery, because, like the enquiry at Quigny and the enquiry at Montenay, the enquiry into the shooting of Richard Selva at Pouilly had come to a dead stop.

Not finally, though. Nosjean didn't believe that for a moment. After all, they'd only just started. As the politicians liked to say, he'd explored every avenue, but there were still a few side roads that could be opened if he tried. He decided to try Georges Ballentou again. It was just possible he might have heard what Selva had been up to. Because he'd clearly been up to something. Even crooks didn't get themselves shot for doing nothing.

Ballentou wasn't at home, but a girl was. She was fair and young and blue-eyed and Nosjean's heart, which was never very stable where attractive girls were concerned, lurched sideways a little. She didn't look like Charlotte Rampling which, as far as Nosjean was concerned was a bit of a disadvantage, but she did look a little like Catherine Deneuve, which more than made up for it. Moreover, she had a smile of the sort that could lift hearts and bring the sun out, and she was friendly and forthcoming and invited Nosjean in at once.

'Coffee?' she asked.

'Coffee would be fine,' Nosjean said.

She left him for the kitchen and he stared around as he waited. Ballentou's house was spotless. It was shabby – after all, Ballentou had spent a long time in prison and he wasn't earning much – but someone had worked hard on it.

'Me.' The voice came from the door and his head jerked round to see the girl standing there with the coffee. 'I know what you're thinking. How come it's so clean? I did it. When his daughter died, he didn't seem to care what happened. I'm her cousin, Imogen Wathus. I came from Epinal and when I got a job here, he said I could have Michelle's room. In return, I look after him. He's a good man.'

Nosjean didn't argue.

They talked for a long time over the coffee. The girl worked as a computor operator at one of the city offices but she managed to make it sound exciting and funny and Nosjean was enchanted by her. He'd just been heavily involved with a girl at the library but she'd decided being a policeman's

wife, with a husband always on duty, wasn't a good invest-
ment and had married a bank clerk instead, so that Nosjean
was particularly susceptible at that moment to a pretty face
and a welcoming smile.

It was quite clear Imogen Wathus was interested in
Nosjean, too. He was good-looking and educated and intelligent, and the two of them seemed to hit it off immediately.

She eventually brought the subject back to Ballentou.

'He's gone to Paris,' she said. 'Something to do with ex-
Prisoners' Aid, he told me. He's hoping to get some money,
I think. He's been before. He'll be back tonight.

'He's gone straight, you know,' she went on. 'No nonsense.
He stays in at night. Except perhaps to walk to the bar for a
beer. Nothing else. He's never out long. Except to go to work.
He tries to grow things in the garden. He's not very good at
it, mind you, and he doesn't know that when he's not here I
do a lot of it for him. But it encourages him. He's cheerful – '
she paused ' – at least he was.'

Nosjean didn't miss the change of feeling.

'Isn't he now?'

She seemed to think she'd said too much. 'He's just
worried,' she insisted. 'That's all. It's nothing.'

'It might be important,' Nosjean argued. 'Somebody might
be trying to put pressure on him. One of his old prison
associates. They do, you know,' he added earnestly.

The girl frowned and Nosjean pressed on. As he'd half
expected, something had come up and he didn't intend to let
go.

'If we know what it is,' he said, 'perhaps we can help. A
lot of these types who've been inside can't get away from
their past because their old friends won't let them "We've
got a little job for you, Georges." "There's something come
up, Georges, where we could use your skill." That sort of
thing.'

'He didn't have any skill. He always got caught.'

Nosjean had to admit the truth of that. 'He might know
something,' he said.

She looked at him pleadingly. 'You really want to help?'

'Our job's not only to arrest criminals. It's to prevent
crime. What's bothering him?'

'I don't know,' she said. 'I think it's what you say – people

143

he used to know.' She paused, debating whether to tell him, then she smiled, like many other girls before her, trusting Nosjean's open honest face. 'He's scared,' she said.

'In what way?'

'He looks under his car every time he goes out.'

'What for?'

'He says he thinks his exhaust's dropping off. But he also looks inside the engine. I suddenly wondered if he was looking for a bomb.'

This, Nosjean thought, was one for the book! Bombs! 'When did this start?' he asked.

'A few days ago. I'm not sure exactly.'

'Can you fix it by anything?'

She thought for a moment. 'Some time after the police questioned him, I think.'

'Why? Because he's been seen talking to us?'

'Would someone try to blow him up because of that?'

Well, they might, Nosjean had to admit. Not under normal circumstances but Ballentou *had* been in prison and he was known to the people who operated with Pépé le Cornet. Had he stumbled across their sphere of operations? Did he know something they preferred him not to know?

'I'll see we have this place watched,' he said.

She looked grateful and smiled. Then her worry returned. 'He won't want that,' she pointed out. 'He likes to think that sort of thing's behind him.'

'We can do it without him knowing. Don't discuss it with him.'

'I don't think he'd want me to.'

She couldn't offer anything in the way of help on Selva but Nosjean spent a pleasant hour listening to her talk before he took his leave. He even managed to arrange to meet her for a meal.

He had Selva's address from the prison authorities and the welfare department. It was in the old part of the city but it was a good area, better than most policemen could afford, so he could only assume that Selva had done well with drugs in the past.

On his way he called in at the Hôtel de Police. Pel was staring at reports – firmly believing as he always did, that the clues were there if he could only find them – and trying to will a hunch to come into his head. He was a great believer in hunches. They didn't provide the details but they often helped the case along.

'Ballentou's scared, Patron,' Nosjean said.

Pel looked up. 'Who says?'

'That girl who's looking after him. His niece. He seems to be afraid of a bomb in his car. She thinks perhaps he's being leaned on.'

'Who by?'

'I don't know. But Pat the Bang's not been turned up yet.'

Pel frowned. '*Why* would Ballentou expect Pat the Bang to put a bomb under *his* car? What does she think?'

'She doesn't think anything, Patron. She's got nothing to do with crime. She's just looking after Ballentou. But she's certain he's scared. I think we ought to have the place watched. We wouldn't want to lose him, would we?'

Pel agreed. 'Fix it,' he said. 'Have a word with Lacocq. He's free. He can do it.'

When Nosjean reached Selva's place, a girl answered the door. She was pale and unhealthy looking as if she didn't like fresh air.

'He's not in,' she said in answer to Nosjean's query.

He wasn't ever likely to be in again either, Nosjean thought, because he was lying in one of the drawers at the mortuary with a hole in his head.

'Know him well?' he asked.

'I live with him,' she answered defiantly.

She gave him her name – Monica Ormot – but seemed at first unwilling to answer questions. Nosjean produced his identity card with its tricolour strip.

'Police?' she said. 'What's he done?'

'At the moment, we're not sure,' Nosjean admitted. 'But we've got a good idea. Can you give us some indication of his movements lately?'

'I don't see why I should. He's trying to stay out of prison so it's none of your business.'

'Sometimes it is. Has he had any visitors lately?'

'No. He prefers to keep himself to himself.'

'Is that what he said?'

'He doesn't want to get involved again. He wants to stay straight.'

Remembering the body in the morgue, Nosjean suspected that he hadn't managed it. 'Do you mean,' he asked, 'that *nobody* ever called to say they were pleased to see him back in circulation?'

'He had a man come to see him a few days ago. That's all.'

'Know his name?'

'No. His car had a German registration, though, and he seemed American. I thought perhaps he was an American soldier serving there.'

'Did he say why he'd come?'

'Dick said he was in electronics and wanted to do some export business here when he came out of the service. Dick was in that line himself before – before he went – ' she paused ' – before he got mixed up with the wrong sort. I think they were planning something. He went to Paris last week to see what the prospects were up there.'

I'll bet he did, Nosjean thought. 'He didn't mention anybody he saw there, did he?'

'No.'

Pépé le Cornet, for a fortune, Nosjean thought. He looked at the girl. She was scruffy, but slim with a good figure.

'What do *you* do?' he asked. 'For a living.'

'I work at Intergrade. I look after the students who come in from the university. It's a student travel bureau. We fix flights abroad for them at cheap rates and put them in touch with student organisations in other countries so that it's easier and cheaper for them.'

'I expect a lot of them come in.'

'Yes. All students.' She looked puzzled. 'Look, what's all this about? Do you know where Dick is? He went off in the car and hasn't been home for a few days and I'm a bit worried. I was expecting him but there's been no message.'

'Don't you read the papers?' Nosjean asked.

'I can't be bothered with them. They're nothing but politics and strikes and demonstrations. Besides, I'm usually too busy.'

Nosjean drew a deep breath. The pattern was blindingly clear. Selva hadn't changed much. He was getting drugs –

doubtless through Pépé le Cornet's organisation – and had a contact with the American army in Germany where there was a ready sale and had been for some time. He was also clearly hoping to make contact with youngsters through this girl, Monica Ormot. What better way than through an organisation that dealt exclusively with students? It opened up a whole field of prospective buyers. Perhaps he was even hoping to use them to bring the stuff back for him from the trips abroad that his girlfriend arranged for them. But someone had found out and murdered him, either for his drugs and the money he'd made from drugs, or because he was muscling in on their territory.

'Well,' the girl said. 'Let's have it! Why do you want to know so much about him?'

Nosjean's anger swelled up. 'I think you'd better sit down,' he said.

She took a lot of convincing. She just didn't believe Nosjean and when he asked if he could search the place she refused. In the end he managed to persuade her with a mixture of powerful arguments and the threat of a search warrant. At the back of the wardrobe, he found a locked tin box. He shook it and held it up.

'I'll have to take this away,' he said. 'I need to know what's inside.'

'No,' she said unwillingly. 'I know where he keeps the key.'

She produced the key from behind a row of books in the living room and Nosjean opened the box. Inside was a plastic bag containing white powder. Alongside it were other smaller plastic bags some of them filled with the same powder.

'What did he use to stretch it?' Nosjean asked.

'What do you mean?'

'That's heroin,' Nosjean said.

'I don't believe you.'

'Have it your own way. Has he been using your flour lately?'

'He asked for some. For snails in the garden, he said.'

'Not for snails,' Nosjean pointed out. 'For this stuff. They use flour, milk powder, sleeping pills, strychnine. You'd be surprised. A gram of heroin in the street sometimes contains no more than ten per cent of the original. They use all kinds of things. They're not fussy.'

She looked at him, horrified. 'Dick wouldn't do that.'

Nosjean's face was blank. 'He's done it. He went to prison for it.'

'He said that was for stealing cars.'

She didn't seem to know whether to be relieved at her escape or shocked at the death of the man she'd been living with. 'I loved him,' she explained. 'I never dreamed. He was so kind, so good.'

There were a lot like that, Nosjean reflected. It was a pity Selva was dead. They might finally have got something on Pépé le Cornet – that something the police had been seeking for years – and they might even have found out the route the drugs took to the American forces in Germany. As it was, they'd come to a dead end again and could only be thankful that Selva was no longer in business.

When Nosjean reached Ballentou's house, Imogen Wathus opened the door wide with a smile. She looked pretty and, after Selva's Monica Ornot, refreshingly healthy and full of life.

'Saw you coming,' she said. 'He's home. Come in. Can I give you a drink this time? Something stronger than coffee.'

He found Imogen Wathus attractive. When his enquiries were finished and he had time, he decided, he would take a real interest in her. Nosjean was an honest young man, intelligent, and not driven by lusts, and his affairs with young women were usually decent and kind. Only work – and plain clothes work could make the uniformed shifts seem like a pensioner's paradise – got in the way.

Ballentou rose slowly as Nosjean appeared, and offered a glass of white wine.

'Coup de blanc?' he said. 'It's a good time for a drink.'

He sat down and Nosjean offered him a cigarette. The girl sat near them, listening.

'Did you get what you were after?' Nosjean asked.

Ballentou looked startled. 'What I was after?'

'Money from the Prisoners' Aid.'

Ballentou's face relaxed into a smile. 'Oh, yes,' he said. 'I got what I wanted. Are you after *me*?'

'Only for help,' Nosjean said.

'That's nice to know. What's the trouble?'

'Nick the Greek,' Nosjean said. 'Pat the Bang. Richard Selva.'

'I heard Selva had been murdered. There was something in the paper about it.'

'Yes,' Nosjean agreed. 'He was. He was found near Pouilly. Shot through the head. FAS Apex 6.35. Two other 6.35s have been found, too. They were used at Montenay.'

'What about the one from Pouilly?'

'That's not turned up.' Nosjean leaned forward. 'A consignment of them from St. Etienne was stolen near Paris. We think Pépé le Cornet was behind it. Have you heard who did it? Nick the Greek, for instance? He likes guns and he works for Pépé.'

Ballentou shrugged. 'If Pépé was in it, you'll never prove it.'

Nosjean agreed. 'No,' he admitted. 'I don't suppose we will. But we're still looking for Pat the Bang. I thought you might know where he is.'

Ballentou shook his head. 'Pity you didn't get around to asking Selva. He'd have known. He was set up with a girl near the University.'

'I've seen her. He was back in drugs.'

Ballentou's eyebrows rose. 'Already?'

'I expect he got them through Pépé. He was in touch with some pusher in the American forces in Germany. Did you know?'

Ballentou's shrug came again. 'You've come to the wrong man. I'm out of touch. I've been working steadily for nearly two years now. I'm in the clear. Imogen looks after me.' He glanced at the girl who smiled. 'There's no reason for me to get mixed up in that sort of thing again.'

Nosjean looked at Imogen Wathus. 'I think he was hoping to make contact with students. His girl was to have been the contact.'

Her face hardened angrily. 'There are some bastards in this world, aren't there?' she said. 'Had he started?'

'I don't think so. Not yet. He seems to have picked up a consignment recently but I don't think he'd finished getting

149

rid of it.' Nosjean looked at Ballentou again. 'Has nobody ever tried to recruit you? They don't give up easily.'

Ballentou gestured. 'No. They've left me alone. I think it's finally got around that I'm not interested. Besides, I'm too old these days.' He leaned over to pour more wine into Nosjean's glass. 'Anyway,' he ended, 'why bother about Selva? He was a pusher. Somebody's done a lot of kids a good turn.'

18

When Pel appeared at the Hôtel de Police the following day, Claudie Darel met him in the corridor.

'Someone to see you, Patron,' she announced.

'God, perhaps?' Pel chose to be heavily amusing. 'The Pope? Or perhaps the President of France to confer on me the Legion of Honour?'

Claudie didn't turn a hair. 'None of those, Patron,' she said without a change of expression. 'Inspector Duval, from the Sureté.'

Pel's mild expression vanished at once. 'What's he want?' he snapped.

'He's interested in the De Mougy business, Patron.'

Inspector Duval was a tall handsome man – since Pel was small and anything but handsome, he disliked him at once – and he was waiting in Pel's office, smoking a pipe that looked as big as a lavatory bowl. He didn't bother to rise as Pel appeared, but he gestured with the pipe.

'Mind?' he asked.

Pel always minded people who could smoke a pipe with the aplomb Inspector Duval showed. Pel would have loved to have smoked a pipe – if only to get out of the habit of smoking cigarettes – but pipe smoking left him with burn holes in his clothes and a mouth as foul as a puppy's basket.

'No,' he lied through his teeth. 'Not at all.'

'You'll know why I'm here, of course,' Duval said. 'The De Mougy business.'

Pel was rapidly coming to the conclusion that there was not one Paris mob but two – one on each side of the law – and that at that moment he'd got them both on his neck.

'Is it considered in Paris,' he snapped, 'that we're incapable down here of handling it or something?'

Duval waved the pipe, scattering sparks all over Pel's

carpet. Pel studied them sourly. He was proud of his carpet. It was a thick one – the sort only chief inspectors and above were allowed – and, having only recently been promoted, he'd barely grown used to it and didn't want it spoiled.

'Strings pulled,' Duval said. 'You know how it is.'

'No, I don't,' Pel said. 'We don't go in for that much down here. Inform me.'

Duval shrugged. 'The Baron's a pal of Carny de Vitage, the Minister. You'll know that.'

'I don't tread the corridors of power,' Pel said. 'I didn't know.'

'Well, that's the way it is.' Duval was stupendously bland and confident. 'He had a word with him. On the telephone. From Deauville. Didn't think things were moving fast enough. Carny got in touch with the Commissioner who promised to have it looked into.'

'It's being looked into,' Pel said. 'By me.'

'Yes, I know. But he wanted more than that.'

Once more, Pel found it hard to understand how someone from Paris without local knowledge could possibly learn more than he and his team could. 'And what do *you* intend to do?' he asked.

'Oh, I'm not going to get in your way,' Duval said.

'I'm glad to hear it.'

'I won't interfere.'

You'd better not, Pel thought.

'I'll just probe a little higher, that's all.' Duval's smile was condescending. 'Higher echelon, so to speak.' What, in God's name, Pel wondered, did that mean? 'Have a word among De Mougy's friends.'

Pel stared at Duval as if he were mad. 'Why question De Mougy's friends?' he demanded. '*They* aren't likely to have robbed him. They have plenty of their own.'

Duval's smile came again. 'Of course,' he agreed. 'But I've got contacts with a few of them.' Duval seemed to regard his work as an exercise in social behaviour. 'Through friends, of course. People I was at university with.'

Hah, Pel thought. Now we have it! Duval had arrived in the police force from university and considered himself an expert. In diplomacy, no doubt. He felt a plain honest-to-

God robbery needed the sort of diplomacy the Foreign Office used when dealing with mad African dictators.

Then, as he stared at Duval, the explanation leapt at him. Duval was the Sergeant Misset of the Sureté. De Mougy had spoken to the Minister demanding action and the Minister had spoken to the Commissioner, and as usual the buck had been passed down the ladder to the man who mattered, and the man who mattered had immediately spotted an opportunity to get out of his hair the least valuable member of his team. It happened all the time. From his military service Pel remembered how, whenever his commanding officer had been asked for assistance in the form of extra men, he had always made a point of sending the most useless. That way, he was implicitly obeying orders while leaving his own unit's efficiency unimpaired. Pel did it himself. Witness Misset.

The grim expression on his face faded. He decided he could handle Duval.

'You're welcome to it,' he said. 'I have two murders on my hands which I consider marginally more important than robbery. Nevertheless, I shall not lose interest in it myself. Have you any information I haven't?'

Duval hadn't.

'See Claudie Darel next door,' Pel advised. 'She'll give you a list of the Baron's acquaintances. They're well known. It'll save you a lot of trouble.'

Duval seemed happy enough and departed, waving his pipe and scattering sparks. As soon as the door had closed, Pel jumped round the room, spry as a spider, slamming his foot down on them before they set the place on fire.

He was still considering the insult and the brilliant way he had handled it, when Darcy appeared. He was looking at his most elegant. He was dressed in a dark grey suit with a high white collar that seemed to saw at his ears. He was shaved to the bone and looked spotless enough to be on his way to an interview with Brigitte Bardot.

'Morning, Patron,' he said breezily. 'It's obvious you're on top of the job.'

Darcy grinned but Pel's face remained expressionless. He didn't find crime a joking matter and, in any case, he wasn't given a lot to hilarity. His sense of humour started only after

153

his first cigarette of the day. By the time he'd reached his second he'd used up his ration.

'Who was it last night?' he asked.

'The one from the university,' Darcy said. 'She's always around.'

'One of these days one of them will catch you.'

Darcy shrugged. 'Any man with any gumption can make a mess of his love life,' he agreed. 'Romantic confession, once the privilege of the wealthy, is now within the reach of all of us. We went to my place for a spot of heavy breathing.'

'Don't you ever get bored with them?'

Darcy's grin came again, wide and full of large white teeth. 'It's my way of convincing myself I'm not in danger of becoming a homosexual,' he said.

'How is it you never look worn out in the morning?'

Darcy smiled. 'I keep fit. I play squash.'

Pel knew about squash. An hour of frenzy then a coronary.

Darcy offered him a cigarette. Pel stared at it worriedly for a moment, then he remembered reading somewhere that, out of every thousand smokers, only a few were killed by lung cancer while an equal number were probably killed on the roads. It was as good an excuse as any, he decided, reaching out.

'Nick the Greek,' Darcy said as he offered his lighter. 'I think we ought to talk to that blonde he's shacked up with.'

'No.' Pel shook his head. 'Don't go near her. He'll bolt. Let him lie fallow for a while. He might bring in one or two others. Such as Pat the Bang. And if he bolts so will Lafarge. I want them all and I want the loot – to say nothing of the type who tipped them off to what the De Mougys were carrying. Because someone certainly did. Come to think of it – ' Pel glanced at the window ' – it's a nice day, Daniel. I think we ought to go and have another word with De Mougy's staff.'

The Château Mougy looked golden in the morning sunshine and Darcy's car rolled up the crushed pebble of the wide drive with a satisfying crunch that made it sound expensive.

'I wonder what it's like to be so wealthy you don't miss a few thousand,' Darcy said.

It had always been Pel's ambition to be so wealthy his

154

relations would go in fear and trembling of him in case he cut them out of his will. He'd often imagined himself when they were awkward, bringing them to heel with a shout of: What's the matter? Don't you want my money? 'I think I could manage to live with it,' he said.

Algieri, the butler, met them at the door with the information that the Baron and his wife had not yet reappeared. He was wearing his coldest look. Pel returned it three-fold.

'The Baron and his wife aren't the ones I'm wanting to see,' he said. 'I'm interested in the staff.'

Algieri gave him a look of loathing that somehow managed to be concealed behind a deferential manner. 'Where do you wish to interview them, Monsieur?'

'Same place as before would do.'

'I'm afraid it's being cleaned at the moment.'

'Then take your pick. The Baronne's bedroom. The Baron's study. Your private bathroom.'

The deferential hatred came again. 'You'd better use the library.'

When they were established, they invited Algieri to sit down.

'Me, sir?'

'You're still staff, aren't you?'

'I've already been interviewed, Monsieur.'

'And now we're going to interview you again.'

Algieri's eyebrows knitted together. Clearly he considered himself superior enough not to be lumped with the housemaids, footmen and gardeners. His world was ministered by the Baron, with himself somewhere just below and all the rest of the household – even including the Baronne and the Baronne's son – suspended somewhere in the void beneath.

Pel had taken a dislike to Algieri and he gave him a thorough grilling. 'You came originally from Marseilles,' he said.

'That's so, Monsieur.'

'Go back often?'

Algieri sniffed. 'Occasionally, Monsieur.'

'Family still live there?'

'I have many relatives in Marseilles and Nice, Monsieur.'

Which was an interesting point. Was Tagliatti's gang in touch with Algieri? Was it Tagliatti, after all, and not Pépé

155

le Cornet? Or was it both? They had been known to co-operate in harness when it suited them – when the job being planned required more men than each could supply or more money to set it up and buy information than either was prepared to raise.

Or if it wasn't Algieri himself who was in touch, was it some member of his family? They might be worth investigating. Pel glanced at Darcy who made a note. Perhaps Algieri, in an attempt to show how important he was – and clearly he considered himself so – had dropped some hint which one of his numerous relatives had picked up.

'When were you last in Marseilles?' Pel asked.

'A month ago, Monsieur. The Baron allows me plenty of leave and I return whenever I can. I like the heat.'

Pel could well understand that. Much as he loved Burgundy – and Pel's love of Burgundy was close to worship – he would have preferred it to be warmer in winter. 'You have a family? Of your own? A wife? Children?'

'I've never married, Monsieur.' Algieri had the look of a priest at the altar. 'I never seem to have had the time.'

Homosexual? The thought crossed Pel's mind. Was he being blackmailed into passing information? 'I've come across butlers who've married members of the staff,' he said shortly. 'Maids. That sort of thing.'

Algieri's look seemed to suggest that marrying a maid would be not far short of sacrilege. It slid off Pel like water off a duck's back and, when Algieri tried to suggest that once again he should look after the Baron's interests by sitting in on the interviews with the rest of the staff, Pel put him firmly in his place at once.

'The Baron's interests won't suffer,' he snapped.

'But I think – '

Pel looked so angry he seemed in danger of a vertical take-off. 'What you think,' he said, 'is of no importance. You're a suspect like everyone else and if you don't disappear I'll have you arrested under Section 63 of the Penal Code.'

Algieri's look contained daggers, bombs and guns. 'The baron would not approve of *that*,' he said.

Pel glared. 'If the Baron objects,' he snarled. 'I'll have *him* arrested too! If necessary, his wife also! *And* all his relations!'

Pel was nothing if not thorough and Algieri disappeared, looking shattered.

As he vanished Darcy grinned. 'Patron,' he said, 'if you'd lived during the Revolution you'd have been at the guillotine every day watching the knife fall on the aristos.'

'I might well,' Pel said, 'have been on the platform pulling the handle.'

Without Algieri around, this time Josso, the chauffeur, was much more forthcoming. He was an ex-soldier who had been recommended to the Baron and he made no bones about the advantages of the job. 'There are six girls employed in this place,' he said cheerfully. 'And the Baron likes them pretty. It saves me going out looking for them.'

'Do you take them out?'

'Yes. But you have to be careful. They get jealous.'

'Do you do *more* than just take them out?' Darcy asked with interest. 'Visit them, perhaps, at night?'

'No,' Josso grinned. 'They share rooms. I'd have the other one making the same demands. Of course – ' the sly grin returned '– some of us have our own rooms. Algieri, of course. The housekeeper. They have apartments. I've got a room over the garage. I get them in there sometimes. Suzy Vince, the Baronne's maid, has a room of her own, too. Not an apartment like Algieri and the housekeeper, but a private room that she doesn't have to share. It's only the skivvies who share rooms. With them it's more difficult.'

'Does Vince ever visit you? Or you her?'

Josso laughed. 'Not likely. Too high and mighty for me.'

Vince, it seemed, considered herself second cousin to the Baronne. She acted like her, behaved like her and dressed like her – sometimes even in the Baronne's old clothes.

'Well, not *that* old,' Josso admitted. 'The Baronne doesn't *have* old clothes. And mostly she doesn't let Vince have them either. She wouldn't fancy one of the servants being seen wearing her cast-offs.'

'And you've never chased her?'

Josso grinned. 'I tried. But I couldn't get her into the car with me. Said she preferred that old bike of hers. She cycles all the time. Great little cycler, Vince. As a kid she wanted to enter the Tour de France but they wouldn't let her because she had boobs and a bum and didn't have legs with muscles like footballs. It would have put the other riders off. Besides, she seemed to prefer the Baronne's company.'

'How do they get on?'

'They fight a bit. They're always fighting.'

'What about?'

'What dress to wear. Vince often thinks she knows better than the Baronne. I don't think she does but she does have ideas.' Josso smiled. 'They always kiss and make up, of course, because the Baronne needs old Vince and old Vince needs the kudos that comes from working for the Baronne.' Josso shrugged. 'Not that it matters to me. There are plenty of others and the grounds here are extensive enough to get lost in. In addition, I have the use of the Baron's cars. They're all big with roomy back seats.'

'Does the Baron know?'

'No. And I hope you won't tell him.'

Josso seemed to be what was known as a card. With the Baron around, he played his rôle dead-pan with an expressionless face. But there was more than was obvious beneath the surface.

'Think he had other bad habits, Patron?' Darcy asked. 'Such as being in touch with crooks? He could be. One bad habit begets another. For girls you need money and he won't get all that much even as a baron's chauffeur. Perhaps he has more girls than he can afford.'

'It's worth thinking about,' Pel agreed.

The housekeeper appeared to have no other interest apart from her job. She had a widowed mother in the village whom she visited whenever possible and spent all her time with her when off duty.

'My father was an engineer,' she said proudly. 'My family weren't poor. Unfortunately, my father made no provision for old age and *I* have to provide for my mother.'

Suzy Vince, the Baronne's maid, was a thin woman just past youth. She was still attractive but had an astringent manner. 'I wouldn't dream of passing on the Baronne's business outside this house,' she said sharply.

'Could it be that you let something slip by accident? Something that could be overheard? In the village shop, for instance?'

'I don't use the village shop,' she retorted coldly. 'I make my purchases in Paris or Dijon or Lyons.'

'Could one of the other staff have overheard you saying something?'

Vince sniffed. 'I never discuss the Baronne's affairs near the other servants.'

Pel studied her. Like the rest of the female staff, she wore a formal grey dress with a white linen collar, something that wasn't uniform but was clearly designed to show she wasn't a De Mougy.

'Do you wear that when you go out?' he asked.

'Of course not, I have other clothes.'

'Do you buy all of them yourself?'

'I don't understand.'

'Perhaps the Baronne – '

'Ah!' she smiled. 'The Baronne passes many of her dresses on to me. We have the same build exactly. I've stood in at the dressmakers for her. I've even bought dresses for her.'

'You must have impeccable taste.'

'I always intended to have.'

'Intended to?'

'I came from a poor family,' Suzy Vince said. 'I always swore I wouldn't end up like my parents. *Or* like my sisters. One's married to a shopkeeper and is fat and lives most of her life in an apron. The second one's married to a man who works on the railway and spends her time washing greasy overalls. The third's married to a layabout and has to work as a daily help. I was the youngest and I had their example before me to make sure I didn't go the same way.'

'You enjoy being here?'

'Of course.'

'Even as a servant?'

'A servant in magnificent surroundings, Monsieur. And I am a *personal* maid. I don't help with the cleaning or in the kitchen. My job's caring for the Baronne's clothes. That's something I enjoy.' Vince smiled and moved her fingers. 'I enjoy the feel of pure silk. Of fine wool. Of mohair and chiffon. The Baronne wears only the best.'

'Why didn't she ever have the jewels photographed?' Pel asked. 'It's usual with anything valuable.'

159

Vince shrugged. 'She thought they were safe. She was like that. Arrogant about things.'

'Did you like her?'

Vince's mouth moved. 'I admired her taste but not her personally. She had a man, did you know? Not the Baron, another one.'

'So I heard.'

'He couldn't trust her and I didn't like her for that.'

There seemed to be an element of spite and resentment behind the statement, as if Vince's attitude to the Baronne veiled her dislike.

'But you liked what she stood for?'

She smiled. 'I liked her clothes. What woman wouldn't? *And* her jewels, I suppose. If I had jewels like that I could live for years in comfort.'

'If you could sell them,' Darcy said.

Her eyebrows moved. 'Would it be difficult?' she asked.

19

Pel opened his conference the following morning with a feeling of frustration. Darcy had checked on the butler, Algieri. All his family seemed to be in service and a lot of them still were, but there was no connection with Maurice Tagliatti or Pépé le Cornet.

Frowning heavily, he listened to what Nosjean had to say. He'd had a break at last. Selva's car had been found and he was hoping it might lead somewhere.

'In the car park at the supermarket at Bornay,' he said. 'It had been there some time. Nobody knows exactly how long but I suppose it arrived there some time shortly after Selva was shot.'

'Who put you on to it?'

'There's a type who keeps an eye on the car park. But it's a big one and that place's open seven days a week so he didn't spot it at first. He walks round occasionally and eventually he noticed it had been there some time. It's a red Citroën. The small model. Cars are often left there, of course, but this had been there longer than most. He decided it ought to be examined. It was locked so he informed the local cops. They opened it and did a bit of checking with the number. It turned out to be Selva's.'

'Find anything?'

Nosjean shrugged. 'Not much, Patron. We found photographs under the seat; one of an old woman, one of a house. It turns out that the woman's his mother and the house is where she lives. We've found Selva's sister and she's identified them. There was also a bill which appears to be from a restaurant where he ate. Two people. Plain fried steak and pommes frites, with a salad and wine. The name of the restaurant isn't clear but he obviously ate there with someone, and I guessed it was that girl he was living with. It was. She said they'd been in a hurry and settled for the bar-restaurant at St. Antoine.'

'Why were they in a hurry? Going somewhere special?'

'No. Just to the cinema. She's worried she's going to be involved now and she's talking. It seems Selva was out all day and arrived home latish and they went for a quick meal. Three days before he was found. So it must have been the night before he was shot. She thought that when he'd paid he just stuck the bill in his pocket and forgot it. There were two cinema ticket stubs in the car, too, so it seems they did go to a film. There was also a man's handkerchief and a stub of pencil. All, I suppose, belonging to Selva and pulled from his pockets. But no wallet. No bank card. No driving licence. Nothing with his name on them.'

'What does it mean to you, mon brave?'

'To me, Patron, it bears out the idea we had that whoever shot Selva made him turn out his pockets first. In the car. Probably made him throw everything on the floor.'

'Because he wanted something?'

'No, Patron. I don't think so. After he shot him, I think he drove the car away and before he parked it at the super-market he went through what had been in Selva's pockets and took away everything that might identify him or might carry fingerprints. He left these other things – a handkerchief, the photographs and so on – because he didn't think they would. I don't think they would have either, if Fingerprints hadn't identified him first. We wouldn't have known where to look and there was nothing identifiable on the photographs. I think whoever shot him was just trying to make him disappear. Trying to hide his identity.'

'Why?'

'So Pépé le Cornet wouldn't know he was dead, perhaps? Selva was Pépé's man. If he'd been murdered, it would be reasonable to expect Pépé to react. Perhaps Pépé would even know who'd done it. Perhaps whoever did it was hoping to prevent him finding out.'

'Nick the Greek?' Pel asked. 'Could it have been him? Have they been falling out? Or Pat the Bang? We haven't turned him up yet. Perhaps he's scared and lying low.'

Nosjean wasn't able to add much more, however. He was moving steadily forward but so far he hadn't achieved a breakthrough. Neither had Bardolle with the Huppert shooting at Montenay, while the De Mougy theft at Quigny was also still simmering. De Troq' had his ear to the ground and Pel had heard that the people there were very impressed by the fact that he was a baron like De Mougy. The idea of a policeman who was a baron seemed to appeal to them.

There was still Inspector Duval, of course, the last of the Paris lot, pursuing his lonely course among Baron De Mougy's friends, but Pel had no doubt that De Troq' was skilful enough – or arrogant enough – to ignore him. Or, if he wasn't, simply to trample him into the ground despite his size. Duval seemed a good-natured enough idiot and probably wouldn't mind.

For the conference, Darcy had set up a projector and Photographic had made slides. As everybody became silent, Darcy began to project pictures of Richard Selva and his known acquaintances.

'Any of them,' Pel said, reading out the names. 'Any of them might know what he was up to, and could lead us to his killer.'

There were pictures of Pépé le Cornet, Maurice Tagliatti and their immediate associates, together with those of the members of their gangs who were known to associate with drug pedlars and people who handled guns. Their names had often cropped up before, even if their faces hadn't.

Misset sat glumly at the back where he couldn't be seen. He was back on the team with a vengeance. Pel's praise over the counterfeit money had been thinly spread and he knew that, even if no one else suspected it, Pel had guessed long since that what Misset had pulled off was sheer luck and not due to any hard work on Misset's part.

It was hard to get Ada out of his mind and he was still far from welcome at home. His mother-in-law had reappeared from Metz and she and his wife seemed to be in process of producing a conspiracy against him with his children. He wondered if he shouldn't have packed up the police and bolted with Ada. The money she'd got out of Poland made his salary look like a rag picker's wage. Yet – at the back of his mind he knew it to be true – she hadn't really been interested in Josephe Misset. She'd been using him as she'd used old Gold-thread, Heinz Horstmann, and Dexter, the

163

American in Warsaw who'd helped her get away. She'd kept him quiet until she was ready to disappear, and she'd had no more intention of falling for him than she had of flying to the moon.

There were still a lot of smiles around the Hôtel de Police and a lot of jokes at Misset's expense. He'd boasted a little to hide his disappointment, letting them know – when Pel wasn't within earshot – that he hadn't found Ada Vocci disappointing. But now he was hunched in his chair, a faraway expression on his face. He looked up, uninterested, as the photograph on the screen changed.

'Nick the Greek,' Darcy was saying. 'His associates will follow.'

Misset's face went red. 'I know him!' he said.

Every eye in the room swung round to him.

'I saw him at the Hôtel Centrale,' Misset said. 'When I was – er – well, working for Major Chaput.'

Pel glared. 'Why in God's name didn't you say so before?'

Misset floundered, caught off-balance. 'Because this is the first time I've seen his picture,' he said.

Pel had to admit the fact. Misset had been involved with other things and had missed the photographs that had been handed round.

'What was he doing?' he demanded.

'Asking about Ada Vocci. He was good and mad, too.'

'What in God's name had he got to do with her?'

'I don't think he had anything, Patron.' Misset suddenly began to feel important again. 'He was looking for a dame, and he'd looked at the register and thought she might have registered as Ada Vocci. He said he was a cop.'

'What happened to him?'

'I don't know, Patron. He said he'd come back but I didn't see him.'

'Get round there,' Pel rapped. 'Find out if he did.'

The conference broke up soon afterwards and Pel and Darcy met in Pel's office.

'Was *Ada Vocci* his contact?' Darcy said. 'Was *she* waiting for him to hand over the jewels? She arrived at the Centrale soon after they were stolen. It's possible.'

'As well as carrying counterfeit notes?' Pel asked. 'It doesn't sound likely.'

164

It didn't either. Passers of counterfeit money wouldn't get involved in a jewel theft any more than jewel thieves would get mixed up with counterfeit money. And it seemed to Pel that whoever had stolen the De Mougy jewels would have more than enough on his plate getting rid of them and wouldn't want to draw attention to himself by getting involved with someone working another racket. By the same token, it didn't seem possible that someone who had pulled off as big a coup as Ada Vocci had would wish to be involved with a thief who had set the district by its ears over a jewel robbery.

'Do you still think he'll turn up at Lafarge's, Patron?' Darcy asked.

'Lafarge's the only one of our suspects who thinks he's totally in the clear. Besides, it's a quiet road where he lives. Just the sort of place to arrange a drop. Has Aimedieu seen anything yet?'

Aimedieu hadn't.

'No visitors?'

'Just his wife and son, Patron.'

'They couldn't be running errands, could they? Taking messages.'

'Doubt it, Patron. The woman seems to be going round the corner to do the shopping, that's all. The boy goes to school and returns at the usual time. They don't appear to have friends.'

'No visitors?'

'No, Patron. No callers, either.'

Misset was back within the hour. He was panting. 'He did come back,' he said. 'And it definitely wasn't Ada Vocci he was after.'

'What happened?'

Misset drew a deep breath.

He'd gone to the girl at the desk and asked, 'Has that good-looking type been back?' and she'd replied. 'The only good-looking type I've noticed is you.'

It had pleased Misset but, with Pel on his neck, he'd forced himself to keep his eye on the ball and demanded details.

'He came back,' the girl at the desk had said. 'He sat in the chair over there and asked me to tip him the wink when Mademoiselle Vocci appeared. When she came down I did.

He stood up, stared at her, then shook his head and turned round and just walked out.'

'Did he speak to her?' Pel asked.

'No. He just walked out. That's all. As if he was no longer interested, she said.'

'So, it wasn't *Ada Vocci* he was hoping to see.'

'It couldn't have been, Patron. When I saw him he was making a hell of a lot of song and dance. If it *had* been her, surely he'd have followed her.'

Pel frowned. 'So if it wasn't Ada Vocci,' he said, 'then it must have been some other woman.'

'His girl?' Darcy suggested. 'Is she double-crossing him?'

'Find out, Daniel!'

Viviane Simoneau, Nick the Greek's girl, was as bewildered as Selva's girl had been. She was sharp-featured but attractive and had created a tidy little home. Nick, it seemed, gave her plenty of money.

'Where does he get it from?' Darcy asked.

'Work, of course. It's his salary. He's well paid.'

'For doing what?'

'He's a salesman. Very high-powered.'

'What's he sell?'

'Perfume. For a Paris firm. They deal with them all. Diorissimo, Nina Ricci. St. Laurent. Chanel. He's good at it too. Shops and stores always have women buyers for that and with his looks they fall heavily.'

It made sense. Nick the Greek could have sold hot coals in Hell if the buyers had been women.

'Are you sure that was what he was doing?'

'Why should I disbelieve him?'

'Plenty of reasons,' Darcy said bluntly. 'Did you know he'd been in jail?'

She stared at him, startled, then she looked angry. 'If that's all you can say about him – ' she began.

Darcy halted her. 'I can say a lot more,' he pointed out. 'He's been involved in armed robbery, housebreaking, hold-ups, bank jobs, drugs, assault, pimping. *Those* women fell for him, too. This time it's jewellery and we think it was part of a gang job.'

'I don't believe you.'

166

Darcy had taken the trouble to bring a photocopy of Nick's record from the files, together with his mug shot. He offered them without a word. She stared at it disbelievingly. After a while she looked up at Darcy.

'Is this really him?'

'Take a look at the picture.'

'He never gave me a hint.'

There seemed to be a lot like her around. Richard Selva had had one, too.

'You're lucky,' Darcy said. 'There've been a few of Nick's girlfriends who've disappeared rather suddenly. To North Africa or South America, we think. You'd probably have gone too. He was probably planning something for you when he'd finished with you.'

She sat down, stunned.

'He was seen at Montenay,' Darcy said. 'What was he doing there?'

'He took me there. He drove me.'

'Why were *you* at Montenay?'

'I used to live there. I went to see Monsieur Huppert.'

'Oh?' Darcy's eyebrows rose. 'Why?'

'Well, I knew him. I knew his wife. I went to say how sorry I was about her being shot and was there anything I could do?'

'Did Huppert know Nick?'

'I don't suppose so. He only met him once.'

'Just once?'

'As far as I know. He was with me.'

'How did they get on?'

'They talked a bit. You know how people do. They seemed to get on all right. That was all. But only because of me, I think.'

Darcy paused. 'Did Nick ever produce any jewels for *you*?'

'He said he'd find me something. To cement the relationship, he said.'

'Stolen, I expect. Where is he now?'

'He went away two days ago. He said he had to go to the south coast. There's a lot of money there and he was hoping to pull something big off.'

'I bet he was.'

167

Her brow wrinkled. 'I still can't believe he's what you say,' she insisted. 'He's innocent, I'm sure.'

'So where is he?'

'Perhaps he heard you were after him and wanted to hide.'

Darcy's eyebrows lifted. 'Innocent people don't hide,' he pointed out.

Darcy came back looking puzzled. 'It isn't her, Patron,' he said. 'She didn't even know Nick was a villain. She thought he was a sales representative.'

'Then who *was* he looking for?'

Darcy frowned then slapped the desk. 'The maid!' he said. 'Suzy Vince. Who else?'

'Of course!' Pel was on his feet at once and reaching for his hat. 'Perfect for Nick the Greek. Just past youth but still hoping. Likes luxury. Likes money and clothes. Doesn't like the Baronne. Somehow Nick got in touch with her and she was the one who tipped him off. She's just the type he likes. Just the sort to fall for his good looks. And she liked jewels. She said so. Especially the Baronne's. Come on, Daniel, let's get out there and pick her up.'

But when they reached the Château Mougy, Suzy Vince had disappeared and the Baron had returned, two metres of angry bone and sinew wanting to know when he was going to get his possessions back.

Pel was as short with him as he was with Pel.

'When you tell us where Suzy Vince is,' he snapped.

The Baron's jaw dropped. 'Was *she* in it?'

'She could be.'

'Well, you're too late. She's disappeared.'

'When?'

'Some damn fool from Paris with a pipe came to see her and started asking questions. Algieri said she seemed scared and soon afterwards she said her sister was ill and she had to go and see her. She's not been back since.'

'Surely you're not interested in Suzy?' the Baronne said. 'She's far too loyal.'

'I think we'd better examine her room nevertheless, Madame,' Pel insisted.

It didn't take more than a quick search to produce two

windcheaters – single thickness, nylon, unpadded and therefore not bulky – which corresponded to the description of those used by the men who had robbed De Mougy.

De Mougy eyed his wife coldly. 'So much for your damned loyalty,' he growled. 'Was she behind it?'

'Not behind it,' Pel said. 'But we think she was the one who tipped off the thieves about what you were carrying when you left to catch the aeroplane to Deauville. We now know two of the thieves and possibly a third, and we'll pick them up. In the meantime, we'd like to question Suzy Vince.'

Nobody had noticed Suzy Vince leave the château but Josso had seen her cycling to the village.

'She had a hold-all with her,' he said.

'We'll find her,' Pel promised.

They did, but not where they expected. Her bicycle was found to have been left with a friend in the village who said she'd caught a bus to the city, claiming she was going to see her sister.

Josso knew where her sister lived and they found her at work in her shop, wearing the apron Suzy Vince had sneered at so much. When they explained what they were after, she called her husband from the garden at the back of the shop to deal with the customers, and led them into the private quarters.

'Yes,' she admitted. 'She came here. She wanted a bed for the night.'

'Had she any luggage?'

'Just a small hold-all with her night things and a small case.'

'What sort of case?'

'Well, it wasn't a case really. It was a flat thing – one of those things wealthy people put their jewels in when they go away. She had it in the hold-all. I saw it when I showed her upstairs.'

'Did she say why she wanted to stay with you?'

'No. I was surprised. Because she's never thought much of me and my husband. I think she was scared.'

'Did she say why?'

'She just said she wanted to stay quietly out of the way for a day or two. I asked if she was in trouble. She said no but I'm not so sure. She seemed nervous. Then this man came.'

'Which man. Did he give a name?'

'No. He just appeared at the door asking for her.'

'What was he like?'

'Tall. Dark. Good-looking. I showed him in. When he came into the room, she was scared stiff of him. I think he was scared too. They started quarrelling.'

'What about?'

'I think she had something of his and he wanted it back. He made her get her clothes and took her outside. He had a car. They drove off. I could see her looking back. I'm sure she was scared.'

'I'm sure she was, too,' Pel said. His wife *had* been right. The jewels *had* been handed over to someone inside the ring of road blocks that had been erected after the hold-up. Suzy Vince had been waiting nearby with her bicycle and Nick and his accomplices had passed them to her with the windcheaters that had disguised them and had then continued to the search at the road block while she had cycled along the forest paths. The area bordered De Mougy land and she was quite capable of the half-day ride. Wasn't she the girl who'd wanted to ride in the Tour de France?

It didn't take five minutes when they returned to check with Pomereu and Inspector Nadauld, of Uniformed Branch, from whom they learned that, yes, indeed, a woman by the name of Suzy Vince had been stopped at the other side of the forest as she had emerged on her cycle. But she had identified herself quite frankly and had been dressed only in a blouse and skirt which couldn't by any stretch of imagination have hidden a lot of money, a jewel case and two windcheaters.

'It's obvious what she did, Patron,' Darcy said. 'She hid it all somewhere – and I bet she knew those woods well enough to know plenty of good places – and picked it up later.'

When they returned to the office. Claudie Darel was waiting for them. 'Assault case, Patron,' she said. 'It seems a bad one. She's in hospital. I think you'll be interested.'

'Who is it?'

'Name of Suzy Vince. Aged thirty-one. No address given. She's unconscious.'

170

'Get out there, Claudie! Sit by her bed. And don't move. We'll relieve you when necessary. Listen to everything she has to say when she comes round.'

As Claudie vanished, Pel turned to Darcy. 'She *did* handle the loot,' he said. 'She was keeping it for Nick and when that damned fool from Paris started asking questions she got scared and bolted. What's more, though she didn't know how dangerous it could be, I think she had the bright idea of disappearing on her own with it. Why else was Nick looking for her? Why else was he in such a temper when Misset saw him at the Hôtel Centrale? He thought she might be there and it was a reasonable assumption. He beat her up because she was double-crossing him.'

He picked up the telephone and rang Madame Bonhomme's number. Aimedieu answered.

'Anybody visited Lafarge?' he asked.

'Nobody, Patron,' Aimedieu said. 'The only people I've seen going in and out are still the wife and son. Lafarge himself hardly ever appears.'

'I suppose he's still there?'

'He's there, Patron. I've seen him through the window.'

'Keep your eyes open. Things are moving.'

Claudie rang soon afterwards.

'She's come round, Patron,' she said. 'She talked.'

'Right. Come in. I'll have you relieved at once.'

When Claudie arrived, she was looking tired. 'It's as you thought, Patron. She agreed to help Nick because she didn't like the Baronne very much. But the chance of wealth was too much of a temptation and she bolted with the loot.'

'What about the jewels? Where are they?'

'I asked her, Patron. I even tried pressing but the doctor wouldn't let me press too hard. But she did say she hadn't got them any longer and when I asked where they were she wouldn't tell me. She's scared stiff and she's obviously been threatened. She admitted having had them but she wouldn't say where they are now.'

'I think I *know* where they are,' Pel said. 'Nick the Greek's got them and he's wondering how to pass them on to Lafarge because while he knows we're watching *him*, he doesn't know we're watching Lafarge. We need a bug on Lafarge's telephone.'

171

Darcy grinned. 'There'll be a public outcry, Patron,' he said. '*We're* not supposed to indulge in dirty tricks like listening in to people's conversations. Only crooks are allowed dirty tricks like that. Judge Brisard would never approve.'

Pel gave him a sour look. 'I'll see Judge Polverari,' he said. 'He has a much more realistic attitude.'

20

Judge Polverari raised no objections. 'Somebody's bound to cry "Foul",' he pointed out. 'Counsel for the defence, for a start, if you pick up Nick the Greek.'

'We'll cross that bridge when we come to it,' Pel said.

'You're supposed to prove the tapped telephone's being used by suspected felons or conspirators, or that it's being used to further illicit enterprises and that the tapping could lead to the apprehension of the felons or the prevention of the furthering of illicit enterprises.'

'If Nick the Greek gets away with the De Mougy loot,' Pel said, 'that's a felony, and if he's plotting with Lafarge for its disposal that's an illicit enterprise.'

'You've convinced me,' Polverari smiled. 'I'll sign your warrant.'

Within an hour, they had a man knocking on Lafarge's door claiming to be a telephone repair man and, because they'd had some trouble on the line, could he have a quick look at the telephone? Ten minutes later he reported to Pel's office that the wire was tapped and that the listening apparatus was set up in an empty building behind Lafarge's house, from which an extra line had been run to the bedroom at Madame Bonhomme's where Aimedieu watched. Brochard joined Aimedieu and a round-the-clock surveillance began.

Almost immediately, Aimedieu called in on Madame Bonhomme's telephone. 'I think Nick's in touch with Lafarge,' he said. 'Someone telephoned him this morning and Lafarge told him to be careful. He sounded as if he might be suspicious and mentioned "telephone repairmen". What do I do?'

'Lafarge won't move in a hurry,' Pel said. 'I don't think he'll dare. Just keep watching. I'll attend to the other thing.'

Darcy found him studying a map of the area round

Lafarge's house. 'Lafarge's worried about our telephone men,' he said. 'Aimedieu's not certain, but he thinks Nick's been in touch and been warned off.'

'What are we going to do? Remove the tap?'

'That won't help. If Lafarge's worried, he's going to be looking over his shoulder all the time from now on. Even if he decides there's nothing wrong with his telephone, he'll still be watching.'

'Suppose we persuade him it's not *him* we're interested in but someone else round there. Georges Ballentou for instance. He must know Ballentou lives there. He's only a couple of streets away in the Rue Louis-Levecque. He and Nick were inside together so he must be aware of him. Suppose we lay on a phoney raid on Ballentou. Think he'll agree?'

'He's been very careful,' Pel said. 'And he's well aware that being well in with us will be an asset in the future. Let's try him.'

Nosjean had visited Ballentou's house more than once – and not always to see Ballentou. His visits had been informal and concerned with Imogen Wathus rather than her uncle. Watched with a certain amount of benign agreement by Ballentou, he even took her out to a meal.

It wasn't hard to persuade himself it was in the line of duty and they talked for five minutes about Ballentou and the shooting of Richard Selva, before going on for the rest of the evening to the more interesting subject of each other.

Imogen Wathus was hardly bigger than a sparrow but she had the appetite of a horse. 'It doesn't seem to make any difference,' she said. 'I try hard to put weight on but I can't manage it.' She smiled. 'Perhaps it was living alone. Perhaps it'll be easier now I've come here to live.'

She had lost her parents as a child and had had to learn very early to look after herself, which was why she had welcomed the chance to share Ballentou's house. 'It just makes you feel wanted,' she said.

Nosjean's heart skipped a beat and he said he couldn't believe that she wasn't wanted.

Her eyes lit up and she smiled again, feeling better and more at home. Her smile managed to make Nosjean feel better too.

'It's funny, isn't it?' she said. 'How some places feel better than others?' She paused. 'I didn't come here just because I got a job here. I had to leave Epinal. There was a man. He let me down. He promised all sorts of things but then he just walked out on me. I began to feel I couldn't rely on anyone and had to have a change. It feels different here. I get on with my uncle and – ' her eyes met Nosjean's ' – well, I just feel it's easier to trust people.'

Thanks to Imogen Wathus, Nosjean had got to know Ballentou fairly well. When Darcy tried his idea on him, he thought the idea would work.

Ballentou was brought in quietly and the whole thing explained.

'All it involves,' Pel said, 'is a big show and then for you to lie low for a day or two.'

Ballentou wasn't very keen. 'I'm trying to pick up a few threads,' he said. 'It isn't easy. Everybody still goes on thinking I'm on the make when I'm not. A thing like this could cause the whole thing to go wrong.'

'We'll attend to that,' Pel pointed out. 'We'll make it right. You can be sure of that.'

Ballentou was still suspicious. 'What do I get out of it?' he asked. 'So far I haven't got much from going straight and staying straight.'

'Well, you won't get your name in the paper,' Pel admitted. 'That's for sure. Because a few of your friends might not agree with you giving aid and comfort to the flics.'

Ballentou smiled and Pel went on. 'But I can arrange for you to be paid and see that you get every help we can give you in the future towards getting a better job. We don't forget people who help. A bit of security and the police behind you in your efforts to rehabilitate yourself ought to be an advantage.'

Ballentou considered. 'I'd want it making clear after it was over and I'd been released that I wasn't guilty of anything. I couldn't afford for anyone to have doubts.'

'That can be done,' Pel said.

'Even a story in the newspapers about me?'

'We don't tell the newspapers what to print, but we'll issue a statement. A good one.'

Ballentou thought it over and nodded. Then he held up

175

his hand. 'There's one other thing. I don't wany anybody to know I've been helping the police.'

'Who's "anybody"?'

'If Nick the Greek's involved in this,' Ballentou said, 'then probably so is Pépé le Cornet. He wouldn't let it go if Nick's picked up.'

'What do you want?'

'Someone keeping an eye on my place.'

Pel glanced at Nosjean. They could hardly say someone had been watching it for some time now.

'We'll attend to it,' he said.

Pel took the matter to the Chief and Judge Polverari and they discussed it back and forth for a while. The Chief wasn't keen that the police should appear to have made a mistake but he was keen to get the De Mougy loot back and in the end he agreed.

The following morning Aimedieu telephoned again. 'Same type rang, Patron. Lafarge told him to be quiet.'

'Any names? Any hint of his identity?'

'No. None.'

'Keep watching,' Pel said. Things had suddenly started going their way. There'd been a bank hold-up in Lyons two weeks before which would give them the excuse they needed. 'And don't get excited if you hear police cars.'

That afternoon, as arranged, two police cars, sirens wailing, raced through the Rue Dolour and slid to a stop in a cloud of dust outside Ballentou's house in the Rue Louis-Levecque. A knot of gaping spectators quickly gathered on the sidewalk, among them, it was noticed, Lafarge's son. Two uniformed men made a show of pushing everybody back then Lacocq and Morell came out with Ballentou, who was putting on a good show of arguing.

Darcy followed them.

'If people *will* talk on the telephone – ' he said loudly to Lacocq.

Imogen followed Ballentou, in tears. As she saw Nosjean among the police, she ran to him.

'What's happening? Why are they taking him away? He's done nothing!'

Nosjean took her arm and pulled her aside. 'He'll be back

176

tonight,' he said quietly. 'He's not being arrested. He's helping us.'

She pounded on his chest with her small fists. 'That's what they always say. "Helping the police with their enquiries." He's behaved himself. He's caused no trouble. I know he hasn't. He's a good man now. He went wrong when he was young but not now. He hasn't been in trouble since the day he was last sent to prison. Only that one time.'

'Which one time?'

'He had a fight.'

'With a warder?'

She shook her head irritatedly. 'It was another prisoner. It was nothing. Just some dispute. You don't know what it's like being in prison.'

Nosjean managed to calm her down. 'He's not being arrested,' he assured her again. 'He'll be back in twenty-four hours.'

Her eyes widened. 'You mean all that shouting's put on?'

'And very well too.'

'Promise me you're not arresting him?'

'Look,' Nosjean said, 'trust me.'

She calmed down at last and gazed up at him. The smile in her eyes had gone and they were puzzled and worried and concerned all at the same time, and in addition there was something else – a *need* to trust Nosjean.

'Can I?'

'What do you think?'

She was silent for a moment, staring at him, beseeching him not to lie to her, then the smile reappeared. It seemed to light up the whole street and made Nosjean's heart skid about under his shirt.

'All right.' She sniffed and dabbed at her tears. 'I trust you.'

That night, Ballentou was quietly taken home. Nosjean got permission to do the driving. During the journey Ballentou was silent, then suddenly he looked at Nosjean.

'Are you serious about Imogen?' he asked.

Nosjean was startled. 'I hardly know her,' he said.

Ballentou laughed. 'That's the way I thought it was,' he said. 'But she's obviously got it bad.'

Nosjean shrugged. 'Well, I'm sorry. I don't move as fast as that. But I'll be honest. I like her very much. I'd like to get to know her better.'

Ballentou touched his arm. 'That'll do for me,' he said. 'I wouldn't like her spirit to be broken like my daughter's was, and she might need someone to look after her.'

'What's wrong with you? You're not that old.'

Ballentou shrugged. 'No. But you never know, do you?'

A statement was issued to the press. The whole lot of them trooped in: Sarrazin, the freelance; Henriot, of *Le Bien Public*, the local rag; Fiabon, of *France Dimanche*. Pel gave them the statement solemnly. 'The hold-up in Lyons,' he said. 'We had reason to suspect the man we picked up but it turned out that it couldn't be him and he's been released. There isn't a stain on his character. We had to have him watched but it turns out there's an explanation. We've now got to search elsewhere.'

'Have you any leads, Chief?' Sarrazin asked.

'Yes, we have. But not in this area.'

Only *Le Bien Public* bothered to use the statement. There was nothing exciting about someone being taken in for questioning over an event that had occurred in Lyons two weeks before and even less when it was found to be a false alarm. *Le Bien Public* ran a small story; the others ignored it.

But it worked. The following afternoon, Aimedieu telephoned from Madame Bonhomme's to say that Lafarge's 'contact' had been on the telephone again.

' "Relax," he said,' Aimedieu reported. ' "It's nothing to do with us." I've got a note of it word for word, Patron. "It was a type down the road," he said. "Georges Ballentou. You'll know him. He was inside with you. The flics took him in, over some job in Lyons. I thought he'd gone straight but it seems he's mixed up with some gang down there. It was *him* they were watching and *his* telephone they were tapping. We're all right." '

'And the reply?'

'Not much, Patron. The other type hardly says anything except "Okay?" Questioning, sort of. Or "yes" and "no".'

That night, it was warm enough for Pel and his wife to

178

take their apéritifs in the garden. Almost immediately, Pel disappeared behind his own face. Madame said nothing. She'd long since learned that when Pel was deep in thought he preferred not to be interrupted. She didn't mind. She was learning to understand her Evariste Clovis Désiré. He was a dedicated policeman and totally absorbed in his job. Leaving him to it, she went to her desk and began to work on her bank statement. When she'd finished, she left it where Pel could see it because she knew that, despite the savings he had been squirreling away for years, he always considered himself on the verge of bankruptcy. It would give him a sense of reassurance to know that Madame's business was thriving and he needn't fear an old age of penury and starvation. She had already learned a lot of little tricks to keep him happy, perhaps the most important of which was not to interrupt when he was preoccupied.

She pottered round the house, singing quietly to herself.

'Le roi a fait battre tambour
Pour voir toutes ses dames,
Et la première qu'il a vue
Lui a ravi son âme.'

'Where do you find them?' Pel had appeared looking worried. Even now that he was married and secure, he was pessimistic enough to feel it might not last.

'Oh, I pick them up,' Madame said. 'Here and there. Have you worked it out? Who shot Madame Huppert. Who shot Selva. Who robbed the Baron de Mougy. Where his wife's jewels are.'

Pel's eyebrows rose. He hadn't realised she'd been so much aware of what was going on.

'Some of it,' he said. 'I know who's got the De Mougy loot but I don't know where he is.'

'Then you've lost him?'

'Not by a long way. I know where he's going to be eventually. It's just a case of waiting.'

'You're good at that.'

Pel nodded. He could sit for hours waiting if he knew something would result. He had, he considered, excellent sitting bones.

Madame smiled to herself. She had long since become

aware of Pel's eccentricities and in a way they had endeared him to her because, beyond his highly efficient exterior, he was a different man, concerned with his failings, the fact that he didn't look like a film star, couldn't stop smoking, worried about money. But, when on a scent, his mind worked in weird and wonderful ways and he was best left to himself.

Nevertheless, her eyes were bright. She found being married to a successful detective intriguing. She loved being involved in the fight against crime. Though it didn't bring in as much money as her salon it was much more exciting. It gave her a feeling of being part of the fight herself, especially when she could put her finger into the pie and give it a little stir.

Bardolle was waiting for Pel when he arrived the following morning. He was excited.

'Patron,' he said. 'I've checked on those four guys Huppert sacked. Douaud, Muller, Redaudineau and Carruolo.' He accepted the cigarette Pel held out and lit it hurriedly, blowing out smoke and waving his arms to clear the air. 'Redaudineau's dead. Booze. Carruolo's returned to Portugal. Muller's in Alsace. Douaud's not doing that kind of work any more. They're all in the clear, Patron. But I found out from Douaud that Tehendu – you remember he was one of the two we had our eye on – once worked for Fabrique d'Armes Automatiques de St. Etienne, the people who make the FAS Apex 6.35s.'

'What!'

Pel was just rising from the desk when the telephone rang. It was Aimedieu telephoning from Madame Bonhomme's and he sounded excited, too.

'Patron,' he said. 'We've got a bite! Somebody rang Lafarge.'

'Nick?'

'Somebody different. He said the goods would be along this evening.'

'Did he say *what* goods?'

'No, Patron. He said he was from the Burgundy Electronics Company and that the video that Lafarge had ordered had come in. Could they send it along this evening?'

'And?'

'Lafarge said, Yes, it would be all right.'

'We'll be there.'

As Pel was about to replace the telephone, Aimedieu's voice came again, urgently. He sounded worried.

'There's something else, Patron,' he said. 'A car's arrived at the end of the road. There's a guy in it reading a paper and smoking a pipe. It looks to me as if he's also watching Lafarge's house.'

'*What!*' Pel saw all their plans ruined. 'Who is it? Nick?'

'No, Patron. I think it's that type from Paris. Duval. I think he's trying to make up his mind to go in and collar Lafarge.'

Pel cursed. 'Listen, Aimedieu,' he said. 'Carefully. Where is he?'

'Just outside. He doesn't know I'm only a metre or two away watching him.'

'For God's sake, keep an eye on him! If he looks like getting out of the car, stop him. Tell him we don't just want Lafarge. We also want Nick the Greek. He's got the loot and he's going to pass it on to Lafarge. But if that damned idiot collars Lafarge, Nick'll disappear with it. Hang on.'

Holding the telephone, he yelled to the sergeants' room. 'Morell! Lacocq! Come with me. We'll want a plain unmarked car.' With the instrument to his ear, Pel gestured to the rest of the room. 'Bardolle! Forget Tehendu. He'll keep. I'll want you, too! Also with an unmarked car. Get Brochard.' He spoke to Aimedieu again. 'Just hold him, Aimedieu.'

'Patron – ' Aimedieu's voice came in a worried bleat ' – he's an inspector, remember. From Paris. I'm just a sergeant. From the provinces. *How* do I stop him?'

'Use your head,' Pel snapped, slamming down the instrument. 'Shoot him if necessary. Between the eyes.'

21

Aimedieu was arguing with Duval when they appeared. They arrived at Madame Bonhomme's by a circuitous route so they wouldn't be seen from Lafarge's house and pulled to a stop by her back door. Aimedieu had Duval against the wall. Aimedieu was pale and worried and Duval was trying to thrust past him, watched by an agitated Madame Bonhomme.

'Name of God, Patron,' Aimedieu said. 'I'm glad you've arrived! I couldn't have kept him much longer.'

Duval stared from one to the other. 'What is this?' he demanded. 'Is this how you usually behave in the provinces? I was about to question a suspect at a house down the road there when this idiot rushed out and said I mustn't. When I demand to know who he is, he says he's just a sergeant. I'm an inspector.'

'And I,' Pel rapped, 'am a *chief* inspector. I think we'd better go inside.'

Duval was still arguing as Pel pushed him ahead of him through Madame Bonhomme's door. When he was still inclined to argue, Bardolle's bulk, crowding up behind, carried him through. Aimedieu went straight back to his lookout post.

'It's all right, Patron,' he said. 'There's no movement. Nobody's noticed anything.'

Madame Bonhomme put her head round the door. 'I can make coffee, if you wish,' she offered. 'I also have tea if any of you gentlemen like it. Also, of course, I have wine, which I imagine you might prefer. Cold wine. It will cool tempers, won't it?'

'That would be splendid, Madame,' Pel said. He advanced on Duval who was obliged to take a step backwards. Finding a chair behind his knees, he collapsed into it.

'I'd like to know what's going one,' he said angrily.

'You will in a second,' Pel said. 'First, let's taste Madame's excellent wine. It'll give us time to recover our wits.'

Duval had no wish to be silent. 'I've discovered that there's a man across the road there who might have been involved in the robbery at Quigny,' he said.

'*How* did you discover?'

'I spoke to the Baronne's maid.'

'You probably also got her beaten up,' Pel said.

He didn't add that she probably deserved it.

He tried to explain. 'Of course he was involved in the robbery at Quigny,' he said sharply. 'We knew that within two days of it happening.'

'Then – ' Duval looked bewildered ' – why haven't you arrested him?'

'Because we're after bigger fish. *And* the jewels. If we pick up Lafarge our man will disappear with the loot. He might even get scared and throw it in the river. And that will help nobody.'

'You *know* he's got the jewels? This man of yours?'

'I'm damned sure he has.'

'Who is he?'

'Arion Nichopopoulos. Known as Nick the Greek.'

The name obviously meant something to Duval because he made no attempt to argue. 'Why do you think he'll come here?' he asked.

'Because we know he's scared of being found with the loot.'

'So what do we do?'

'We wait.'

'How long?'

'As long as necessary.'

Duval took some convincing. Like most Paris police, he believed that everybody in the provinces was a half-wit. But they eventually got through to him and, finally, it became plain that his chief wish was not to be pushed out and return to Paris without being able to claim he had been in at the kill. In the end, they suggested he should relieve Brochard and maintain watch with Aimedieu so that he'd be there when Nick the Greek turned up.

'I can recommend it,' Aimedieu said. 'Madame's a good cook.'

When Duval finally agreed, Pel knew he was already

working out ways of writing his report so that he could claim most of the credit for himself. He didn't blame him. Nobody could blame a cop for looking after his future. After all, nobody else would.

'Patron!' Brochard said. The tape recorder had been set in motion by Lafarge picking up the telephone. 'Someone's calling.'

They crowded round the loudspeaker.

'You know who this is?' The squawky voice came clearly.

'Yes.' Lafarge's voice came back. 'It's all right. It's safe.'

'Tonight, then. After dark.'

'Have you made arrangements?'

'Yes. Paris has organised it. We pass them on to Charlot. He'll be waiting in the car on the road to Besançon. A blue Citroën. Number 4319 HA 75. He then heads north for Paris. You continue south. I'm going to Perpignan. If we're picked up, we're clean. We come together for the pickings a month from now.'

'I'd rather keep the stuff.' Lafarge's voice was nervous.

'The Boss's fixed it this way.'

'Suppose they pick us up on route?'

'Why should they? All you have to do is drive nice and gently towards Besançon. Slowly. Never exceeding the speed limit and wearing seat belts, so they've no reason to worry you. Charlot will be waiting in the square at Lissy-sur-Ille. You park alongside and pass the stuff across. He drives off. You drive off. I drive off. It's over and done in ten seconds.'

'I'll be ready.'

'What about your family?'

Lafarge laughed. 'Gone to mother's in Vichy for a holiday.'

'Do they know anything?'

'Nothing. When they come back I'll be somewhere else.'

'Right. After dark, then. At 9.30.'

There was a click and the conversation finished.

'Let's hear it again,' Pel said.

Brochard rewound the tape and restarted it. They listened carefully then Pel turned to Duval. 'Satisfied?'

To his credit, Duval didn't argue. 'Of course, Chief,' he said. 'How do I help?'

Pel managed a smile. It was somewhat bleak but it acknowledged that he had accepted Duval.

'What do you wish?'

'I want to be first inside.'

Pel hesitated. He had a suspicion that if there were shooting – and there might well be – that Duval would get himself shot. Ah, well, he thought, better Duval than one of his own boys.

'Very well,' he said. 'I shall be behind you.'

'What about the suspects?'

'We allow them to take the stuff – '

'Away?'

'We can cover the square at Lissy,' Pel said. 'Our people will pick up our friend, Charlot, whoever he is, watch his car and grab the lot as they hand over. We'll have them tailed from here to Lissy.' He turned to Darcy. 'Arrange it, Daniel. Different cars to take over from each other so they don't know they're followed. And have that square at Lissy well covered. A car ready to seal every entrance so they can't bolt. As soon as Nick and Lafarge enter it, block the exits so they can't get out again.'

Darcy left nothing to chance, and even went to Lissy to make sure the local police knew exactly what they had to do. Everybody had been called in. He left De Troq' and Bardolle in Lissy to take care of things, then headed back towards the city.

'All set, Patron,' he announced. 'The main road's narrow there and only one of the entrances into the square is really wide. They've arranged for a lorry to block that, so there'll be no getting past. How about here?'

'Nosjean and I will go in behind Duval as soon as they leave. I want that house going through with a fine-toothed comb. I think Pépé le Cornet's the man Nick calls the Boss and there might be something in there that will connect him to it. I want it clearing as soon as they leave.'

'Give them half an hour,' Darcy suggested. 'In case they forget something and come back.'

'They won't come back,' Pel said. 'They sounded too confident. Someone's sewed this one up good and tight.'

It took some doing for Pel to sit still and appear not to be over-excited. He didn't take kindly to sitting still when things were moving to a climax, but he had long since learned that a man who couldn't delegate could make a hash of an arrest and he trusted his squad, especially Darcy, Nosjean and De Troq'.

He telephoned home, saying he'd be late, and sat down to go through the reports on his desk on the shootings at Pouilly and Montenay. He hadn't, he felt, given them his full attention with the De Mougy thing hanging over him. But that was the way it always was. To cope with everything, a man needed two heads. After tonight, he hoped, they could forget De Mougy, but as Claudie brought him coffee and Cadet Martin brought him beer while he sat reading Bardolle's report, he still managed to work his way through a whole pack of cigarettes. Despite what Bardolle had turned up about Tehendu, it didn't make sense. Why would Tehendu shoot Madame Huppert who'd given him a chance? Was Tehendu some sort of stooge for the Paris mob?

Out at Madame Bonhomme's, Aimedieu and Duval stared through the curtains until their eyes ached with concentrating. Nothing was moving and Aimedieu began to wonder if they'd been tricked. It had happened before.

At six o'clock Pel arrived with Nosjean. Madame Bonhomme let then in, quivering with excitement. Then Lagé appeared.

'Everything ready?' Pel asked.

'Car waiting, Patron,' Lagé reported. 'Another one in sight of it in case something goes wrong. They'll pick them up when we radio they're on their way.'

At 9.30 p.m., when it was well and truly dark, the tape recorder clicked and the spools started turning. Aimedieu's head lifted.

'Patron!'

They crowded round, listening. It was the same voice they'd heard before.

Lafarge answered and the first voice spoke again. 'All clear?'

'Not a soul in sight. Where are you?'

'Round the corner in the Rue Armand-de-Léon. I've got my car parked there. I'll be outside the door in two minutes. Be ready.'

'That's Nick,' Pel said quietly.

Two minutes later they saw a car slide quietly to a stop outside Lafarge's house. Nothing flashy – a small modest Renault that wouldn't attract attention.

'Is that him?' Madame Bonhomme asked eagerly.

'I think it is, Madame,' Pel said. 'Now I'd be grateful if you'd sit in your kitchen – just in case there's trouble.'

'What sort of trouble?'

'These are vicious crooks, Madame. Their kind have been known to use firearms.'

She disappeared as instructed, but she seemed very unwilling.

By the light of a solitary street lamp they saw a figure leave the car and go into Lafarge's house. It was too far and too faint to tell who it was but the figure was young and tall and straight and carried a canvas hold-all.

'That's Nick,' Nosjean said.

'Patron.' It was Aimedieu. 'They're coming out again.'

A figure appeared at the door opposite.

'That's Lafarge,' Aimedieu said.

'You sure? We don't want any mistakes.'

'Patron, I've been watching that place for days. I know the way he draws breath.'

The tall, straight figure reappeared, but it was Lafarge who was now holding the canvas bag. The two men talked together for a few seconds, then Lafarge climbed into the car. Nick slapped the bonnet and waved, then turned and began to walk quickly away.

Pel picked up the microphone of the radio. 'Lagé. Nick's on his way towards his car. Let him get round the corner then pick him up.'

'Right, Patron.'

As Nick vanished they heard the little Renault's engine start and saw the lights come on, then it moved slowly away.

'Warn everyone.'

As Aimedieu began to call up on the car radio band, Pel reached for his own radio. Within seconds he was speaking to Darcy.

'They're on their way!'

As the little Renault that Lafarge was driving moved out of the Rue Dolour, it was picked up by a Mercedes waiting

187

on the main road. Finding a place two cars behind, the Merc followed the Renault out of the city.

The radio crackled. 'Patron, I think he's suspicious. He keeps slowing down.'

'When does Bardolle take over?'

'Outside the city.'

'Right. Stick with them. They'll lose interest when they see your lights disappear.'

As the red Renault left the city, it began to head towards Lissy-sur-Ille. As it put the city outskirts behind it, the Mercedes dropped behind and a big Citroën took over.

After a couple of dozen kilometres, the radio squawked worriedly. Bardolle's voice came. 'He's stopped, Patron. In the lay-by at Rolandpont.'

'Any other car there?'

'No, Patron. Just a lorry. It's a big lay-by. Made out of the old road when they straightened the corner.'

'Where are you?'

'Other end. We coasted in without lights. He probably hasn't seen us.'

'Any contact with the lorry?'

'No, Patron. I can see him quite plainly. He hasn't left the car.'

'Make a note of the lay-by and the lorry's number. Keep him in sight.'

'He's got out, Patron. He's pretending to take a leak. But his eyes are all over the place, I'll bet. He's making sure nobody's following.'

Three times on the way to Lissy the red Renault stopped. But every time the car that pulled into the lay-by behind it was a different one. After the second time, the driver of the Renault didn't bother to get out.

By this time the voice was Lacocq's. 'I think he's satisfied he's not being followed, Patron. He's not worried any more. We're close to Lissy and I think he feels he's safe.'

'Keep following. He'll be picked up outside Lissy.'

After a while the red Renault moved off again. The Peugeot 604 which was tailing it now crept quietly out of the lay-by where Lafarge had stopped, keeping its lights out until two or three cars had passed, then it switched its lights on and took up a position two cars behind, keeping the Renault in sight all the time.

At the outskirts of Lissy, a fawn-coloured British Rover with white lights and carrying a GB plate took over. It was driven by a policeman from Lissy and the car was one which had been stolen and recovered. The policeman considered it a brainwave to use a foreign car without the yellow French lights.

The red Renault moved slowly into Lissy, heading through the narrow streets towards the square. As it entered the square a heavy lorry without lights edged forward and parked across the entrance just out of sight. A policeman climbed out of the back with a red lantern, ready to halt approaching cars. At the same time, the other entrances to the square were sealed by other cars, all out of sight. The man in the red Renault suspected nothing and coasted to a stop alongside a large Citroën which was parked in front of the church. Inside it, two men were smoking but, as the Renault stopped close alongside, the driver stubbed out his cigarette and began to wind down his window. Lafarge in the red Renault wound his window down, too, and the canvas hold-all was handed across the intervening space. The window was wound up again, the Citroën's engine started and the two cars were just about to leave when a car which had been parked outside a bar opposite came to life, jerked forward, narrowly missed an old man who was heading for the bar, roared across the square, and came to a stop immediately behind the Citroën and the Renault, blocking their exit.

Three heads turned and three white faces were caught in the glow of headlights. Then three doors opened and the occupants of the cars leapt out. Immediately a search light was switched on in a window above the street, pinpointing them like butterflies pinned to a board.

'Hold it! Police! Don't move!'

The iron voice of a loud-hailer rang out in the narrow square. The old man on the way to the bar stopped dead and turned, wondering what was happening, as men emerged from doorways and parked cars. They were all armed. Windows opened and lights were switched on in bedrooms.

'Drop the bag!'

189

The driver of the Citroën dropped the hold-all. Darcy appeared and smiled at the Citroën's passenger.

'Pat Boum,' he said. 'We wondered where you'd got to. Right, you lot, faces to the wall. Hands flat against it.'

The three men turned, leaning on their hands. Darcy, his gun in his hand, approached them cautiously, backed up by half a dozen other men. De Troq' kicked the feet of the three men wider apart so that they couldn't move without an effort. Hands patted their bodies. A Luger appeared from a shoulder holster under the Citroën driver's arm. Pat the Bang's pocket produced another. Lafarge was unarmed. Darcy picked up the canvas hold-all and, taking it to the front of the car, opened it in front of the headlights. Immediately he caught the glitter of jewellery.

'All right, boys. I think we've got them.'

Pel was waiting by the radio at Madame Bonhomme's. Across the road, a police car stood outside Lafarge's house, where the door stood wide open. The lights were all on. Nosjean and Duval and two policemen were going through the place carefully, watched by a handcuffed and sullen Nick the Greek.

As the radio squawked, Pel snatched up the microphone. Darcy's voice came. 'We have them, Patron.'

'And the jewels?'

'Those, too. It's over, Patron. We've picked up Pat the Bang. Ballentou was wrong when he said he and Nick wouldn't work together. They *were* doing. He was the type who met Lafarge – Charles Arnemor, you'll be pleased to know. Pépé le Cornet's sidekick. He was to take the sparklers back to Paris just as Nick said. We've got the connection to Pépé.'

'But not Pépé,' Pel said. 'He'll swear it had nothing to do with him and he'll have an alibi to prove it.'

Darcy sounded cheerful, nevertheless. 'All the same, Patron, we can give him a bad time. He'll probably decide to keep out of our diocese after this. After all, Arnemor's his right hand man. He won't enjoy seeing him go to jail.'

'Neither,' Pel said dryly, 'will Arnemor.'

As he replaced the microphone, Nosjean arrived.

'I've searched Nick's place, Patron,' he said.

'Find anything?'

'Yes. Explosives. Two kilos.'

'Enough to blow a car inside-out. Who's he after?'

'Ballentou's the one who's been scared.'

'What about De Mougy's money?'

'No sign of it, Patron. I expect that's been dispersed long since.'

Pel shrugged. 'De Mougy can afford to lose it. And he'll be happy enough to get his heirlooms back.'

As Pel turned away, he saw Madame Bonhomme watching him.

'Is it over?' she asked.

Pel nodded. 'It's over, Madame. You can have your house back.'

She beamed and produced a bottle of wine. 'I think, Chief Inspector, that we ought to have a drink. You, Pierre Aimedieu – ' Pierre, Pel noticed, not just Aimedieu ' – and all the other gentlemen.'

'There are a lot of them, Madame,' Pel pointed out gravely. 'And policemen are inclined to drink a lot.'

'Never mind. There's more where this came from. And I've become very attached to them. Especially to Pierre Aimedieu. He's promised to visit me and, to an old woman living alone and unable to go out much, you can't imagine what that means.'

Pel took the glass she offered him. 'We owe you a considerable debt, Madame,' he said. 'How can we repay you?'

She smiled. 'Well, when it comes up before the magistrates, I'd appreciate a seat in the public gallery.'

'I think we can do better than that,' Pel said. 'You'll be called as a witness to the theft of the bicycle that set the whole thing off and the magistrates will be able to compliment you personally from the bench.' She beamed with pleasure and Pel went on. 'But that isn't very much, Madame. What else might we do?'

'I'd like to have a look round Police Headquarters and see how things work. And I'd like a ride in a police car.'

Pel was surprised. He'd expected something much more sophisticated. A tour round the Hôtel de Police and a ride in a police car, followed by a testimonial from the Chief and a meal in the police canteen had been what they'd intended for young Petitbois, whose bicycle, retained for so long, had provided the first clue. Nevertheless . . .

His serious face cracked in a smile. 'Would you object to a companion, Madame?' he asked.

22

With Lafarge, Nick the Greek, Pat Boum and Charles Arnemor behind bars at 72, Rue d'Auxonne, there was time to draw breath. Duval had written his report under Pel's direction so that some credit – but not much! – was given to Duval himself. The insurance investigator, Briand, and Major Chaput had headed back to Paris. Once more there was elbow room in Burgundy to turn round and examine the outstanding cases of murder.

They had made no progress with the shootings, however. Occupied with the murder of Selva, Nosjean had been thinking. Like Pel, he was inclined to brood a lot and, also like Pel, he was good at sitting still and letting his mind work.

Nosjean's mind had worked a great deal as he recalled everything that had been said to him. Someone had shot Richard Selva. That was clear. But who? The same man who had shot Madame Huppert? Nosjean found it hard to believe. For one thing, Madame Huppert had been shot at roughly the same time as Selva and it didn't seem possible, unless he were Superman, that the murderer could have got across the city in time. But both bullets were 6.35s. Which was a large coincidence. And could the murderer *somehow* have got across the city? Could Doc Misset have got his times wrong? An hour wrong, even half an hour, and the murderer *could* have made it. But, if he had, *why* had he? Why shoot two people as unlike each other as Madame Huppert and Richard Selva? One a perfectly normal housewife and businesswoman, the other known to be on the fringe of the Paris mob, part of Pépé le Cornet's set-up, a man who dealt with drugs. It didn't make sense.

While Nosjean brooded on Selva and Pel brooded on Madame Huppert, everybody else was congratulating themselves on what had happened on the De Mougy case, so that there was a lot of noise in the sergeants' room and a lot of cheerful backslapping. Misset came in for more teasing. Now that the counterfeit money business had been cleared up, photographs of Ada Vocci were again being passed round and Misset was making the most of it.

'She's a bit of all right,' Brochard said. 'How did you get the information out of her, Misset?'

Misset made modest movements. 'How do you think I got it?' he said.

'I know how you get most things. In bed.'

'Well,' Misset said, 'if it's there you grab it, don't you?'

Pel listened with a blank face to the exchanges, part of the celebrations without being in them. Returning to his office, he found someone had placed Didier's application to join the police on his desk. Attached to it was a note from the Chief. '*You know this boy, I believe. Comments?*'

Pel studied the application. Following their talk, Didier had tidied the application up a little, but not much, and Pel remembered his comment. 'Why make a fuss when you know everything's all right? When you're aiming for something and can reach it easily, just go straight for it.' It was exactly what Didier had done. He'd got it all down but there wasn't a lot extra. For a moment, Pel studied the form, wondering if it could be improved, but then he realised that there was little that could be added. Didier had it all in – without elaboration and all quite clear – and in the end Pel simply added a note. '*I know this boy. He has all the right attributes. Of good steady character.*' Finally, he drew attention to the application itself. '*He appears to be a boy with a great deal of calm confidence, who knows exactly what he's after, knows he can get it, and sets out his stall without fuss. He could be a very good policeman.*'

If that didn't get Didier into uniform, he thought, nothing would.

At breakfast next day Pel brooded a little, thinking about the Huppert business. It troubled him because there still seemed so much to clear up despite Bardolle's discovery about Tehendu having once worked for the firm that had produced the 6.35s.

It was obvious that whoever had shot the Hupperts had acquired his weapons from the stolen consignment from St.

Etienne and that *could* mean Tehendu, because the 6.35 was a small calibre weapon which ruled out a professional gunman who would never be bothered with such a small gun. Was the shooting only intended as a threat, then? Something some lunatic like Démy could have thought up, but which had gone wrong and resulted in Madame Huppert's death. But why use two different guns – same type, same calibre – on two different people within two minutes and within two or three steps of each other? It didn't make sense. Had the killer tried to shoot only Huppert, missed and killed his wife by accident and then tried again in the forge, and again failed to do any more than wound Huppert? Which, Pel thought, was possibly all he had intended to do in the first place. To frighten him. But why? And why *two* guns? Had he felt the first gun was inaccurate and thought his aim would be better with the second? Had he been short of ammunition, as Ballistics had suggested? Why shoot at Huppert, anyway? Why go into the forge where he could easily have been trapped if Huppert had had the sense to slam the door and lock it? If it were Tehendu, he'd know all that. And why hadn't the dog barked? Why hadn't it bitten him? That was what it was there for. It had almost bitten Pel and, until Huppert had got rid of it, almost bitten everybody else who'd visited the place.

Pel's thoughts were ranging over the whole cast of characters. Tehendu? Madame Gruye? She had an interest in Huppert's business. Could *she* have shot Madame Huppert because she disliked her? Had she and Madame Huppert quarrelled? Démy? He was clearly a little unbalanced and he knew about guns. Could he have done the shooting for some strange twisted reason or because he admired Madame Huppert? Had she rejected his advances? Or had *he* been trying to get rid of Huppert because he wanted Madame Huppert and shot Madame Huppert by mistake? Nick the Greek? He had talked to Huppert. His girlfriend had said so. Could *he* have had some reason for shooting at Madame Huppert? Or at Huppert and hitting Madame Huppert by mistake?

What seemed most likely was that the bullet had been directed at Huppert and had hit his wife instead. But it was hard to believe that the shooting had been done by a burglar. There was nothing to steal and no money on the premises.

The firm was too insignificant. Was Huppert somehow mixed up with Nick the Greek? Was there something hidden there they didn't know about? And what was the connection with the shooting at Pouilly and the death of Richard Selva, who'd been shot by a gun that must surely have come from the same stolen consignment as the guns that had done the shooting at Montenay? There was clearly *some* connection.

Pel lit a cigarette without even noticing and only woke up to the fact as he crushed it out. It would be nice once in a while, he thought, to have a case that was easy. He didn't want to be a big shot or famous, or a tycoon who wanted to rule the world. He just wanted to live in peace, stop smoking and have easier cases. One that was so neat, for instance, it became known after him. By his name, *Un Pel*. A slick neat solution that every policeman in France would know and admire.

He smiled. It would be nice to be immortalised in that way. Then he frowned. There were other aspects to it, of course. In the last century, a certain Monsieur Poubelle had decided that Paris house refuse should be collected instead of thrown in the gutters and had thoughtfully set about providing bins for it. It was certain *he* hadn't expected that they would eventually take his name – poubelles, garbage cans.

Pel wrenched his mind back to the shooting. It had all started just when he was thinking everything was quiet. At Quigny-par-la-Butte, with that damned church that chimed twice. The whole period had been full of unexpected things. Clocks that chimed twice. Jewels that vanished. More guns than made sense. Dogs that didn't bark and didn't grab what was in front of them. And Didier – he thought about Didier again and what he'd said when he'd first appeared with his application at Pel's house. *When you're aiming for something and can reach it easily, just go straight for it.* Why hadn't the dog?

His wife looked up.

'What's worrying you?' she asked.

He explained. 'The dog didn't bark,' he said. 'And it didn't bite anyone.'

'Perhaps the man with the gun wasn't in the yard,' Madame suggested.

Pel frowned. 'What do you mean?'

196

'Perhaps there was nobody to bark at. Perhaps there was only Huppert. It never barked at him, you said.'

'Huppert was there,' Pel agreed. 'Of course, he was.'

'But perhaps the man with the gun wasn't.'

Pel thought for a moment, remembering Didier again: *When you're aiming for something and can reach it easily, just go straight for it.* The words went round in his head. It was roughly what Misset had said, though Misset's words had been boastful and bombastic: *If it's there, why not grab it?*

If it's there, why not grab it?

Pel paused, frowning. 'If it's there,' he murmured out loud, 'why not grab it?'

His eyes lit up. 'Yes, he was,' he said. 'The man with the gun *was* there! He was there all the time.'

He wolfed his croissants and announced that he had to go at once. At the Hôtel de Police, he sat at his desk, staring at the pistols that had been recovered from the canal. Bardolle was waiting with his list of everybody who had worked for Huppert. Pel paid particular attention to the name of Tehendu. He looked over the list of the men who'd been fired by Huppert over the years and finally the notes he'd made on his next door neighbour, Démy. Then he smoked two cigarettes in rapid succession, pushed the file at Bardolle and rose to his feet.

'Let's go to Montenay,' he said.

They spent part of the morning talking to Huppert's neighbours.

'The dog?' they said as Pel questioned them. 'No, we heard no dog.'

'Wasn't that odd?' Pel asked. 'It seemed to bark at strangers.'

A man who lived opposite frowned. 'Yes, it did,' he admitted. 'If anyone went near the place, it woke the whole street. I once even got out my gun, thinking the place was being broken into, and found a couple of kids kissing. It was the only dark spot in the street and they just wanted to say goodnight in private.'

Once again, Démy insisted that he hadn't heard the dog bark on the night of the shooting.

'But you *did* hear Huppert call his wife to come down because there was somebody in the yard.'

'No, I didn't,' Démy said. 'I heard him shout: "Come down. Somebody wants you." That's what he said. I'm sure of it now.'

'You knew he had a pistol, you said.'

'He once threatened to use it to shoot me.'

'Why?'

'I threw a brick through his window.'

'Did you ever offer to shoot *him*?'

'No.'

'Not even a month ago?'

'You don't think *I* shot at the fool, do you?' Démy asked.

'I think many things,' Pel said. 'You knew he had a pistol.'

'His wife showed it to me.'

'When was that?'

'When she was scared. When I offered her mine.'

'Where was Huppert?'

'He was in Morocco.'

'Doing what?'

'Selling. At least that's what he said. I think he was having a holiday. His case had "Hotel Miramar" on the label. I saw it with my binoculars. It's a posh place. I stayed there once myself. Old Gruye went too.'

'Where?'

'To Morocco.'

'With Huppert?'

'Certainly not with me.'

'Does she usually go away with him?'

'She went that time. I saw him pick her up at the end of the street. Her case was marked "Hotel Miramar", too.'

'She doesn't strike me as the type,' Pel said.

'She doesn't strike *me* as the type either,' Démy admitted. 'But you never can tell, can you?'

Pel paused, studying Démy, then went on slowly. 'You said once that Huppert's wife was interested in you. What made you think that?'

'I told you. The way she looked at me.'

'You couldn't have been misreading her expression?'

Démy shrugged.

'And you were interested in her?'

198

'Of course. Sympathy chiefly. Huppert put on her.'

'And when he went to Morocco you went round at her suggestion to comfort her.'

'No, I didn't,' Démy said. 'I went round to turn the electricity off.'

Pel was startled. 'To turn the electricity off?'

Démy explained. 'He had to go to Morocco on some business deal. I told you. Some wrought-iron for some Arab. You know what they're like. They love wrought-iron and they're the ones with all the money these days, aren't they? It was during August when everybody was on holiday and there was only Madame Huppert next door.' Démy frowned. 'He'd left in a hurry for the airport, she said, but just before he went he'd been doing something in the forge and he'd forgotten to turn off the electricity. He'd telephoned from the airport asking her to do it for him. "I've left the power on," he said. "Switch it off." At least, that's what she told me he said.'

'But she didn't switch it off? Why not?'

'It had one of those skull-and-crossed-bones warning signs alongside it to indicate danger, and she was scared.'

'Why? I thought she was the one with the brains.'

'She was. But she thought it didn't look right – that it had been tampered with. I was just about to switch it off for her, when *I* decided it didn't look right, too.'

'Why not?'

'There seemed to be more wires than there should be. And there's a lot of power goes in to that workshop. They have an electric furnace and a three-phase supply and step-up transformers to bump it up. In the end I put on rubber boots and gloves. *Then* I switched it off. There was a flash and a hell of a bang and all the lights went out. All the way along the street, too. An hour later, when the electricity people had arrived, Huppert turned up. When we told him what had happened he went pale. "Oh, my God," he said to his wife. "I might have killed you." Then he said he'd been worried about the main power switch and had been trying to do some temporary repairs on it. To keep the place going until he could get the electricity people in when he came back from Morocco. It had worried him, though, and he'd decided at the airport that he'd better come back and do the job himself and catch a later flight. At least – ' Démy's lip wrinkled ' – that's what he said. I think it was an attempt to kill me.'

Pel went into Huppert's forge and stood for a long time staring at the main switches. They were well labelled and had a huge skull-and-crossed-bones sign alongside. There appeared to be nothing wrong with the switch, and the electricity was on so that the factory hands could work in another part of the building.

The forge was still taped off, but there were men moving about the premises. Pel studied the chalk marks they'd found on the floor and on the bench, the marks Huppert said had been made by one of his work-people. They fascinated him. They were almost obliterated by this time but they were still visible and, finding a piece of chalk in a drawer, Pel bent and made them clear. Darcy and Bardolle watched, puzzled.

'That'll do, I think,' Pel said.

Followed by the other two, he crossed the yard to the office where they could see Huppert at the desk. Madame Gruye was with him, working the old tape recorder with the home-made pedal device. They could hear Huppert's voice coming out of it, calm and clear, between the bursts of typing. Pel watched them for a while until they became aware of his presence.

'When are you going to be finished?' Huppert asked. 'This place can't function without the forge.'

'It won't be long now,' Pel said. 'I'm just having a last look round.'

Huppert shrugged. 'Help yourself then,' he said. 'You'll have to excuse us, though. We have things to do.'

Pel continued to watch as Madame Gruye worked the pedal of the tape recorder. He seemed fasincated by the way the pressure of her foot on the home-made pedal switched it on and off.

'Work's the best way to get over what happened,' Huppert said. He tossed down his pen and rose. 'We'll be going to the kitchen in a minute or two for a bite of lunch. Fancy joining us?'

As Huppert and Connie Gruye disappeared, Pel remained standing in the office door, staring at the tape recorder. Bardolle and Darcy looked at each other and Darcy shrugged.

Huppert and Madame Gruye were tucking into their lunch by this time and the smell of fried steak came through the window. Madame Gruye was pouring wine and Huppert was breaking a piece of bread from a baguette. An hour later, when they had finished, from the door of the forge Pel saw them rise and saw Huppert head for the office. As Huppert reached it, Pel saw him stare in surprise, then they heard him call Madame Gruye.

Pel appeared in the doorway.

'Something wrong?' he asked.

'Someone's stolen the tape recorder,' Huppert said. 'We were only down the corridor.' He looked at Pel. 'And you were – '

'In the forge.'

'What's happened to it? Did you see anyone?'

'It'll turn up,' Pel said. 'Don't worry. I'll see it does. But there are a few things that puzzle me. Chief among them, what *was* your intruder after?'

Huppert shrugged.

'Tell me again: This towel you had. What was it for?'

'I told you. It was a cold night. I snatched it up, shoved it round my neck like a scarf and tucked the ends into my jacket.'

'And then what?'

'Well, when the bullet hit me, I used it to wrap round the wound.'

'It was fortunate you had it.'

'Yes, it was.'

'Why did the thief enter the yard, do you think? The kitchen light was on. Your wife's light in the bedroom was on. You were reading in the office. It seems a silly time to attempt a burglary.'

Huppert shrugged again. 'Well, you know how they are.'

'Yes, I do,' Pel agreed. Only too well, he thought. Burglars usually had more sense than to enter premises when people were about. 'You didn't turn on the yard light, you said?'

'No. Perhaps because I thought it would mean he would see *me* better.'

'But you grabbed your pistol?'

'That's right.'

'First strapping on the belt with the holster. Didn't that take time?'

Huppert looked puzzled. 'It seemed sense. Somewhere to put the pistol. Weapons are heavy.'

'Then you called your wife down?'

'Yes.'

'Why?' Pel frowned. 'When there was danger?'

'I've told you. To telephone the police.'

'But you have a telephone by your bed. I've seen it. Why not from there?'

'I expect I just didn't think.'

Pel nodded. 'Where was the intruder when he fired?'

'Over by the pump. I told you before.'

'You're sure about that?'

'Quite sure.'

'Then you went into the forge. That was a dangerous thing to do.'

'I suppose I didn't think much about that either. We've had burglars before and I wanted to catch this one.'

'He fired at you. If I'd been a burglar I'd have kept quiet. And you fired back. We found two ejected cartridges in the forge that came from your pistol.'

Huppert nodded his agreement. 'Yes. I fired twice. So did he.'

'You were standing in the doorway. Against the light. That was very stupid.'

'I suppose it was.'

'Let's go over it again,' Pel said.

'We've been over it half a dozen times already.'

'Let's try once more. To get it clear. A man broke into the yard. But he left no traces. No fingerprints. No footprints. The dog didn't bark so you didn't hear him at first. He took his time. He got into the factory to find a set of bolt shearers, cut a hole in the grille then carefully put the bolt shearers back in the workshop. He then came into the yard. That was when you heard him and decided he was near the pump. He shot at you as you appeared and you fired back at the flame of his gun. Then, instead of turning to run, as you'd expect he would, he hid in the forge and you went after him. You enter the forge. He doesn't fire at you immediately but when *you* fire he fires back and you're wounded. That right?'

202

'That's right.'

'You wrap the towel round the wound and run for the house. It's then you find your wife.'

'That's correct.'

'All this takes no more than a minute or two.'

'Exactly.'

'During which time he escapes.' Pel frowned. 'You remember the ejected cartridge cases we found?'

'Of course. I found one myself and handed it to your sergeant.'

'Very helpful,' Pel agreed. 'Ballistics said that those cartridge cases came from two pistols of the same type. Not the same pistol – two different ones.'

'How can you tell?'

'Because we found the pistols. In the canal where they'd been thrown.'

Huppert's eyebrows rose. 'I didn't hear about that.'

'Nobody did. We kept it quiet. It's what's known as tactics. Ballistics, however, say that two pistols, even the same type, even with adjoining serial numbers, never have the same characteristics in the rifling grooves and the marks made by the firing pin. There was a murder in England some sixty years ago when a policeman was shot by a Webley and Scott revolver. The English police tried 14,000 Webley and Scotts – there were a lot about at the time because it was just after the first war – and not one had the same characteristics as any of the others. Now – ' Pel leaned forward ' – let's do a bit of reconstruction.'

'Again?'

Pel ignored the comment. 'You heard the disturbance outside, so you snatched up a towel for your neck, together with your pistol and its holster and went outside. But the man had left no sign of himself. Your dog didn't bite him. It didn't even bark. *Why* didn't it bark? Why didn't it grab him?'

Huppert seemed hypnotised. 'I don't know.'

'*I* know,' Pel said. 'It didn't bark because it knew the man in the yard. I stood near that pump, where you said the intruder fired from, and I had to bolt into the forge because if I hadn't the dog would have grabbed *me*. It was well within reach. So if the intruder had been someone it didn't know, and if he'd stood near the pump, it would have raised hell,

203

wouldn't it, and very likely savaged him? It ought to have grabbed him easily, but it didn't, did it?'

'Perhaps,' Huppert whispered, 'he wasn't near the pump. Perhaps I made a mistake.'

'Yes, you did, my friend,' Pel said gently. 'I'll explain. You wrapped that towel round your neck, knowing perfectly well you were going to be shot. You needed it to staunch the blood.'

Huppert was pale. 'How could I know I was going to be shot?'

'You'd already had one go at your wife, hadn't you? You'd hoped she'd kill herself turning off the electricity, but your next door neighbour arrived and had enough sense to take precautions. That's why you came home from the airport – not to check, but because you expected to find your wife dead. Despite what Démy thinks, it wasn't him you were after. It was your wife.'

'No.'

'You also set up that earlier shooting incident a month ago. So that the police would believe your story about an intruder when it happened again. Isn't that true?'

'No.'

'Then why didn't you just grab your gun and run outside? Why bother to put on a towel and the belt carrying the holster? You were taking your time *if* you wanted to catch anyone.'

'I didn't think.'

'No, you didn't. And the belt was somewhere to stuff the second gun, wasn't it? *And* the third. There *were* three guns, weren't there? Your own old one and two new ones. You used one of the new ones to shoot your wife. She guessed what you were up to, and when she saw you in the yard she turned and ran and the bullet hit her in the back.'

'I didn't shoot her.'

'I think you did. And she knew you had. Because you'd tried to electrocute her and she knew it even if Démy didn't. When the doctor spoke to her before he sent her to the hospital she said: "Jacques", didn't she? Doctor Lachasse thought she was asking for you. But she wasn't, was she? She was trying to accuse you. She was going to say: "Jacques did it." But she couldn't manage it. Not then or ever. She died before she could give a statement.'

Huppert was staring, fascinated, at Pel. Madame Gruye stood behind him, bulky, silent and brooding.

'You shot at this so-called intruder you talk about with your own gun – the one you'd always had – but you obviously couldn't shoot your wife with that one, could you, so you shot her with a different one, one you'd managed to buy. But you still had to use another – a third pistol – to shoot yourself. You couldn't shoot yourself with your own old pistol. That would have looked *too* fishy. But you also couldn't shoot yourself with the pistol you used to shoot your wife because you hadn't time.'

'Time?' Huppert looked bewildered. 'Why would I shoot myself? I might have missed and killed myself.'

'Missed?' Pel asked. 'When you were holding it in your hand and could have put it to your arm to make sure.'

'I wasn't – ' Huppert stopped dead. 'The police would have found powder burns on my shirt.'

'They didn't do that,' Pel explained, 'because you didn't hold the pistol close enough. You knew about the powder burns so you didn't even *hold* the pistol. Let's go into the forge and look. You too, Madame. I'd like you to identify your tape recorder.'

Huppert's face was ashen as he saw the tape recorder standing on the bench close to where they had found the unexplained chalk marks. The home-made spring pedal that worked the tape recorder was on the floor, attached by its cable to a set of clamps on a laboratory retort stand, which had been fastened in position alongside the tape recorder by the vise on the bench.

'What's all that for?' Huppert asked nervously.

'It's the device you made to work the tape recorder,' Pel pointed out. 'I found it works other things too.' He gestured at the marks on the floor. 'I want you to stand there. With your feet inside the chalk marks.'

Huppert was pushed forward unwillingly until the toes of his shoes were inside the curved marks.

'Fit exactly, don't they?' Pel pointed out cheerfully. 'Just one more thing.' He took Huppert's hand and lifted the arm that had been wounded so that Huppert's fingers rested between the chalk marks on the bench. 'There,' he said. 'Right, Bardolle, carry on.'

Bardolle produced a pistol from his pocket. It was an Apex 6.35. without a trigger guard.

'One of those we found in the canal,' Pel pointed out.

Bardolle was securing the pistol upside down in the clamps that were held upright by the vise. When he had it secure, he slotted the strip of plastic that had worked the tape recorder switch over the trigger. It dropped neatly into place.

'It fits very well, you'll notice,' Pel pointed out. 'That's why the trigger guard was sawn off, isn't it? With the trigger guard still there it wouldn't have worked because the trigger guard would have been in the way and jammed it. It was fortunate you had all the equipment you needed right here at your disposal. Vise. Hacksaw. Everything.'

Huppert's face was grey.

'Now,' Pel said. 'If you notice, that pistol's now aiming directly at your left arm. If I were to press the pedal with my foot, the bullet would strike you exactly where the bullet struck you when you were wounded. You could work that pedal yourself from where you stand, couldn't you?'

'No.' Huppert's voice was only a whisper. 'It can't be done.'

'I think it can.' Giving Huppert a little push, Pel had him standing with his right foot where his left foot had previously been. 'If you were to press that pedal now, though,' he said, 'the bullet would strike you – where?'

'In the chest,' Darcy said cheerfully. 'It would kill you. Stone dead,' he added.

'No.' Huppert's eyes were like saucers and his voice came out in a croak. 'It's not possible.'

'Try it.'

'No.'

'Then, I will.'

Pel reached out with his foot and stamped on the pedal. As the pressure worked the cable, the piece of plastic slotted over the trigger of the gun jerked. Huppert gave a yell and collapsed.

Pel looked down at him. 'If that gun had been loaded,' he pointed out, 'you'd have been dead, wouldn't you? But if you'd been standing where I first placed you, with both feet in the marks you'd made, and your hand on the mark on the bench you'd have been merely wounded in the arm, as you were. And as you staggered back – doubtless in some pain – your foot would come off the pedal and the pressure would be released. Meanwhile, as the breech returned, the cartridge would be ejected. It was neat. It suddenly occurred to you that what would work that old-fashioned tape recorder would also work a gun. You probably experimented with a rod down the barrel to make sure the bullet didn't do too much damage. Your mistake, my friend, was in not shooting yourself with the same pistol you used to shoot your wife. But that was impossible, wasn't it? You'd thought it all out and you knew you wouldn't have time before the alarm was raised to fasten *that* pistol into this device and line it up safely so that it would only slightly wound you and not kill you. You had to do that beforehand because it needed time and care.'

Huppert stared at him, fascinated, and he went on smoothly. 'Judging by the cartridge cases we found, you fired twice at yourself. The first one missed. Probably because you hadn't the courage to stand in the proper place. But you made no mistake with the second. *That* must have taken courage. It must also have been painful. But I suppose it wasn't so bad because it barely nicked your arm and you had the towel round your neck to wrap round it, didn't you? It made things all right.'

Huppert was still on the floor, sobbing now. 'It did,' he moaned. 'It did.'

'Not quite,' Pel said. 'But nearly. You went to your wife and realised she was still alive. But you decided she was dying and unconscious and you came back out here. Even with one hand it was possible to unfasten the vise, tuck the pedal and cable under your arm and use your good hand to carry the tape recorder back to the office before telephoning the police.' He looked at Connie Gruye. 'And doubtless you were on hand in good time to fix it all up the next day before anybody noticed it had been dismantled. It doesn't take long, we found.'

She gave him a bitter look and he bent over Huppert again. 'Where did you get this pistol?'

'This man came. With Viviane Simoneau. When she came to ask about my wife. I'd met him once in the bar and I knew he'd been in jail. I asked him. In a roundabout way. He said he knew of a consignment that had been stolen.'

'And it was done because Madame Gruye told you to, wasn't it? Because she wanted to control this firm. Because, although nobody believed it, she was your mistress and what she said went. You even got rid of the dog because she told you to. Isn't that correct?'

'Yes,' Huppert's moan was barely audible. 'Yes.'

'And she threw the guns in the canal for you, when you couldn't do it yourself because of your arm?'

'Yes. Yes. My wife had found she'd been helping herself to cash and wanted to get rid of her. We fixed it up together.'

Madame Gruye was staring at Huppert with eyes that were like stones. 'You miserable worm,' she snapped.

Pel gestured. 'Let's go,' he said. 'You as well, Madame. We'll need you, too. As an accessory before and after the fact.'

23

Nosjean was still brooding over the Selva murder. The connection between *that* shooting and the Huppert shooting obviously existed somehow, but it just didn't make sense. It made even less sense when Nosjean appeared in the Hôtel de Police and found Huppert and Madame Gruye in the charge office being faced with the murder of Madame Huppert.

Darcy explained, and a lot of Nosjean's questions were answered at once. And, as they were, he recalled something that had been said to him some days earlier. Returning to the sergeants' room, he sat staring at the telephone for a long time. Eventually, he picked it up and dialed the number of the prison at Number 72, Rue d'Auxonne.

'Dick Selva,' he said. 'Did you ever have any trouble with him while he was there?'

'No. People like him are only too anxious to get out and start again. He behaved himself. He got remission for good behaviour. There was just the one incident.'

'What incident was that?'

'He got into a fight.'

'Who with?' Nosjean asked.

'So,' Pel was saying, 'we don't have a mad pistoleer careering round the city shooting at people. They were separate cases entirely. Huppert shot his wife because he was having an affaire with Connie Gruye who was egging him on because she'd worked at the place for years and wanted to be part of it. But suddenly there was no chance because Huppert's wife had found her dipping her hand into the till and was all for getting rid of her.'

'It takes some accepting,' the Chief said.

But it was true all right. People murdered each other for all sorts of reasons. A woman they'd arrested recently had tried to hammer her husband's head flat simply because he snored. A man had shot a workmate because he worked too hard and was considered a bad example. Another had shot his neighbour because they'd lived next door to each other for years and he'd grown tired of him. Because of a snore. Because a man worked too hard. Because someone lacked neighbourliness. It didn't make it too hard to believe that Huppert had murdered his wife because Connie Gruye had told him to. Yet the firm she'd wanted to run wasn't Metaux de Dijon or some other vast organisation. Just a miserable little outfit which brought in barely sufficient to keep its owner.

Pel shrugged. 'We'll just have to think again about Pouilly,' he said.

Nosjean had just appeared. 'There's no need, Patron,' he pointed out. 'Not now. They are connected. In a way.'

Pel's head turned and he swung his chair round.

'It was Ballentou.' Nosjean's face was grim. 'He had the best motive in the world. His daughter dead from drugs, and Selva a pusher, as he well knew. Selva might even have been the one who got her on to drugs.'

Pel didn't blink. 'And the 6.35 he used?'

'From the same source as Huppert's, Patron. Pépé le Cornet. Ballentou knew a consignment had been stolen, because we told him, so he went to Paris to arrange to get one. He knew where to go. But when Pépé learned Selva had been shot it didn't take him long to put two and two together.'

'He was taking a risk, mon brave.'

Nosjean shrugged. 'I don't think he cared much, Patron. After his family had gone. But the idea had been in his mind for some time, I think. Selva arrived at Number 72 while he was in there and he was beaten up. Who by? By a man who was never in trouble in jail apart from that one incident – Ballentou.'

Pel sat back in his chair. 'And the bombs he was scared of?'

'He'd removed Selva. Selva was Pépé's man. As soon as they'd cleared the De Mougy stuff and things were quiet again, I reckon Pat Boum was going to get rid of him. Nick must have known he'd shot Selva – in the same way, I suppose, that he must have known Huppert shot Madame

Huppert. Because he knew where the guns had come from. He'd provided two of them and he guessed the other had come from the same source. I don't suppose he was worried about Madame Huppert being shot, but he was worried about Selva, because Selva was Pépé's man. That's why they had that explosive. It was for Pat the Bang to use.'

'And now?'

'I'm going to bring him in.'

Pel nodded. He'd met Imogen Wathus and heard of Nosjean's interest. 'I don't think you'll find it easy, mon brave,' he said.

As Ballentou climbed into the police car, watched by Aimedieu, Imogen Wathus was beating Nosjean's chest.

'You lied to me!' she was saying, heartbroken and despairing. 'You only looked at me to get at him.'

'No,' Nosjean said. 'That's not true. I didn't even know then.'

She didn't believe him, of course, and tried to pull the police away as they thrust Ballentou into the car. She hadn't believed it when Ballentou had admitted it. Not even when he'd explained how he'd watched Selva for days, and finally got into his car with him outside his flat before he could protest, and forced him with the 6.35 to drive out to Pouilly, where he'd forced him to turn out his pockets before opening the car door and, as Leguyader of Forensic had suggested, putting the gun to his head and blowing him out. He had driven the car away, checked what Selva had taken from his pockets and removed everything that might identify him, leaving only the things the police had found. He had then cleaned the car of fingerprints and left it in the car park at the supermarket, knowing it might be some time before it was noticed. He had hitched a lift home. He'd tried to hide Selva's identity, he said, because he'd guessed the 6.35 might lead to him, and the method of his daughter's dying would clinch the suspicion. He had gone to Paris to pick up the gun, and again later, pretending to visit the Prisoners' Aid Society, to deflect suspicion.

Ballentou told the whole story in his usual quiet self-effacing manner, no excuses, no complaints, as ready as he always had been to accept what was coming to him. Imogen listened with scarcely a protest, but when it was all finished it made no difference. She still refused to believe it. She refused to believe it even when Ballentou produced the 6.35 whose number, sure enough, indicated it was part of the consignment from St. Etienne.

It wasn't that she disbelieved Ballentou; it was Nosjean she disbelieved. She just couldn't accept that he hadn't been using her, and her face was full of lost illusions.

'You did it deliberately,' she wailed. 'I thought you meant what you said! But you didn't! All you were doing was hoping to make an arrest!'

Nosjean sighed as he climbed into the car with Aimedieu and closed the door. There were no winners in police work, he reflected. Only a lot of losers.

The final episode of the tangled Huppert, Selva and Vocci cases came the following morning.

Misset arrived late. There was nothing unusual in that because Misset rarely arrived on time, but this morning he was heavy-footed, scowling and feeling as if he'd been orphaned. His wife wasn't speaking to him and his children clearly didn't think much of him, either. Now that Ada Vocci had gone, there didn't seem to be much left. His car was still out of action and he trudged towards the Hôtel de Police feeling as if he'd been filleted.

As he passed through the front door, the man on the desk looked up. 'The Patron's asking for you,' he said.

Misset scowled. 'Tell him I've just been knocked down by a bus.'

He picked up the newspaper the man on the desk had been reading and immediately the headline caught his eye.

Russian Defects to West. Red Spy Net Bared by File.

Misset regarded it sadly. So there *had* been a spy! Chaput had been right after all!

But it hadn't been Ada Vocci. The route had been roughly the same, but it hadn't been Ada alone who had passed along it, and the Americans had got the file in the end. And it hadn't even been a female spy but a good strong male colonel by the name Chaput had mentioned – Spolianski – and he had passed through the Iron Curtain between East and West by the simple expedient of walking nervelessly through one

212

of the check-points with a forged pass and civilian clothes, and had promptly gone to ground in Holland until he could get the best price for the contents of the file which he'd sewn in separate sheets round the lining of his overcoat.

Misset sighed and was about to hand the paper back when another large headline sharing the top of the front page caught his attention. Occupied with the Russian defector, he hadn't noticed it at first and it hit him like a clenched fist. *Counterfeit Money Arrest. Man Found With Fortune In Notes.* His eyes ran down the type. Gold-thread, Heinz Horstmann himself, had been picked up on the frontier with Switzerland at Basle with a white suitcase full of phoney dollars.

'Thanks for the paper.' The man at the desk waxed sarcastic and reached out.

Misset thrust his hand away, goggling at the print. 'Hang on!' he said. 'Hang on!'

It was the real dope on Ada at last. All those stories about her husband and her father had been just a lot of hogwash. It wasn't an Italian businessman's profits at all. It wasn't even a Polish patriot's gleanings from the Russians. It was a great wad of excellent counterfeit dollars she'd picked up somewhere at the other side of the Iron Curtain. Even the Russians had crooks, it seemed. No wonder she wasn't eager to have too many people know too much about her. No wonder she'd never dared claim political asylum. No wonder she'd disappeared. She must have had an instinct for it. And poor old Gold-thread, trying to make a quick dollar, had swiped the case and got landed. And, with Counterfeit Currency in Paris crowing because Gold-thread was in gaol, Ada was in the clear. Apart from Misset, there was no one now who knew the truth about her.

Given another day or two, she'd be somewhere like Brazil. And, name of God, Misset thought, his mind revolving nostalgically round the big bed in the Hôtel Centrale, good luck to her!

As he put the newspaper down, the man at the desk snatched it up. 'They're still wanting to see you,' he pointed out acidly.

'Too late,' Misset said cheerfully. 'I've just taken an over-dose of sleeping pills. Who's "they"?'

'That cop. The type from Paris.'

213

The news wiped the smile off Misset's face at once. 'Is *he* back? What's he want?'

'I expect they're waiting to demote you.'

For a moment, Misset wondered if he should bolt. He could always say he'd been delayed clearing something up. But they'd catch up with him in the end.

He dragged himself upstairs. Briand was waiting in Pel's room. Pel himself appeared from Darcy's office a moment later, his face full of unrelenting dislike.

Briand rose and looked at Misset. 'Ah!' he said. 'Sergeant Misset!'

Misset decided they'd found out what he'd been up to with Ada Vocci, and that the following week he'd be back in uniform coping with the traffic round the Porte Guillaume.

But Briand kicked off with enthusiasm. 'You'll have heard that a man has been arrested at Basle by the Swiss police?'

Misset answered warily, giving nothing away. 'I read something about it.'

Briand beamed. 'It's the money I told you about. We've discovered now where it comes from. We've got the full story.'

Misset waited and Briand gestured.

'It's part of a stock of counterfeit dollars made in Warsaw some years ago,' he explained. 'It was originally intended to disrupt the Western economy. During the last bout when the Russians and the Western bloc were at each other's throats. But the idea was abandoned with the thawing of relations and, when a large proportion of it was stolen, the Russians passed the information across. At the moment they're anxious not to give offence. It won't last long, of course, but there you are.'

'And where did I come in?' Misset asked cautiously.

Briand gestured cheerfully. 'Didn't *you* sort it out? The Polish woman who arrived here was an official of their Treasury Department, it seems, and handled deals of this sort for their government. She has several passports and speaks several languages perfectly. Horstmann was an associate who helped her get the money out and they'd split up to get it over the frontier. Unfortunately, a large proportion of it's already been cashed and disappeared. That's been lost and will have to be stood by the taxpayer and the Gnomes of

214

Zurich. She knew what to do because she was based at the bank that held the counterfeit notes.'

Good old Ada, Misset thought nostalgically. Always a game little bird.

'As for you – ' Briand went on ' – you can give us some of the information we need. Her name was – ' Briand leaned over and passed over a piece of paper apologetically '– it's spelled A.D.E.L.I.N.A W.O.J.C.I.E.C.H.O.W.S.K.I.'

'Holy Mother of God,' Misset breathed. Nobody who could look like Ada could without her clothes on could possibly be called Adelina Wojciechowski.

Briand smiled. 'We must celebrate. It's thanks to you they bolted, I suppose.'

'Yes.' Misset wasn't slow to take advantage of Briand's mistake. 'I kept having a drink with her. I soon saw what was going on. She said she was a widow.'

'She was unmarried,' Briand said. 'It's a pity we didn't pick her up, of course, particularly as she'd also got a lot of industrial diamonds she'd smuggled out.'

Misset jumped. 'What!'

'Half a million francs worth. They were in the strong room where the money was kept and, as a senior official, she had access to those too. She helped herself to them – as an extra, you might say. It's a pity we lost them!'

Misset's heart sank. Holy Mother of God, he thought, what had he overlooked? Half a million francs worth of diamonds! Enough for him to bolt to Brazil and live in luxury for the rest of his life. And in safety, too, because Brazil had a distinct disinclination to deport people. Half a million francs. He groaned. And he'd had the opportunity to search Ada's room, and he'd missed them!

Briand was still lauding Misset to the skies, and Misset was trying to look as pleased as a bitch that had given birth to a litter of ten pups while inside he was writhing with pain at what had escaped his notice. Half a million francs, he thought again.

His mind was far away as he listened to Briand droning on. Half a million francs and Brazil had started him thinking again of Ada Vocci, with her smooth skin and the scent of her perfume. To say nothing of the way they'd always cheerfully pushed poor old Serafino under the bed.

'It's a pity about the diamonds,' Briand went on. 'Because *they* weren't counterfeit. They were genuine. It would have been quite a haul.'

Misset tried to look as if he'd fought tooth and nail to prevent them disappearing. Pel gave him a glance of contempt.

'Didn't you say she wasn't married?' he asked.

'That's right,' Briand agreed.

'Then why,' Pel asked silkily, 'was she carrying round an urn containing the ashes of her husband?'

Yes, Misset thought. Why was she? What *was* in that damned urn she carried around with her all the time? She never let it out of her sight.

'It had a false bottom . . .' Misset began, but then he caught his breath. Name of God! He almost passed out with supressed rage, as it suddenly dawned on him. And he'd never realised! The ingenuity of it! If he'd only known.

'What urn?' Briand was asking.

'She carried it about with her,' Misset said quickly. 'It was full of dust and crystals. She said they were perfume. To make the old bastard's last resting place more pleasant.'

'But they weren't *all* perfume, were they?' Pel said. 'Some of them were – '

'Diamonds!' Misset said.

If only he'd known. He'd had a dozen opportunities to help himself to the urn. Ada would never have been able to complain to the police. Clearly poor old Gold-thread hadn't been aware of this twist in the scenario either, or he'd never have left the urn behind when he'd bolted with the suitcase of counterfeit notes.

He forced himself back to the present with an effort. Briand was staring at him. 'And what happened to this urn?' he asked sharply.

Pel was already heading for the safe. Producing the urn, he set it on the desk and lifted the lid. Together they stared inside at the mixture of perfumed dust and crystals. Putting his hand inside, Pel produced a few of the dusty crystals, placed them on his desk and tapped them with the butt of his gun. They crumbled to powder.

'Well, *they're* not diamonds,' Briand said gloomily.

Pel was undismayed. 'Doubtless they're at the bottom.'

216

'It's going to be a job to separate them.'

'Probably not as difficult as you think.' Pel rang for Claudie and demanded a bowl of hot water. 'And would you have some tights you can spare?' he asked. 'I'm sure Inspector Briand will be happy to replace them.'

She came back a little later with a bowl of steaming water and a nylon stocking. Pel took the stocking from her, emptied the contents of the urn into it and tied it in a knot.

'So nothing gets out,' he said, plunging it into the hot water.

They didn't have to wait long. The crystals dissolved quickly and vanished with the dust. Pel fished the knotted stocking out to empty the contents on to his blotter. Among the perfumed scum, there was a sediment of dullish stones.

Pel looked up. 'I think we've found your diamonds,' he said.